T0354936

Destiny
Lends A Hand

Destiny
Lends A Hand

By James E. Davis

Order this book online at www.trafford.com
or email orders@trafford.com

Most Trafford titles are also available at major online book retailers.

Printed in the United States of America.

ISBN: 978-1-4269-6199-1 (sc)
ISBN: 978-1-4269-6198-4 (e)

Trafford rev. 04/20/2011

 www.trafford.com

North America & International
toll-free: 1 888 232 4444 (USA & Canada)
phone: 250 383 6864 ♦ fax: 812 355 4082

INTRODUCTION

This book (Destiny Lends A Hand) is purely fiction; although the City of Detroit and the counties mentioned are real, this book is in no way meant as an insult to them. The characters and their actions are totally fiction. Any resemblance in this book to the lives and actions of anyone living or deceased is pure coincidental. None of this book can be used or copied without written permission of the Author.

Copy writes pending

James E. Davis   Author

I especially want to dedicate this book to my sons Kevin and Nicholas, and my wife Rene', I'm sure I've driven you all a little bit crazy these last few years and I'm glad you still talk to me. It's been a long haul but it's finally done. Thank you guys very much, I love you.

CHAPTER ONE

Shawn read the letter again for the third or was it the fourth time he hadn't been counting, between getting his coffee and checking out the ruckus in the street, he'd forgotten how many times. It was the middle of summer the second week of July 1985, and the teenagers in the neighborhood were still celebrating the fourth with an occasional firecracker breaking the evening silence. One mild explosion drew his attention to the front window and as he glanced out at the sidewalk he saw a young man toss something up against his business sign, he thought it was another firecracker, and good thing the young man's timing was off because it bounced away from his sign before exploding detonating with the deep concussion of a hand grenade. As the echoing sound of the m-80 blasted through the neighborhood Shawn knew chasing after the culprit would be ridiculous so he just shook his head and surveyed the damage. He was sure the punk's intention was to blow the glass out of the sign but the only fatality was one of the lights, now the words "Law office" had disappeared so the sign read, "Cassidy & Investigations", leaving a nice large black space between Cassidy and the "&". So much for light bulbs Shawn thought as he turned back to reading the letter.

He fanned through the ten one hundred dollar bills mentally counting them, "yeah there's ten," he said shaking his head. Money accompanied the letter, which really shocked him, it was usually like pulling teeth trying to get money from a client, this one was flooding him with it and he wasn't even sure he'd take the case. He let his thoughts tighten around the writer's request as his eyes became glued to the handwriting examining it with x-ray vision.

It wasn't as though he needed the money. Oh lots of people including his girl friend thought he was fighting poverty but he kept his financial situation very private. Finally, by this time in his life, he'd learnt how to make a substantial amount of money trading in the stock market. His uncle taught him how to work the market in his favor, he also taught him how to hold on to the money he made. At this time in his life he had a stock portfolio filled with a few dozen of the best dividend paying stocks in the market. His uncle had taught him well, very well in fact, so now instead of throwing good money after bad and loosing as he'd been doing for so long, his trading theories were netting him quite a hefty sum. His investments were multiplying and he was learning how to hide his profits from probing eyes. After three years of his own trading and earning mediocre returns his uncle taught him how to trade the options market, and how to keep at least fifty percent of his portfolio in blue chip stocks paying high dividends. And once he learnt how to trade options, with the short selling of stocks, he increased his earnings ten fold. Now he loved it. He learnt stocks go down faster than they go up, and when a company goes bust someone makes a killing as the stock goes to zero, why shouldn't it be him making that killing?

He scanned the letter again sentence by sentence then word by word looking for anything in the writing he'd possibly seen before. Sure, there were the same letters putting the words together pulling at his thoughts, but the penmanship was something he'd never seen before. The letters were written with such flair and grace that he wondered if a princess had written it. He shook his head and changed his thoughts back to the writer's request.

Forest and Beth Foust had been found dead in their home some weeks back, "yes I remember reading about that in The Detroit Free Press," he replied to the letter writer. He remembered reading about it just a minute or so before turning to the financial section giving that headline a hollow response. Now, recalling the story he'd read, he remembered Forest had been accused of killing his wife Beth after she supposedly landed a blow across his noggin with a ball bat. Case closed he surmised at the time and then he quickly turned to the financial section without giving the matter another second of interest.

"They're wrong," the writer stated. These words stood out from the page as if flashing neon. He wondered how this person was so sure of it.

"She's probably a girlfriend madly in love with him," Shawn retorted aloud as if there was someone in the office listening to him and willing to discuss the matter, there wasn't. "She thinks it's beyond him to do such a thing. She's probably in love with him and can't believe he'd do it. Well sweetheart, people do funny things when they get hit with a ball bat." He tossed the letter lightly to the center of his desk. "I'm afraid you just don't want to look at the facts," he added with a look of conviction to the jury.

As he remembered it, Forest was found lying on his bed with a very large bump protruding from the side of his head, and he was very dead. The main fact pointing at his guilt was, he'd been all cleaned up and she was still lying on the floor covered with blood. It's quite impossible to bludgeon someone to death without getting blood on yourself. The detective in charge of the investigation figured Forest had come home drunk, got into a fight with Beth, she hit him with a ball bat and he returned the favor by killing her. There was no other evidence giving merit to anything such as a break in or any one else being present in the house pointing to other possibilities for the murders, leaving Forest looking very guilty of the whole damn mess. Beth was found dead lying on the kitchen floor, bludgeoned and very bloody. Following the blood trail, it looked as if he had chased her through three different rooms of the house beating her every inch of the way, then finishing the job in the kitchen.

The detective heading the case concluded that after killing Beth Forest had showered and changed clothes, probably planning to go to the hospital but he lay down for a moment and fell asleep, never to wake again "He must not have realized he had a serious concussion. Didn't his mother tell him you shouldn't go to sleep after being hit in the head like that?" Shawn asked himself with confusion. "He had the time to clean up and change clothes, he had to be coherent enough to do all that, SO WHY THE HELL DIDN'T HE CALL AN AMBULANCE?" Shawn questioned out loud. "MAKES SENSE" he replied answering for the invisible partner he'd been bouncing his questions off from. He'd remembered seeing a follow up story in the Free Press a week or so later which gave the detective's theory about the case, and the folder was closed. He remembered telling himself, they finally got one right. "What with all the facts they had to sift through" he'd remembered with a laugh.

There was no love lost between Shawn and any of Detroit's Police Departments. Oh, there were a few officers he was on friendly terms with, but a very few. Being a Private Detective creates a stink most police officers hate, especially commanders and police detectives. Digging into their cases pissed a lot of them off, especially if the case was still open, and that happened quite often with Shawn. The last five or six years had turned the faces of many of these officers against him, officers that had once treated him like a friend when he was an attorney in the public defenders office. Now the word detest came to Shawn's mind before the word friend did when these people crossed his mind.

When Forest was found the coroner figuered he'd been dead about twenty hours. They established Beth had been dead a few hours longer, only because the watch on her wrist had been smashed and stopped during the beating. "Maybe if Forest had received medical attention right away he'd still be alive." Who knows? Shawn questioned with a shake of his head. Alive, but in prison.

Hadn't he learnt you don't go to sleep with a head injury, especially one that bad? Shawn questioned again shaking his head in disbelief.

"I need your help, please." He read again. He had a huge soft spot when it came to women, they could twist him around their fingers without even trying, and he was sure this had to be a woman; And a very classy one at that. The stationary the letter was written on wasn't something you'd buy at K-Mart it had to be special ordered from one of the best stores in HOLLYWOOD, and the envelope added a regal tone. You couldn't find this stationary in any ordinary store, not even in Detroit. The handwriting was something he'd never seen before either. If there was a word for, "better than fancy," it definitely described hers. He imagined a beautiful blond, or maybe a tall redhead, about thirty-five or so, sitting in front of a large mahogany desk putting this letter together her hand floating across the paper with words flowing from the tip of her pen, while with her other hand she pulled one hundred dollar bills from a pile of them setting in front of her.

It was said Forest had lots of money, but it was never found. "She probably has it, or he probably knew how to hide it," Shawn concluded with thoughts of his own success flashing through his mind. It was said Forest had an heir living somewhere in Michigan, he'd been divorced some years back but that part of his life hadn't been dug into enough after the murders, the detective had too many cases to work on when this happened, so the heir remained a mystery. So did the heir have his money or maybe this lady had it all. Shawn couldn't remember reading if the heir had ever been found or not. He put the bills back into the envelope and studied the newspaper clippings she'd sent along with the letter. There was a picture of Forest and Beth together from some time back but the clipping didn't do either of them any justice what so ever. Beth was thirty-five years old, but this photo made her look sixty. "So much for newspaper clippings," Shawn claimed. Forest had just turned fifty. She must have been after his money Shawn figured, "damn gold digger" he mumbled. There was a statement in the letter that really surprised him though; she said Forest didn't drink. "Didn't they do an autopsy?" He asked his invisible partner. "They must have," he replied answering his own question. Someone was wrong some where. "Maybe after getting hit that way he decided to start drinking? Maybe the detective figured he'd have to be drunk to beat the hell out of such a fine lady?" Now there were too many "maybes" tugging at his mind. Suddenly from no where a picture of Forest clubbing Beth to death flashed smack into his minds eye and he jumped seeing blood flying and Beth scrambling to get away from him, he quickly shook it away looking around for blood spatter on his desk, and then he continued reading.

"I've known Forest for a few years and believe me when I say he wouldn't have done such a terrible thing; I know what I'm talking about. Forest didn't drink. He loved me too much to ever do anything that would damage our relationship."

"Yeah, this is definitely from a tall blond," he concluded as he tucked it all back into the envelope and put it away in a secret drawer of his desk.

Thinking back to the first time he'd read the story in the newspaper he remembered wondering how they had determined Forest was drunk when he killed her? Compared to when the bodies were found and the story was plastered across the front page of the newspaper there hadn't been enough time for an autopsy. Either the reporter added his own thoughts as facts or the investigator used his nose to gather crucial evidence and reported it as fact. There hadn't been time for an autopsy. It wouldn't be the first time facts became distorted and never corrected. After twenty-four hours all information in the newspaper becomes gospel right? You just can't find out who the hell said so, if any of it seams wrong tuff shit. Bullshit reporters don't have to reveal their sources, so the whole damn thing could be a lie. "So where's the clothes Forest was wearing? I mean, there should have been some clothing laying around somewhere with Beth's blood all over them?"

Maybe Beth discovered the girlfriend, or maybe he just came home late and she'd been holding dinner for him Shawn wondered? "I'm sure as hell not going to tell this young lady she could be the reason Beth clubbed him over the head." He tucked it all in for the night.

Heading for the restaurant across the street from his office he took in a deep breath of the night air and decided to leave the letter alone 'til tomorrow. After all, Monday morning would be a better time for starting a new case, even though the letter had been sitting in his mailbox for two, or had it been three days? "I guess I should get my mail more often," he commented walking along. He was in dire need of some hot chocolate and a chocolate covered long john. This combination would usually fire up his collective investigative skills, he claims jokingly. "I'll sleep on it and maybe tomorrow I'll just send the money back." But he failed to realize he had no return address. "Maybe Forest forgot to put the seat down?" Shawn wondered aloud, adding another maybe to his list of questions making light of the situation as he walked along to the restaurant. He couldn't stop thinking about the letter though. "What ever it was it sure got him killed," Shawn concluded.

He pointed to the biggest long john on the tray, getting a very recognized smile from Angela the waitress as she poured his usual large cup of hot chocolate and delivered both to his usual booth towards the back of the room.

"I'm going to ask Shelly if you taste like chocolate?" she said still wearing the big smile she'd produced once seeing him in the doorway. Seeing him always brought a smile to her face and this evening it was definitely needed. Shawn was always very polite to her and this evening she'd been putting up with so many jackasses thinking they were in a bar room that she was sick of it. Flirting with Shawn always made her day.

"You'll have to wait a few days to work on that," he replied, handing her payment for his order with a generous tip.

"If I could get all the jackasses that come in here to tip me as well as you do Shawn I could make a damn good living." Then with another pleasing smile she returned to the kitchen and began delivering orders to various tables, Shawn noticed the smile was now missing. As she placed the food at a booth along the far wall he heard a well-known male voice make a rude suggestion to her. He wouldn't have blamed her if she'd dumped the plate on his head, but she just walked away.

The clientele here was mostly lawyers, court officers, and occasionally a judge would stop in. They all made him sick. That was why he'd taken a booth out of their eyesight; he didn't want to vomit good food. Listening to their chatter reminded him of being in his high school locker room. The jackasses were always there.

The voice he'd heard making the rude comment was that of James T. Hunter, an attorney he'd had the displeasure of teaching how to win a jury. Hunter came out of law school able to file briefs, and that was about it. It took him about a year but he taught Hunter how to take control of a jury, how to grab it by the throat and keep it if there was one shred of evidence in his favor. The one thing Shawn taught and enforced to all of his students was you work the case to find the truth, not just to win. Hunter couldn't have negotiated a case between two dogs when he started, but when Shawn finished with him he was one of the best lawyers in the public defenders office. Shawn left the public defenders office in 1982; and in 83 Hunter lucked out and secured a job as an Assistant District Attorney. That's when Shawn found out he was putting people in jail and prison weather they were guilty or not. He had to win no matter what. In his mind every one he tried was guilty; he just had to sway the jury to get his guilty verdict. And because of Shawn's fabulous training he'd become damn good at that. It made Shawn sick. Hunter wouldn't check the facts, or look for the truth. He just went for the win. And that's when Shawn refused to train another attorney as long as he lived.

When he confronted Hunter about his outrageous activities Hunter just boasted, "that's the name of the game Shawn." When he told Hunter this wasn't a game, Hunter just smiled. Shawn wanted to throttle him right then and there.

"So where's Shelly been keeping herself?" Angela asked while wiping down the booth behind him. Shawn turned to her quickly noticing her smile had now found its way back.

"She's in Chicago at some big conference," he replied wiping chocolate from the corner of his lips.

"How long will she be there?"

"A couple of weeks, depending on how long it takes for the speakers to run out of steam. Really, I think it's their way of getting a summer break all expenses paid. I don't think they really teach anything."

"Well, if you get cold while she's gone..." Angela whispered, giving him an even bigger smile along with a quick lick of her lips. It wasn't the first time she'd offered to address his needs while Shelly was away or just ignoring him. Angela hoped some day he'd say yes and she'd be able to hold his naked body in her arms and make him forget all about the lady dangling him on her string. She had met Shelly a couple of years back, and once in a while she'd be with him when he'd stop in for dinner or his usual snack. But most of the time he'd come in alone. Angela new he'd been trying to get Shelly to marry him; that was no secret. And she knew he'd been working on that for a few years but it wasn't happening. She couldn't understand why not. She knew if he'd ask her she'd say yes in a heartbeat.

"She sure loves her work doesn't she?"

"Well, she's good at it. If you're ever in trouble, she's the best lawyer in town."

"C'mon, better than you? I don't think so." Now she had moved to his booth taking the seat across from him and she was sitting with her elbows on the table her chin resting on her fists, her look expressing more of the conversation than her words. Someone yelled for more coffee so with a sigh she gave him another sweet smile and left to tend the customer. Two minutes later she looked to his table but he was gone. He must have slipped out the back door she figured as she wiped down his booth. Under his cup he'd left a ten-dollar bill.

Angela was a very attractive brunette with a body he wouldn't mind exploring, and if he hadn't been in love with Shelly he'd probably have taken her up on her offer by now, but Shelly consumed every love making thought his body and mind produced, to him playing around was out of the question.

He'd met Shelly during his first year of law school. Cooley was the only school either of them could afford, but they both graduated at the top of their class. Shelly graduated Summa Cum Laude. She made it very clear that some day she wanted to become a judge, and before dying HOPEFULLY serve on the Supreme Court. High expectations SHE KNEW IT, and she'd bust her butt as a trial lawyer until she made it. They fell in love after a few months of hot passionate study sessions, and after graduation both of them joined the Public Defenders Office in Detroit. They dated heavily during law school and those first few years working in Detroit, but after Shawn quit the Public Defenders Office their dating took a sharp down hill turn. She claimed it was only because she was too busy. He loved her very much, so he put up with her rough schedule, even though sometimes it hurt. He wasn't about to destroy his chances with her. Their relationship was stronger before because they'd worked so close together he told himself over and over. He didn't feel as though she'd been dangling him on a string, but every one else did. Tomorrow might put a new light on things he'd always say.

After leaving the Public Defenders Office, he opened his own law practice, and worked on getting his Private Investigators license. Training new law school graduates on how to conduct themselves in a courtroom in front of an arrogant judge had been quite profitable, until the episode with Hunter. He quit training every one after that.

By then the request for his investigative skills had increased considerably, especially from insurance companies. Hell, he'd just wound up a month long case looking for a grand champion poodle that came up missing. The insurance company was on the hook for one hundred thousand dollars if this animal wasn't returned. Stud fee for this dog started at five hundred dollars and his pups could demand three to five hundred dollars for a female and up to a thousand for a champion male. His champion bloodline was worth a lot, especially when held for ransom.

And his luck pulled him through. He'd been sitting in a coffee shop two miles from the airport when he over heard two men complaining about a big white dog they'd been fighting with, and one of them had been bitten. The dog was a large white poodle. He offered to buy the men breakfast and possibly end up with a client and a dog bite case and his brilliant offer obtained some very crucial information. The dog he was looking for could be on its way to Europe. The two men worked at the airport and they'd been trying to put the dog into a cage for flying on an airplane. Well, he lost no time checking out the airport and he found the dog he was searching for caged up and waiting for his flight only minutes before he'd be placed into the cargo hold of a Boeing 747 on its way to Japan not Europe, but just as far away he'd never have found it. It's surprising what you can learn when you stop for a cup of hot chocolate he beamed tucking away his finders fee.

Now, the few friends he had that knew about it teased him calling him the Dogcatcher. He'd just laugh it off though. "What the hell, a ten percent finders fee, ten grand for one months work, call me what ever you want," he'd say shrugging his shoulders.

He often wondered if he should tell Shelly just how much money he had tucked away. He wanted her to marry him, but he didn't want money to be the catalyst for her saying yes. Although, her thinking he was almost broke did seem to be one of the reasons she was pulling away. Or maybe it was the way he conducted himself? He questioned.

He had serious problems relating with most judges and other lawyers, he thought most of them were pompous fools. He'd seen too many guilty defendants set free on technicalities, while other defendants that should be put on probation, end up in jail. Too many judges were afraid of having their rulings overturned.

So they handed out light sentences when certain defendants should have gone to prison. Once Shawn pissed off one judge they all took a disliking to him, well most of them anyway. When he quit the public defenders office in 1982 he tried to get Shelly to leave Detroit with him, but she wouldn't. She was too afraid to begin all over some place else. So he stayed in Detroit. In the last few years she'd witnessed all sorts of wrong doings in the court system and understood what pissed him off so much, but she still stayed because she was sure she could help correct it.

Allowing a guilty defendant to walk because of a minor detail just because some judge was afraid of having his decision over turned was stupid. But if it were a defendant of Shawn's, most judges would come down hard. He knew his defendants were being treated badly because of him. It wasn't legal but the judges could do what they damn well wanted to.

Shawn held the record in Detroit for being the first attorney with the most trips to jail for contempt of court. He never failed to tell a judge he was full of shit, if that was what came to mind as he was defending his client. One time a judge called his client an idiot. Shawn asked the judge how he expected to get respect if he didn't give respect, and the judge said it was his courtroom and he could say and do anything he wanted. Shawn told the judge he was also a jackass. That got him cited for contempt of court with three days in jail. After that Shawn would request approaching the bench when he got pissed. Then, after the judge would cover the microphone he'd whisper his remarks. It didn't keep him from being held in contempt, but it usually kept his stay in jail to one night.

When he returned from breakfast the following morning his thoughts settled back to the letter he'd received from his mystery client. It has to be from someone in high society he questioned, he was sure of it. "Possibly a judge's wife," he entertained with a laugh. That would necessitate anonymity. There was no return address on the envelope or any hint of where in the world the letter could have come from, which cancelled his idea about sending the money back. It could have come from someone in Wayne County or one of the surrounding counties; that sort of nailed it down to about a million people or more. "Just anyone is not going to send me that much money without knowing me!" he blurted. They have to know I'll either take the case or hold the money and give it all back, his thoughts tugged.

"There's at least fifty other Private Investigators in Detroit, but every one of them would probably spend the money and wait for the client to call, they wouldn't spend one minute on the case. Yeah, this person knows me." He paused as if waiting for that silent partner to agree with him, but he didn't.

There was a light knock on his door then the mailman walked in flipping through a bundle of mail in his hand, which he slowly handed to Shawn.

"I figured all this wouldn't fit in your box. You know you could put in one of them there slots in your door," the old man advised, "at least then your mail would be inside once I delivered it. We've had a rash of boxes being pulled off from outside walls and mail being scattered all over hell."

Shawn recalled seeing the teenager throwing firecrackers last evening and thought to himself he probably knew the culprits tearing the boxes off.

"Do you ever collect your mail the morning I deliver it?" he questioned in a pleading tone.

"Sometimes," Shawn replied, remembering how full it was Sunday morning when he'd gathered it. He was guilty of ignoring some things, and gathering the mail was one of them. The mailman continued scolding him for his lack of attention to their diligent effort for delivery, telling him he could either learn to collect his mail daily or put a mail slot in his front door so the mail would at least be inside not setting out where it could be stolen.

Shawn half listened, while he thumbed through the bundle of envelopes the old man had given him, not expecting to see another one from his mystery client but there it was. He wondered if Mike could tell him when the first letter had been delivered, knowing Thursday had been the last day he collected it before Sunday.

"Mike, do you remember delivering another envelope that looks like this one?" Mike was getting close to retirement age and had been delivering mail in this neighborhood for years; Shawn figured he'd probably started his area from day one.

"Got yourself an expensive girlfriend there?" the old man asked peering over the rims of his glasses. He reminded Shawn of his old high school principal, chewing him out and sticking his nose where it wasn't welcome. The question required a yes or no answer and that was all. He knew Mike also recognized the envelope as being from expensive stationary and it must have peaked his imagination. Suddenly Shawn wished he hadn't asked him anything while Mike stood scratching his head and staring at the ceiling as if that would improve his memory, Shawn was becoming infuriated.

"MIKE!" Shawn half shouted hoping to speed up his attempt at recovering information.

"Now hold on, today's Monday," he replied still scratching his head. "I didn't deliver on Saturday, the sub did." Shawn's eyes were rolling, he wished he'd have just said bye Mike, now he was harboring on becoming rude.

"Friday, yep it was Friday. AND YOUR DAMN BOX WAS FULL THEN!" he blurted back.

Shawn quickly thanked him and ushered him out the door leaving him still scratching his head, it was more than he wanted to deal with. "Ok, maybe it was Wednesday when I collected it last." Shawn mumbled to himself feeling a little guilty. Many times he'd be fed up with someone but he'd still hold his tongue, unless it was with a judge. He was glad he held it with Mike.

Dropping the rest of the mail on his desk, he kept the letter from the mystery client in his hand while he poured himself a cup of coffee and toyed with his thoughts. "Mr. Cassidy, please send back my money, you have ignored my request long enough. He sat down and began stirring his coffee as he held the letter up to the light coming through the window, trying to see if there was more money inside. He couldn't tell. When he finally opened it and unfolded the letter, more hundred-dollar bills fell to his desk. "Well, I can cancel that thought," he said, picking up the money. He counted out another ten bills of the same denomination to go along with the first ten. "Shit, two thousand dollars and I haven't even agreed to take the case yet." Again there was no return address. He began reading this letter hoping there'd be instructions on how or where to contact the client if he did decided to take the case.

Dear Shawn;

I know your usual fee is two hundred dollars per day; I will pay you one thousand dollars a day. I think you're being cheated at your usual rate.

"Well isn't she a sweetheart," he mumbled with a big smile and continued.

I have listed a few people you might try talking with, they might help your investigation. Their names and addresses are also included. I'm sure you'll be surprised about what you find. As I've said, Forest was a very gentle man, not capable of what they have accused him of. I wish I could meet with you and discuss this matter openly, but that is out of the question; I must remain incognito.

I will keep a close watch on you though, not because of any distrust, I wouldn't have hired you if I didn't trust you. I will watch close in case you need additional funds or further information that I may be able to offer. If you are unable to prove my request, at least I'll know you've tried your best.

Thank You Shawn.

There was a page included with a couple of names with addresses on it, but nothing he recognized, and still no instructions on how to contact this client.

"WHO THE HELL IS THIS?" he blurted out waving the letter in the air above his head. "I still think she's some judge's wife, wouldn't that be a kicker?" His voice echoed with a laugh, as if there was someone in the room to answer him. "Forest having an affair with some judges wife, wouldn't that be the shits?

He counted the money again then read the letter over a few more times trying to place a face to the profile he'd created, but no one appeared.

He wished Shelly was home so he could run all this through her mind, she usually had a better perspective on weird shit like this; and to Shawn this was as weird as it could get.

When he and Shelly met they became friends right away, and by graduation marriage seemed to be in the not to distant future. He couldn't put his finger on it, but he was sure quitting the Public Defenders Office had put a damper on those plans. They still dated, but not as often. She always had work to do which pulled her away. The sex was still very good, when he could get her to stay long enough to get past foreplay. Many times it was dinner then, "I have to go, I need to be relaxed for court tomorrow." He would offer a full body massage to help her relax, and sometimes she'd say yes, but not lately. He was sure she wasn't seeing anyone else. He knew she'd been seen out having dinner with the Mayor and different judges, judges Shawn hated. Sometimes she'd be seen hanging on to the arm of some state senator or congressman, but that was done so she could build her reputation working towards a judgeship. Shawn understood. He didn't approve but he understood.

He liked running his cases through her mind, weather she could help him or not wasn't an issue with him. He did it to include her in his life. He'd watch paint dry with her if she'd ask him to. She'd usually provide him with some very good information whenever he included her, sometimes information he already had, but he wouldn't tell her that. Most of the time he just wanted to hear her voice, and know she was still there for him.

Sometimes if he had nothing to do he'd disguise himself and sit in the courtroom while she pleaded a case. He wouldn't want her to know he was there for fear she'd think he was spying on her. And this one day he was very glad he'd sat in. After she'd won a tough case that had dragged on for months, her boss put his arm around her and whispered something into her ear, she quickly pushed him away, which made him feel good. He wished he could have heard that whisper; it really bugged the shit out of him not knowing what was said. But he'd never ask. He'd wondered about her relationship with her boss, but from the way she pushed him away she definitely wasn't involved with him, screw the whisper.

He loved watching her in the courtroom though. Her mind worked so fast. She could make someone forget their own name while she twisted their thoughts around getting to the truth; she always went for the truth. Even though sometimes it lost her the case. She would say, "Justice won, as it should have." Often he'd be awe struck by her actions in court and the ability she projected. He told himself to stick around until she told him to leave, even if he became old and gray waiting; as long as she still accepted his company he'd wait forever.

The second letter contained a colored photograph of Beth and Forest standing beside each other. It must have been taken during good times, Shawn told himself because they were holding each other and smiling. They actually look happy, he thought as he stared at the photo. The black and white photograph in the newspaper hadn't done either of them any justice, Beth was a very beautiful lady he realized eyeing the colored picture. He could see why Forest was immediately found guilty; you just don't beat the hell out of a lady as beautiful as this and get away with it. Even if she just burnt the hell out of your t-bone.

Hoping someone recorded the date it was taken he turned the picture over, and there at the top edge was written June 21st 1983. The picture was two years old.

He knew from the clippings that Forest was fifteen years older than Beth. At the time it amazed him that Forest was able to get such a young lady to marry him. This photo answered that question too. For being fifty years old Forest looked damn good. He must have been a body builder because he looked mighty fine in his tight fitting tee shirt and the age of thirty- five seemed to fit him better. His face had that stern but gentle look, and the letter writer was right, he didn't look like a killer, but looks can be deceiving.

Beth was very pretty. She had long blond hair, in this picture it was up in a very attractive bun but he was sure if it had been down it would reach her waist. She had bluish green eyes and a cute little nose, and she was tall, as tall as Forest and he looked to be at least six foot or more. She had the face of an angel, and the look in her eyes as she gazed at him said Forest I love you very very much, if you could believe a look. The longer Shawn examined the picture he knew a jury would have convicted Forest in a second if it had gone that far. You just don't bludgeon to death a lady that looks this beautiful.

"So what the hell did happen?" he asked himself as he pondered over the various pieces of material. "And that's exactly what this lady wants to know," he said picking up the letter and dropping it back to the center of his desk with a hard shake of his head.

Picking up his phone he dialed the number of the hardware store across the street, he could just make out the number on their window from where he sat.

"Hello, "this is Shawn Cassidy, I'm in the law office across the street from you."

"Yes Mr. Cassidy, what can I do for you?" an elderly mans voice softly asked.

"Does your store install mail slots in doors?"

"We certainly do."

"Could you install one in my front door?"

"Would you like that today?"

"If that's possible, I can stick around."

"I'll send my son right over to see what you need."

Next he dialed the number of the local pizza parlor; today he'd be eating in. With money like this coming in the mail he figured he might as well try and protect it. Besides, he didn't want to finance the destruction of the neighborhood. "If someone found this kind of money lying in my mailbox that would sure buy lots of firecrackers and m-80's," he mumbled while waiting to place his order.

CHAPTER TWO

His mail slot could have been finished by two that afternoon, or definitely by three; but Shawn kept interrupting the young man doing the work offering to share his pizza and bugging him about the neighborhood hoodlums. Did he know who the boys were he'd seen throwing the firecrackers? No he didn't. Did he have any idea who was pulling off the mailboxes in the area? No idea what so ever. Shawn asked question after question which made the young man feel as though he was on the witness stand. The last nail was put in place around four PM and the young man was on his way back to the store, wiping sweat from his brow and trying to convince Shawn it was from the summer heat. His Eyes lit up when Shawn paid the bill fifty dollars too much and said keep the change, then he figured listening to Shawn wasn't all that bad.

Once the young man left Shawn took a few pieces of his mail and dropped them through the outside mail slot watching as they landed perfectly into the plastic tray mounted on the inside of the door. He was getting board but he retrieved them and did it again. Suddenly he had an uneasy feeling as though he was being watched, but after taking a quick look around the neighborhood he dismissed it. Probably if anyone was watching him they'd just think he was a little bit crazy and he'd feel a little ridiculous, but he did it again, just once, and went back into his office. Yes, it would protect his mail just fine and he wondered why he'd never thought of it himself? Mike had given him a very good idea so he made a mental note to add a few more dollars to his mailman Christmas fund. With the amount of money being sent to him in the mail this mail slot would be better than the old box mounted out side of the building. His mail would be much safer unless some one broke down the door.

His boredom was becoming worse and he found himself wishing Shelly were home so he could call her and work on getting a date for the evening. It wouldn't have been so bad but it had already been three weeks since they'd been out together and now it would be another two weeks for sure. He dialed the number of his friend Tony whom he hadn't talked with in a couple of days, but he wasn't home either. He was in the process of leaving a silly message on his machine when Tony's wife answered.

"Hello Mr. Cassidy," Correen said in a very professional tone. "I think I'm going to need your help."

"And what can I do for you this evening Mrs. Breen?" he replied, playing the professional to the hilt.

"I need you to help me find my cat," she said with a slight snicker, which he knew was directed towards his recent animal recovery. He joined her laughter knowing she was just teasing.

"Well Mrs. Breen, my rates have gone up," thinking about his mystery client he couldn't help himself, he had to say it. "A thousand dollars a day."

"Wow, I think she can stay lost," Correen replied with more laughter. "She's not worth two cents right now. I just spent fifty dollars to get her fixed; now she runs away. A thousand dollars a day, are you trying to scare business away?"

"No, I have a mystery client and that's what she's paying me."

"A mystery client?" her voice quickly took on a surprised "you're kidding me" tone and he knew a quick explanation would ease her frown.

"Yeah, I've gotten two letters from this lady and each one of them has contained a thousand dollars, she's almost begging me to take this case but she won't or can't tell me who she is, so she says"

"Are you going to?"

"I'll probably dig into it for a couple of days, what else do I have to do hunt for missing cats?"

"I can pay you with dinner," she replied trying her best to muffle the sudden burst of laughter blasting from her lips.

The three of them had been friends since high school, first him and Tony, and when Tony finally won over Correen's lovely heart the three of them became the best of friends. Tony insisted Correen learn Martial Arts so she could protect herself if it ever became necessary, and she learnt very well. Many times the three of them sparred together and both of the guys feared the day she might really cut loose and kick their butts.

When Tony and Correen finally tied the knot Shawn stood by their sides guarding the rings and passing them forward when the request was made. It was a small wedding, actually very small. At Tony's request Shawn agreed to be the best man and ring bearer, while Correen's best friend stood as her maid of honor. The reception was even smaller, the foursome had a small dinner planned together and the preacher was invited but declined once the twenty-dollar bill was placed into his hand. The only thing they could figure was he'd expected much more after saying he'd do the ceremony for free.

They were like family and Correen was quite aware of Shawn's financial situation, she knew he'd only take a fee he thought was reasonable, and a thousand dollars a day was ridiculous. A client could offer him ten thousand dollars a day, but she knew if he didn't feel right about it he wouldn't take it. Shawn controlled their stock portfolio as well as his own and she was quite aware of the value of both of them and the money he needed to get by.

"Now that's the best offer I've had in a long while" he said, his taste buds already savoring her fine cooking. I haven't had a home cooked meal in a couple of weeks. I'll see what I can do. Tell that husband of yours to give me a call will you?" After a few more minutes of small talk they said good-bye and Shawn was back to being board.

He entertained more thoughts about his mystery client, then jotting down the address he made a mental note that he might stop by if he was in the neighborhood, knowing all along that was where he was headed anyway. As he locked his office door he made a visual scan of the nearby area checking to see if anyone was watching, when he was satisfied there wasn't he flipped his mail door open a few more times just for grins, then he jumped into his one of a kind Ford Firebird Convertible and headed for the city of Warren.

Seabring Cassidy owned the largest automobile dealership in the city of Detroit and in 1954 an engineer about to loose his job with The Ford Motor Co. came up with an idea to save his position. In an agreement with the General Manager of the design department Harrison Frost went to Cassidy Motors and sort of bribed Seabring into financing him into designing a fancy new 1955 automobile. The truth of the matter, the engineer had been fired for being too good at designing. Other engineers lacked his explosive ideas when it came to designing and their disgruntled attitudes disturbed the General Manager. If Harrison could find a way to cover his salary for one year he could continue working on the automobile he was presently designing. He headed strait for the largest Ford dealer in the state, Cassidy Motors.

Seabring was an easy target and was more than happy to join Harrison in building and designing a new 1955 Ford vehicle. If his design were accepted it would be built and displayed at the 1956 Detroit Auto. Show. And it would also be considered as the starting pace car at the 1956 running of the Indy. 500.

Catch number one; Seabring had to pay twelve thousand dollars towards the development of the vehicle, if he wanted a model for himself. Shawn's father jumped on it. He would have jumped on it if they had requested a hundred thousand dollars. What he didn't know was, the twelve thousand was the amount of money needed to cover Harrison's wages for one year. If he would have known about the deception it wouldn't have mattered one bit, he loved being offered the chance to collaborate with a Ford Factory engineer. In agreement with Harrison's General Manager, if he could succeed with this new vehicle it would pave the way for him getting hired permanently by Ford Motor Co. as long as he found a way to secure his wages, Ford would cover all the cost of manufacturing.

Shawn's father was allowed to add his own ideas to some of the make up of the car, but 90% of the car was still the Harrison's design. He was good at making other people think his ideas were their ideas. Shawn's father believed he designed most of the vehicle and he never missed a chance to brag about it. Harrison did use some of Seabring's ideas though, like making the vehicle two foot longer than he had figured in the first design. Harrison gave Seabring the go ahead for naming their vehicle, and he quickly came up with the Ford Firebird. Well, the engineer for the Thunder Bird blew his stack, and the name was finally scrapped, along with the model once two and only two of them were completed. Shawn's father did get to have his car, but the name had to be changed to the Ford Concept Firebird. Finally, after two and only two of the vehicles were made, the whole idea was scrapped. There were numerous arguments with Seabring, he wanted to buy just enough Ford stock so he'd have a say about the manufacture of the new vehicles so their design could be put back on manufacturing status, but it didn't work.

The automobile was beautiful. Seabring's was a white convertible with white leather interior. The top was an off white leaning towards a light tan. It had a newly designed four-speed transmission with a newly developed 390 v-8 engine, another first from the engine department. The dashboard had a gauge for everything. It had been designed for an airplane and added a real touch of class to the interior of the car.

It had a tachometer, which was a first; other engineers said it was a waste of space. It had a high temperature gauge, a low temperature gauge, a battery voltage and generator output gauge, and an oil pressure gauge. It had indicator lights that told the driver if a headlight or taillight had failed. The jack wasn't the usual bumper lift type, but a hydraulic bottle type with spots designed in the frame at each corner of the under carriage to prevent any possibilities of ever slipping. Shawn's father was the first to place the spare tire mounted on the rear bumper covered with a chrome shield. He talked the engineers into making a chrome cover which encased the tire completely, that request cost him an extra five hundred dollars. Another unnecessary item other engineers claimed. "What the hell is the trunk for, if not to house the spare tire?"

"It's too ostentatious," chief engineers charged. The main reason the new automobile came under attack from other engineers was they hated Sebring's money and attitude; it was his car, his plan. If he would have left his pride to home, who knows? There might have been Ford Firebirds for everyone to drive. They never even tried to put a price on the automobile. It was put on display at the 1956 Detroit Auto. Show with hopes of generating enough orders to place the vehicle back on manufacturing status. That didn't work out though. There weren't enough orders because Ford couldn't come up with a reasonable price for the vehicle; and other engineers sabotaged the project out of jealousy.

But the vehicle was welcomed as the starting pace car at the Indy 500 that year. From there Seabring's car was placed in the show room at Cassidy Ford in Detroit, where it stayed until Seabring Cassidy died in May of 1982. It had less than one hundred miles on it.

It had been taken out once in a while for parades and special occasions, started and let run every day, but the raised turntable it perched on became its stationary home.

Seabring spent thousands of dollars building a platform to show it off, and hundreds more keeping every one at arms length from the vehicle. He had a raised walkway built around the car with a wrought iron railing shielding it so People could look but not touch. If he wasn't there to drive it to the wash and wax station his employees were to push it by hand.

Shawn had been given the task of cleaning, waxing, and pulling minor maintenance on the vehicle. Not because he was the chosen one as a prince taking care of a jewel, but because if something was neglected, scratched, or broken, his father could take him home and beat his ass. Shawn learnt very quickly how to keep the vehicle spotless and shining, at least by the third ass whipping. He actually fell in love with it, the car that is. Being seven years old and getting his behind blistered if the damn thing was found having any dust on it was too much. One day he confided in his uncle Tim about what would happen if the vehicle was found dirty. Tim was flabbergasted.

Tim was Shawn's uncle on his mothers side, her only brother, and Seabring's partner in Cassidy Ford. He wasn't a full partner though he only owned about forty percent of the business. Seabring held on to sixty percent so he could stay in charge of everything. When Tim found out what Seabring had been doing to Shawn, he would stay late or come in very early and clean the car himself. Shawn never received another beating, for that anyway.

Shawn's mother had died during childbirth, thanks to an incompetent staff at Ford Hospital in Detroit. She was left alone for about five minutes during Shawn's delivery and when the attending nurse returned to her room she wasn't breathing. The quick response from a surgeon passing through the hall saved Shawn's life, and ended Seabring's. Once Shawn was removed from the birth canal, blood began circulating properly through his mother's body again, but Delores was brain dead. When she died, Seabring died inside. He brought Shawn home from the hospital but would never allow himself to become attached to him. He blamed Shawn for her death, and secretly wished the baby had died along with her so he wouldn't have to be reminded of her every day of his life. Shawn looked so much like her. The pain became so bad that he began abusing Shawn physically, that's when Sebring and Tim had their first falling out.

"Have you been beating that boy?" Tim questioned one morning. His tone cut into Sebring like a knife.

"Is that what he told you?"

"No, I caught him in the bathroom with his pants down, he's all bruised on his backside, I tried for over fifteen minutes to get him to tell me what happened, HE WOULDN'T TELL ME A DAMN THING!" Tim lied, his voice getting louder. "THE LOOK ON YOUR FACE TOLD ME EVERYTHING I NEED TO KNOW!"

"I haven't…"

Tim quickly cut him short. "YOU LAY ONE MORE HAND ON THAT YOUNGSTER AND I'LL BEAT YOU TO DEATH!"

"YOU'RE NOT BIG ENOUGH!" Seabring yelled back.

"I'LL GET ME A GOD DAMNED 2X4 AND WE'LL SEE!" Seabring knew Tim would do just that, so he walked away without another word. He finally realized he had to stop whipping on Shawn. On that day Sebring's friendship with Tim almost ended, a friendship that began in grade school and had never included as much as an argument 'til then; now it almost came to blows. Customers fled the Dealership that morning hearing the argument between the two men, and employees stood fast by the telephones ready to call for an ambulance. Everyone was sure the argument would come to blows. From then on there was a dark cloud over their relationship and the dealership. From that day forward things at Cassidy Ford Motors continued but suffered along with their friendship, never to regain its usual composure.

Seabring's verbal abuse towards Shawn never stopped, but he talked to Shawn a lot less after that, so it was somewhat of an improvement.

After that day Shawn's grand parents and Uncle Tim helped more to raise him, taking as much of the pressure off Seabring as they could. Years later when Seabring was thinking about the future of Cassidy Ford and wondering what would happen if heaven forbid he died before Tim, he asked Tim to keep the car on display if God forbid he was to die or something like that, and Tim assured him he would. All the while he was planning to sell the car to Shawn for one dollar, if Shawn wanted it. And Shawn did.

Shawn turned down Beckwith Street taking another look at the address he'd written on the piece of scratch paper in his pocket. "1489," he said aloud while tapping his fingers along the steering wheel to a Country Tune by George Jones he'd been listening to. He quickly pulled over to the curb checking the numbers on the even numbered side of the street. He knew he was in the 1400 block by the 1488 and 1496 numbers he could see on that side. There was only one house on the odd numbered side and it took up the whole damn block, he couldn't believe that was the house he was looking for. He made a complete circle around the block to be sure before pulling into the wide circle driveway of a mansion that had to be at least four thousand square foot or larger, he was quite shocked.

"Information you could have included in one of your letters!" he blurted to his mystery client. As he pulled up to the front of this beautiful mansion now he could see the numbers "1489" in large gold lettering above the front door.

As he drove in he marveled at the wide cement drive that had to be at least sixteen foot across allowing two cars to pass each other with plenty of room between them. The house was a large two-story with fancy trim on the gable ends and under the soffits. There were four tall pillars across the front holding up a large porch, and each of the pillars had its own large light shining over an array of beautiful flowers in the front yard, and he wondered if Beth had a green thumb. The property took up the whole city block and every foot of it was covered with flowers, well groomed bushes, or fine manicured green grass. As he took in the complete view he noticed at every corner of the property there were large antique lampposts.

"Marking the boundaries no doubt," he said talking to himself. There was also a well-tailored city sidewalk outlining the property on all sides, including the lamppost area. Shawn was impressed. "He must have put in the sidewalk too," Shawn remarked, after noticing the sidewalk across the street and down the block to be at least twenty years old or more and in serious need of repair. "This guy spent thousands just nursing the property," Shawn prattled in amazement.

He took a walk through the plush green grass around to the rear of the house finding that to be as elegant as the front and included its own wide driveway to the street behind the house. There were two garages, a large two car connected to the house, and another three car about a hundred foot behind the house. The back garage measured at least forty foot long by thirty-six foot deep. He walked along peaking into the small windows of the back garage and he could see various classic vehicles parked inside. There was a wide dog kennel running along the south end of the building facing the house, it was empty now but from the left over turds here and there he imagined it probably housed some pretty large dogs at one time, used to scare people from bothering his cars no doubt, Shawn figured.

In his mind he compared the house to the large brownstone he had grown up in on the east side of the county in Grosse Pointe Farms. He thought that house was large until seeing this home. He could probably fit that house inside this one at least three times for starters he muttered in his mind

As he walked around the house he tried every door checking to see if they were locked, they were. After trying the front door he pushed the doorbell just for the hell of it, and a beautiful sound of chimes filled the air for ten seconds or so, but no one came to the door, he was sure the place was vacant.

His lock picks were tucked in a hiding place under his front seat, and as he went to get them he felt a sprinkle of rain hit his face. He decided to put up the cars top before grabbing his tools and returning to the house but while he was unsnapping the cover he heard what sounded like the side door of the house open and shut again. He figured at any moment someone would walk up behind him and ask what the hell he'd been up to, but no one showed. When he finished latching the top in place and putting up the windows he cancelled the idea of grabbing his lock picks and walked back around the house to the side door. He was sure that was where the sound had come from and he was right. Having a good eye for details he'd remembered seeing some leaves against the bottom of that door before, but now they were a foot or so away from it. Someone had come out through that door and kicked those leaves away, and that someone knew he was there. Whoever it was their intent was to avoid him and he wondered why? Now it was beginning a steady rain so he returned to his car and sat for a while listening to the radio. He wondered if he waited there long enough if the person he heard come out of the house would return and at least come back and talk to him, but after about a half hour or so he gave up and decided to go home. He'd return the following morning.

"Maybe then it'll be dry," he told his imaginary partner. It was getting dark now anyway and even though the client was paying a thousand dollars a day, it wasn't worth getting shot for. People around Detroit sometimes shoot first and asked questions later, and he wasn't about to get shot. He pulled slowly out of the drive expecting to see someone walking along the sidewalk some where in the area, but he saw no one. He decided to drive around the block a couple of times and look the property over again from a distance and possibly see somebody walking along.

The lighting for the yard was beautifully designed, both front and back. The way it lit up the flowers and walkways at night presented a safe and welcoming exposure. As he drove back along the east side he saw a shadowy figure walking between the house and outer garage then it quickly disappeared. He knew this was the person from the house and decided there was no reason to put his life in danger. Even though the lighting was fabulous, between the buildings it was dark, and it was raining too damn much and he didn't feel like getting wet. He headed for home.

Most of the shootings or stabbings reported in Detroit usually happened at night when people were being stupid or doing something foolish, he tried his best not to be foolish. As he pulled away from the mansion he momentarily rested his right hand on the 357 revolver tucked against his side. Everything here could wait until the following day, he told himself, maybe this person would be more willing to talk to him in the daylight.

CHAPTER THREE

"You've got to understand Shawn, a part of him died when your mother died," his uncle Tim touted, while they both sipped on a beer at Shawn's father's house after Seabring's funeral.

"I hate mom for dieing," Shawn said, wiping tears from his eyes. The tears most people thought were for his father were for his mother; he wished he could have felt her arms around him at least once in his life especially today. Not because they'd just finished burying his father, but because he was crying and he couldn't justify the tears being for him.

It was May 4th 1982; the day of Seabring Cassidy's funeral, he had died suddenly from a massive heart attack on the morning of May 1ST. Shawn hadn't talked to his father in over three years; to him it was as though he was at the funeral of a stranger. In reality he realized now he and his father would never settle any of the hate between them, and a part of his life had been nothing but a blur. A man he figured was too stubborn to die was now laid to rest, and they never even knew each other.

He had held some hope in his heart that some day when his father was old and gray they'd have a long needed talk about why he'd been such an asshole all of his life. He'd get a chance to tell his father he loved him but never liked him. But now that would never happen. He promised himself if he were lucky enough to have children he'd be the center of their lives. He'd never follow in his father's footsteps. Now he cried because he wasn't able to know his mother or his father, and it hurt him very much. His children would be loved and taught to love, if he could just get the women he loved to marry him.

"Well she didn't die on purpose" Tim said after taking another long swallow of beer. "God, if you could have heard her making all the plans to bring you home," Tim cried. "Sure, he brought you home from the hospital and did his best to raise you; but seeing your face every day made him wish for your mother. It hurt'im. You look so damn much like her. I know it's hard for you to understand but he's been dead for years," his uncle carried on.

"It seems to me my mother dieing should have made him love me that much more. Why couldn't he just once have put his arms around me?" Shawn begged. "He didn't have to

say he loved me! God damn it, just put his arms around me."
The discussion wasn't helping Shawn understand things any better.

"Did you ever hate me for being born?"

Tim quickly took him into his arms as he had many times through the years, and they both stood crying. "No son, I've never regretted you being born, I love you as if you were my own." Shawn had never heard about any of this from his uncle before, and as much as he loved his uncle he still wished his father could have loved him too.

"Christ, you've been more of a father to me than he ever was. You've never called me the names he did."

"I wish you could have known him before," Tim said giving Sebring a defense Shawn wasn't about to agree with.

"You mean before he turned into an asshole!"

"He loved you, he just didn't know how to show it. You think you and your buddy Tony raised some hell around the streets of Detroit? We terrorized this town back in our day. Your father pulled me out of so many scrapes I can't count'em. We used to start fights just for the hell of it. He was always there for me, and I backed his ass up plenty of times too, plenty of times!" he said, whipping his empty beer bottle against the bricks of the Brownstone.

"I not only lost a wonderful sister when you were born, but I lost one hell of a good friend. I didn't know the man that brought you home from that hospital! God damn it! Oh, there were many times when I thought things were going fine, then things would take a one eighty and I'd be in the dark." Shawn handed Tim his empty bottle and he whipped that against the wall of the Brownstone as if it was his job to do so. "Do you think it's been easy for me putting up with him these last thirty some years? He's been ten different people! I never knew who the hell I was talking with. His moods changed like the fucking weather. We used to be so close. After your mom died there were so many times when I thought I knew what was going on, and then he'd do a flip flop and I'd be left hanging! Like when he started that car deal, the one on that fucking God damn round fucking turn table," Tim stammered while he opened another beer, he was getting pretty hammered.

Shawn had never seen his Uncle worked up like this, he figured with his Dad gone Tim wouldn't have to worry about reprisals. Maybe getting drunk would allow him to clear up those years of holding his tongue.

"I really thought designing that car was going to snap him out of his shit fuck mood. He never let me in on one part of it. Well fuck! I'm part of Cassidy Ford too. I feel like he walked all over me on that project. That project. SHIT! When I found out he'd been beating you if that fucking thing was dirty," Tim said stuttering. "I told hhhimm if if he did it again I'd take a fucking 2x4 to his fucking head!" Tim was on his way to getting very plastered and things he'd held in for years were rushing to the surface.

Shawn wrapped his arms around his uncle's shoulders squeezing him almost tight enough to cut off his wind. He was taller and about forty pounds heavier than his uncle and it was all solid muscle. He knew Tim was letting go of things he'd had bottled up for years and now was a good time he guessed.

He wasn't there when Tim confronted his father about spanking him, and he didn't know until this day, the of Sebring's funeral why his father had quit beating on him. He knew it must have taken a lot for his uncle to confront his father that way, now he was surprised the business stayed together as well as it had after Tim pulled it off. Shawn had seen his father fire people just for disagreeing with him. Sebring was a man you didn't want to cross.

They started another case of beer clearing up some more of the fog they'd been through the last thirty years. Somewhere in the middle of that case Tim asked Shawn why he couldn't take care of his own damn empties, so Shawn began smashing his empties against the wall. And before Tim left him that night he sold him the car.

"That car's for sale," he said, tossing his last empty bottle against the wall and flinging his suit coat over his left shoulder. Shawn just looked at'im, he wondered just how many thousands of dollars he'd have to dig up to take possession of that one of a kind vehicle. He knew Hugh Heffner, the creator of Playboy Magazine, at one time had offered his father fifty thousand dollars for the car, and after getting a fat "NO" Heff Said, when you're ready to sell it call me with a price. "It's yours for a buck if you want it!" Tim offered loudly. Shawn's eyes widened and his jaw dropped to the ground. He couldn't believe what he'd heard. Don't worry; it's not the booze talking. I mean it. It's yours if you want it."

Now Shawn knew just how his uncle would get back at his father, the Partner he'd hassled with for so many years. The Partner that screwed him over so many times, oh, the money part had always been divided up fair enough, Tim had never argued with that side of the business. It was everything else. Seabring had made many deals with people and companies around Detroit and neighboring cities, deals that before being completed should have been discussed with both Partners'. But Seabring seamed to think Tim's part of the Partnership was to follow his orders and share the profits. Which really wasn't all that bad of a deal. But Tim wanted to be a "hands on" Partner and that meant in on everything. But Seabring never let him in on everything, and it really became worse after Shawn was born, but Tim allowed Seabring to get away with it and he was pissed at himself for doing that, because it got way out of hand and it was really his own fault.

Shawn knew his uncle was aware of the stock portfolio he'd acquired, not right to the dollar but his uncle knew fifty thousand wouldn't even put a dent in it. To allow the son he'd kicked out his home to purchase his most prized possession for one dollar? That would be ludicrous. And now he knew just how his uncle would get back at his father.

His Uncle Tim knew he would drive the car and every body that ever knew Seabring Cassidy would find out. The son of Seabring Cassidy driving the car that had been glorified and displayed up on that turntable for almost thirty years; They would all flip. And Seabring would too. He'd probably roll over, and over in his grave. Your damn right he'd drive the car, he wouldn't leave it up on that damn turntable so people could gawk at it. He'd put it up during the winter, but during the rest of the year he'd drive the hell out of it, and that would make his father turn over, and over, and over, and… He smiled like he'd never smiled before thinking about all that dust coming up from the ground at the cemetery.

"Thanks Uncle Tim," he whispered as Tim hugged him good-by.

Seabring had most of his assets tied up in Cassidy Ford, which automatically went to Tim in the event of his death. That would make his uncle a very wealthy millionaire; the only thing Shawn inherited was the house, which he sold to the first bidder for sixty thousand dollars, and it was worth much more than that.

Shawn was startled from his dreams Tuesday morning by the ringing of the telephone; he slapped his alarm clock when the nuisance hit his ears, but he saw 6:38 staring at him and it was set for 7:00. Then he realized it was the phone and not the clock.

"Yeah," he answered half asleep.

"Good morning sleepy head."

Hearing Shelly's voice brought every fiber of his body to attention.

"Hi," he quickly replied, trying to hide his excitement.

"You sound tired; would you rather I let you go back to sleep and call back later?"

"NO! No, I was just getting up, I'm on my second snooze anyway," he said lying while fluffing his pillows and settling in for what he hoped would be a lengthy chat.

"I don't have long I just wanted to say HI and let you know I'm definitely going to be here for ten days though. This thing drags along but it's really very interesting; there are four U.S. Senators here and about a dozen judges that are supposed to speak at these lectures. I want to hear them all, I'm so excited. It's free so I might as well stay and hear them all."

He wanted to say I miss the hell out of you and can't wait to see you, the hell with all those pompous ass holes. But he was afraid to. He reached up shutting off the alarm knowing if it went off she'd know he was lying about being awake already. Any more he didn't know what to say, or do, to keep from pushing her away. To him she was already smarter and more professional than any of them put together. There wasn't a thing they could teach or tell her that would make or break her career.

This call was shocking to him though, it wasn't very often she'd call him, not like when their relationship was first starting. Back then she'd call him after a date and they'd talk for hours. She must have told him her career plans a thousand times and each time he'd listen as if it was the first time he'd heard'em. Now his thoughts quickly searched for the best way to keep her talking.

"Hey, I've got a real screwy case I'd like to pass through your brain as soon as you've got time," he burst with enthusiasm. He was hoping she'd read his excitement as being for the case and not his real love sick motive.

"What is it? C'mon tell me." The excitement in her voice was what he wanted to hear, so he quickly continued.

"I've got a lot I need to run by you, are you sure you've got time?" he asked, listening to her soft breathing and wishing she was lying right next to him.

"Give me a quick file," she requested, still speaking in her soft cheerful tone.

"Mystery client, willing to pay in advance, I'm sure she's a girlfriend of the guy she wants me to prove innocent of murder."

"Is he in prison?"

"No, he's dead."

There was a long pause from her end of the line and he could hear someone in the background urging her to hang up and come on. Shut the hell up, Shawn shot in his mind, he was trying his best to be mysterious and he didn't need anyone distracting her. She'd said a quick file. He wanted to peak her interest and by the silence from her end of the line, he was sure he had.

"Honey?" he questioned. He wished he could see the faces she was making, he knew when she put herself through a serious thought process she'd twist her pretty face into many different shapes as if her thinking caused it.

"Why...How...?" came from her end of the line and he could almost see the faces she was making.

"Confusing isn't it?" Shawn replied, trying to shield his voice from the laughter on his smiling face. His hope was to pull her into his life more and more and this case was pointing in that direction. Shelly liked investigative puzzles and he was trying to make this case as puzzling as he could to her. "This lady believes her friend has been wrongly convicted of murder and she's hoping I can clear his name." He heard the jerk in the background again and wanted to yell at him and tell'im to shut the fuck up.

"How long has he been dead?"

"A little over five months. He was found dead at the scene of the victim's murder."

There was another long pause from her end of the line and the jerk was getting louder.

"Do I know about this murder? I mean, did it happen in Detroit?"

"Yeah, well Warren." Warren was a suburb of Detroit bordering the northwestern edge of Wayne County with most of the city covering the southwestern corner of Macomb County, the county just north of Wayne. But it was all Detroit.

"The ball bat murder?"

"Murders, sweetheart. They never proved it went down the way Warren Cops claimed. Come on, how many times have you had a defendant almost hung by circumstantial evidence?"

"Shawn?"

He could detect a smidgen of doubt creeping into her voice as the defense mechanism for his client kicked in. He thought quickly about more reasons for her to join him in the investigation and now there were others telling her to hurry up. "Come on now, someone could have broken in and murdered them both, take the client's side and work up a defense. I mean if you were here. I could sure use your input. I'd like to be sure I've covered all the angles before I give up. Like, what happened to the clothes he was supposed to be wearing when he beat her to death? There was no mention of finding blood-covered clothing showing he'd changed after killing her."

"But Shawn, he was all cleaned up and she was still a mess, don't you think he'd have called the police or at least an ambulance?"

"What if his head wound made him forget she was even there?" There was another long pause.

"You mean after beating her to death he forgets she's there?"

"I don't know, that's what we need to figure out."

"Well, it is better than chasing after dogs," she said with a laugh. He could hear the people in the background getting worse yelling their cab was there. "I've got to run, hey, does that mean you'll be able to take me out for dinner when I get back?"

"You bet," he said hoping he just locked in a date for as soon as she came home. "You know that invitation's always open." He wondered if she refused his invitations because she thought he couldn't afford it.

"Ok it's a date as soon as I get back, ok?"

He wanted to yell "great," but he controlled his enthusiasm so he wouldn't scare her; after all he'd have to wait better than a week. He thought about telling her he'd drive to Chicago, but he held on to that thought too.

"Ok, I'll see you when you get back. I love you." He heard the click of her phone closing the connection and knew she'd missed hearing his last few words.

"Damn you!" Shelly barked as a man in their group pulled his hand away from the phone. He'd taken it upon himself to end her call.

"The taxi's waiting," he said pulling her towards the cab. As much as she wanted to tell him to fuck off, she held her tongue and hoped Shawn would understand. She wanted to tell him she loved him before hanging up, but that would have to wait. She didn't know why but she was missing him, something was irritating her but she couldn't put her finger on it. She always felt good after talking with Shawn and now she was feeling very warm inside. The jackass that cut off her call didn't know how lucky he was. She sat back and enjoyed the ride to the auditorium where dozens of important judges and various state senators were gathered to feed these young lawyers their polished wisdom.

As he placed the phone back onto its cradle he took a long look at the eight by ten picture of her setting on his nightstand. Some how he had to convince this beautiful creature he'd die without her. He mentally undressed her as he closed his eyes and settled back onto his pillow. His thoughts began throwing precise pictures of her in front of his minds eye and her beautiful naked body seemed to be within his touch and coming closer, her soft breast peaking through the strands of her long dark hair, her tongue slowly wetting those little pink lips of hers as she kissed his face and glided down his chest. There was a time she'd kiss him from top to bottom covering every inch of his six foot three solid bronze body, but that had been a while back, a long while back. Some how her career became the most important thing in her life and he had no idea how he could compete with it. To slip in front of it for just a while. All he knew now was he wanted and needed her, and he'd wait in line forever if need be. It was time for a cold shower.

He liked it when she said, "Give me a quick file." She had a system in her mind where, if she were really interested, she'd create a mental file and never lose it. Her thoughts would be continually putting information into that file as if there were a separate brain working on it with an investigator. She was amazing that way.

As he showered he thought about when he first met her. She impressed the hell out of him in college the way she'd recite case law almost word for word. They'd be in study group and she'd pull facts from her mind files time and time again and they'd always be right. Other students would challenge her on the information but he never did. One day over coffee he did ask how she kept so much information separated and she told him about how she created a mental filing system on everything she wanted to remember and how she keyed the information in her mind. She had total recall of everything she filed in this manner. If she didn't file it she might forget it, and if she didn't file it, it usually meant she didn't care. It wasn't worth remembering she'd say.

By their last year in college when in study group, if she said she was looking at the file and there was nothing in her hand, every one shut up and listened, there was no more challenges.

After passing the Bar they both secured employment with the city of Detroit's Public Defenders Office. Their relationship continued hot and steamy until he quit his job in 82, then it slowly dwindled to dating once in a while. She claimed she wanted her career well anchored before settling down. But now he just couldn't establish weather it would be him she'd be settling down with, once she reached that goal.

At times during the last couple of years when he had nothing to do he'd disguise himself and sit in the back of the courtroom just to watch her work. He always made sure he kept his distance so she couldn't look him in the eyes; that would be a dead give away. He didn't want her to know he was there. There was no mistaking who was hiding behind the deep blue eyes he had, she'd know it was him the second she locked eyes with him. Lately it seemed to be the only way he could get to see her on his terms, she just couldn't find the time for a date. She was a workaholic.

Many times he sat watching in awe as she conducted her defense for a client, often telling himself she was much better then he was. Maybe he was somewhat biased. Today her whole attitude surprised him he thought as he showered and dressed. Her call ignited a fire inside him which after his shower settled down leaving a burst of energy which he expelled as he took the time to vacuum and wash his dirty dishes, pick up his dirty clothes, and start a load of wash before going to the office.

His office was located in the front of a beautiful Two Story Brownstone he'd purchased in 1982 with the funds acquired from the sale of his father's house. This house was located on the east side of Detroit in the suburb of Grosse Pointe Farms. The outside was beautiful, the inside needed to be gutted and completely remodeled.

"I can't believe you're moving back to the ritzy neighborhood" his friend Tony had said laughing when

Shawn told him about his plans, but he knew Shawn had made a very good investment.

"It's the cat's ass" Shawn said. I'll have my home and office at the same place; I can go to the office in my skivvies if I want to. They both laughed at that, while Shawn continued telling him the rest of his plans for the remodeling. It took him a few months but the house was completed by New Years Eve and he began business from his new office on January 2nd 1983.

So now he sat at his desk contemplating his moves for the day. He needed to call and have his sign repaired, at least the lights had lasted a couple of years. There were no new phone calls waiting on his answering machine to take him in another direction, no new cases to call on. If he wanted to work on something today it would have to be the Beth Foust murder. He wanted to look the house over again and possibly talk to whomever the person was living there. He was sure he could get some information from the investigating officers at Warren's Third Precinct, the station in charge of that neighborhood. He wasn't sure of whom the chief of that precinct was, but he was sure he knew who would know.

He smiled as Tony's heavy breathing came over the telephone. "Did I interrupt something?" he asked half laughing and hoping he had.

"Yeah, but not what you think," Tony replied. "I was working out, you know I wouldn't answer if I was busy with Correen, Tony interruptus will never happen."

"You wait till that baby gets here, you think you're in charge now? You won't even know who Tony is, it'll be Tony never gets started" Shawn continued still laughing. His wife Correen was in her forth month of pregnancy for their first child and Shawn knew Tony had no idea what he was in for.

"Don't scare me, please tell me you're kidding!" Tony blurted, suddenly going all-serious.

"Sure, I'm kidding," Shawn replied lying to him, he figured it was something better found out after the baby was born. "You might consider having your mother-in-law move in for awhile to prevent "Tony interruptus" he teased.

"You're just full of fun this morning," Tony claimed, thanking Shawn for his input. "Is there anything I can help you with, set you up with a dog or cat to go looking for? Or should I hang up now and continue my workout?"

Shawn knew he was kidding, their many years of friendship were filled with almost daily teasing back and forth.

"Do you know who the Third Precinct chief is over in Warren," Shawn asked getting serious.

"Yeah, funny you should ask, one of your old friends Starkway, he's…"

"Lieutenant Starkway?" Shawn shot back with a wrinkled look and sounding quite shocked.

"It's Captain Starkway now, he was promoted when he took over that position. You need to read more of the newspaper than just the financial section," Tony scolded.

"That's what I have you for. Besides, I haven't talked to Starkway in years. As I remember it, he hates private snouts."

"Shit, he might not even be there," Tony continued. "He's gained so much weight he has trouble getting around. He's been sick a lot, misses quite a lot of work. He used to be on a bowling league with another one of your friends."

Shawn could tell Tony was now having fun at his expense.

"And just who the hell would that be?" Shawn asked but afraid of the answer.

"Judge Forth." Tony knew that name would bring feelings of grief to Shawn's mind, he paused waiting for any comments. Surprisingly there were none so he continued; he figured Shawn was just holding his tongue. "He's put on so much weight he was unable to continue bowling, so Hunter took his place."

There was Hunter again. It amazed him how he could go so long without seeing or hearing about someone, then the assholes pop up everywhere. Something was up.

"Some days Starkway is lucky to make it out of bed. Forth hated his guts anyway, didn't want'im on the team. I think he wished Starkway sick and got his wish."

"How'd you find that out, Forth hating him I mean?"

"His wife told me after the funeral, you'd have known that too if you would have went with me like I asked you to."

"Remember! He was your friend not mine!" Shawn replied sharply.

Tony had many friends in Detroit, and Judge Forth had been one of them. Tony would put up with a lot more CRAP from people than Shawn would, mainly because he didn't have to work with them. Shawn had a habit of saying what he felt, no matter whom he was talking too; many times his honesty demanded no bullshit, and bullshit was what came from the mouths of many of the people in the court system. Judge Forth was one of the people Shawn knew was full of shit and he wasted no time letting him know it.

"Your mouth will get you killed one of these days" Tony told him many times, but it hasn't helped him change his ways.

Tony knew what Shawn was getting at. When the shit hit the fan back in 82, and Judge Thomas Hinkley tried putting the screws to Shawn by pulling his license to practice law, Judge Forth could have helped him, but he wouldn't. District Court Judge Collin Therman came to Shawn's rescue and put a stop to the trumped up charges Hinkley was claiming; but Shawn quit the Public Defenders office anyway. Things quickly died down around the courthouse as the jerks went looking for the next putz to run out of town; but for Shawn the hate lingered, slowly skidding to a parasol of grudges he managed to control. Tony wondered if all the jerks involved in screwing Shawn over had to die before Shawn would let it all go.

Shawn knew Judge Forth very well; thanks to him Shawn had spent many nights in jail for contempt of court. His only consolation at the sound of his name was he'd died from a heart attack a few months back.

"I know," Tony replied with an apologetic tone. "I try my best to make friends and not piss everybody off, and yes I know you saw these bastards in a different light. You know I don't fault you one bit for the way you conduct your business. I'm just glad you had the common sense to learn martial arts, because with that mouth of yours you definitely need to know how to defend yourself," Tony finished with a thundering laugh. "If he's there, find some way to give him a complement, be nice to him. He'll be ok if you just hold your tongue." Tony knew Shawn was guilty of making bad statements with just a look. "And smile when you see him."

"So I can't say he's a dumb stupid cop?"

"Sure, he'll be expecting that from a P.I." Tony replied with more laughter. He knew Shawn could be polite as a priest when he wanted to. "What are you working on anyway?"

Along with Shelly, Tony and Correen were the only people, well plus Uncle Tim, Shawn would tell everything about what was going on in his life, with no worries of his personal information ever being passed around. He would trust these people with his entire life if it were necessary. They were his "reference team," and sometimes his "break my mental block team."

"Do you remember that double homicide on the west side a few months back? Warren cop's determined they killed each other."

"The ball bat murders, yeah I remember."

"Well, I've got a client that believes Forest has been framed. He's the husband."

"The mystery client paying you one G. per day, I guess it's better than chasing after dogs," Tony said laughing. "I do remember reading about that. It all sounded screwy to me," Tony replied, his breathing becoming more pronounced. Shawn knew he'd continued his workout.

"I'm going to come over and spar with you tonight or tomorrow night."

"Sounds good, I need someone that can keep up with me. Let me know, I'll fix dinner."

"Did your cat come back?"

"The damn thing was in the house all the time. Hiding somewhere. I think it was afraid we were going to take it back to the vet."

"Ok," Shawn concluded hanging up the phone. Now he had his morning plan in gear, at least part of it. While he chewed on a pencil he mentally asked his stomach what it would like to digest during the morning hours, then dropping the pencil and jumping to his feet he headed for the restaurant across the street. As he locked his door he had to flip his new mail box cover open a couple times just for grins.

CHAPTER FOUR

Tony began planning his future in Martial Arts shortly after he and Shawn graduated from High School. While Shawn began college, Tony started out as an instructor in karate and other Martial Arts training techniques. And after twelve years of diligent effort and Shawn's financial influence, he too had an impressive financial statement, most of which was hidden away following Shawn's instructions. Though he made most of his money in the field of Martial Arts, Shawn had added a hefty sum to his portfolio by trading his profits in the stock market.

Tony started first as a trainer and within a few short years he managed to open his own academe for Martial Arts Training, and to date he owns seven schools scattered across four different counties, and trails close behind Chuck Norris in winning famous world title events. Millionaire status didn't impress him or Shawn, they both managed to hide it very well and keep it to themselves, to talk with either of them you'd never know what their financial situation was.

Shawn managed both his and Tony's financial accounts and was quite successful at it, once his Uncle Tim showed him how. Tony knew Shawn was making him money in the market, and he left it at that. He didn't understand anything about Wall Street or buying stocks so he left that completely up to Shawn. When Shawn told him he sold stocks they didn't own he couldn't understand that and refused to listen.

"Shorting the market, what the hell is that? Is it legal? He questioned severely. When Shawn assured him it was he remarked, "you do the trading I'll spend the money."

His schools demanded a lot of his time; leaving less and less time for him and Shawn to spend together, so whenever they could get together a long workout would be first on the agenda. Working out with students was satisfactory with Tony; but sparring with Shawn was the best. Over twelve years of working out with him was priceless.

He began training Shawn during their senior year in high school; his five foot eight one hundred and fifty pound frame put Shawn, "The Destroyer" Cassidy, on the matt so many times it made him laugh to think about it. The Destroyer part came from Shawn himself claiming he'd probably hurt Tony if he gave it everything he had.

"I'll hurt you, I'm a hell of a lot bigger than you are if you haven't noticed, I'll destroy you."

He's never let Shawn live that down, but today, he could give Shawn everything he had and Shawn would still be standing asking for more. He liked that.

Shawn walked into the Third Precinct hoping this was one morning Starkway was able to get out of bed. A lady officer met him as she was just returning to her desk. She was a large woman almost six foot tall probably about 180 pounds with very little fat that Shawn could see. He bet with himself that she was in her late thirties and single he added, noting the bare ring finger on her left hand. She looked to be solid as a prizefighter he thought as he gave her a quick hard look. I'll bet there's no fat on that body, he told himself, nothing noticeable anyway.

Placing her coffee on a makeshift coaster she gave him a smile.

"What can I do for you sir?" she asked, reaching for a claim sheet assuming he was there to file some sort of request for their assistance.

"Is Captain Starkway available", he asked returning her smile.

"Can I tell'im who's asking?" her smile reflecting in her cheerful voice.

"He knows me," Shawn continued, extending his hand to her hoping for a nice handshake. "My name's Shawn Cassidy I'm a PI here in Detroit."

The cheerful look on her face immediately changed to a wrinkled frown, "police officer in charge". Shawn sensed she was about to snap back the hand she had extended for him to shake as his words bombarded her ears. It was a reaction he'd seen many times. Quickly before she could withdraw her hand he snatched it up into his palm and induced a mild but locking squeeze which she returned showing no resistance. He was a bit surprised at the strength she had but he thought she probably knew when she was licked and fought back showing a quick wit. He was right, when he let go of her hand she quickly returned it to her side wiping it on her pants as her eyes scanned the hallway hoping no other officer caught her shaking the hand of a PI.

"It's not catching" Shawn added, his smile growing bigger as he slowly returned his hand to his side. I don't think I'd ever want to be frisked by those hands, he told himself.

"The Captain is following up on an important homicide," she lied, the smile now missing from both her face and her voice. "He won't be available for some time", she said, shifting her eyes back to her desk and fumbling with other paper work. It was certain she disliked private investigators, probably because of things she'd heard. She wasn't old enough to harbor bad feelings through experience, and Shawn hated that. She instantly showed him her stupidity; disliking him without knowing him, he hated people like that.

She ignored him while she fiddled with items on her desk and sipped her coffee. He knew she was hoping he'd leave, but he stood patiently waiting to see if she'd get tired of him standing there and talk to him anyway. While he stood there he thought to himself, yeah the fat ass couldn't even get out of bed this morning. He was going to ask to see the next in charge when down the hall a door opened and a very large man walked out into the hallway and continued down towards the coffee stand at the end of the hall.

She remembered Shawn had said Starkway knew him, so she knew Shawn was about to say something about him being there and what the hell was she trying to prove. As she looked down the hall she felt Shawn's questioning look even without seeing his face. She quickly left her desk hoping Shawn wouldn't follow, then she could warn her captain there was a PI in the outer office, he could go back to his office or slip out the back. As she whispered to him he turned in Shawn's direction.

"God-damn fucking PI's" Shawn heard him say.

While Shawn waited to see what would happen next, he allowed his eyes to scan the walls around the outer office. There were various plaques showing his years of loyal service to different police agencies, and a few bowling trophies collecting dust along with them. Other shelves contained pictures of various Captains from the past. But one picture on the top shelf caught his eye and prepared him for his beginning statement to Starkway, if he chose to meet with him. It was one of the bowling team accepting an award for winning first place some five years back. Judge Forth stood with his arm around Starkway's shoulders. This picture made it look like they were very close friends. With the amount of dust on the photograph Shawn figured Starkway had probably forgotten all about it. He needed to be sure of the date so he could be close but not right on, being right on would tell Starkway he'd seen the picture. Squinting through the dust he could see the numbers 1981 on the base of the plaque.

Suddenly Shawn heard heavy footsteps coming down the hall and he knew they weren't the lady officer's, he walked towards the exit door as if he was headed out but Starkway called to him.

"Cassidy?" Shawn quickly turned away from the exit and looked towards the voice, the man was huge. Even though he stood about six foot tall the weight he was carrying had to be at least four hundred pounds or more. Every step made him breath heavy and he was covered in sweat, his white shirt was almost soaked. Shawn reached out offering his hand and for a split second he wondered if Starkway would even take it? But before his thought was finished Starkway reached out snatching his hand from the air.

"Cassidy what the hell brings you into my neck of the woods?" Shawn allowed him to grasp his hand and squeeze it like he was wrenching the head off from a snake, it hurt a little, but letting him take control of the handshake would put him in control of the conversation and that's what Shawn wanted him to think. His theory was, you allow your opponent to feel superior to you and he'll be totally off guard. When a man trying to show his strength shakes a wimpy hand, he immediately thinks this guy's a pussy.

"Captain," Shawn blurted, quickly giving him the respect Tony advised. "Judge Forth told me you were the force behind the team, took'em to glory in 80, was it?" Shawn asked, pouring on the charm.

Accepting Shawn's hand Starkway followed full shot right into his conversation as he tried to squeeze the blood from the hand he was gripping.

"It was 81 and I was the only one rolled a perfect game," he boasted, as his mind quickly sprang to bowling and his face lit up like a candle. He momentarily forgot he was talking to a PI. Walking over to the shelves Shawn had been searching moments earlier he grunted with a little difficulty and reached up taking the photo of that winning night into his hand. Wiping the dust off with his sweaty shirtsleeve he then held it up so he and Shawn could admire it.

"That was a great night, I had two games of 296 and one perfect-game, 300." He paused letting his mind go back to that spectacular evening. "Yes sir that was one hell of a night," he said, looking very proud.

"Judge Forth wished he could bowl as well as you sir," Shawn went on, charging Starkway's ego with as much charm as he dared. "He really hated it when you had to step down."

The look on the captain's face slowly changed to one of sadness, looking over his glasses he replied in a very low tone, "he's not with us any more, did you know."

"Yes, I know, I attended his funeral," Shawn said quietly, sadly lying through his teeth. He immediately realized he should have asked Tony if Starkway had been there, but now it was too late.

"I wasn't able to make it," Starkway continued, "I was quite sick at the time, I've been afflicted with diabetes you know".

"OH, I'm sorry, I didn't know," Shawn said apologizing, now he was really feeling guilty. Another fact I could have used before coming here he thought to himself.

"I keep it in check with insulin but if I could get my weight down and under control it would sure help."

"There's just too many good restaurants around Detroit" Shawn said, putting the blame for his obesity anywhere but on him.

"Well, you didn't come here to discuss my bowling attributes" he said, placing the photograph back on the shelf. "What can I do for you Shawn?"

Shawn was quite surprised. Starkway's tone was mild, almost sounding apologetic. Maybe because he just squeezed all the blood from my hand Shawn wondered.

"Oh just a silly thing I'd rather not even bother you with it," Shawn continued, hoping the chief would grab the chance to help him anyway, and it did.

"Hey," he said taking Shawn along to his office, "A friend of the judge is a friend of mine." Before pulling his door shut behind them he turned to the female officer at the front desk.

"Pam, would you bring us some coffee please, oh, and would you dust off those shelves up there when you get a chance." Her smile had returned, telling Shawn she was directly connected to her boss' influences.

The next hour of conversation got him copies of the investigation, plus photos of the crime scene, and before he left he was given the key to the front door of 1489 Beckwith Street.

"There's no one living there now but the place is being kept up by the people they hired before their deaths. He's supposed to have family somewhere here in Michigan, haven't found any yet but we're still looking. We've been making sure the bills get paid though, there's plenty of money left in the estate and we didn't want the place getting run down and the heir suing the city. I don't think you'll find anything that will change the outcome of the investigation though, I'm sure everything happened there just the way its been reported. But you're welcome to look maybe you'll find a link to the missing heir.

"Is there a mortgage on the home?"

"NO, Mr. Foust purchased everything with cash and it was paid off the year it was built. Beth had quite a lot of money; she had a couple of exercise joints down in the big city. The place is too nice to let it get run down, and there's plenty of money to allow the maintenance so we keep it going. There have been plenty of interested people wanting to buy the place."

"How much do you think the place is worth?" Shawn asked him after taking his last sip of coffee.

"I don't know I've never seen it."

"You're kidding me, not even a picture?"

"Those crappy ones in the paper? Nothing I could really put a price on."

"Well it's a mansion, I'd say three and a half to four hundred thousand, at least. Maybe more if you don't mind someone having been murdered in it."

"I'll have to swing by sometime," Starkway assured him.

When Shawn finally left the Third Precinct he had a totally different picture of Jason Starkway. He wondered if it was Tony's suggestion or the reference he made about Judge Forth that put Starkway in his hip pocket? Well, it didn't really matter, he just knew he had to treat Jason more like a friend and see if things progressed in that direction. There was a huge smile on his face now, he hadn't taken any time in the past to get to know the man, now he felt he wasn't quite the bastard everyone thought he was, including himself.

He was on his way back to Beckwith Street wondering as he drove along if the person that came out of the house the night before would be there. Starkway had said the house was empty, well he was wrong about that but Shawn hadn't told him so. Probably one of the maintenance people taking advantage of the house being empty and parking their ass in it, he thought as he pulled into the drive.

He fantasized about coming home to this place as he parked and removed himself from his car. He gave the grounds another once over before approaching the front door; the property was also very impressive in the daylight. He didn't bother ringing the bell he had the key and any cop coming to answer a complaint would have to be from the Third Precinct. There wasn't any alarm to worry about, but if there were a problem and someone called the police they'd be on his side if Pam were on her toes. Maybe she'd look at him different now, seeing how Starkway treated him so well.

He knew every officer on the Sheriffs Department, some of them were friends with him, mainly because a lot of them new Tony. If one of them showed up that'd be ok. He filled his mind with these thoughts wondering who'd show up first if he had to use force, as he filled his right hand with the nine mil Parked where his 357 usually called home.

He could hear Starkway asking him why the hell he hadn't asked for backup, knowing the house could possibly have unwanted visitors. He hoped if someone were there they'd be too damned scared of being shot and just freeze. He quickly remembered two years earlier when he'd broken a mans arm stopping him from running out the door of a home he was visiting, someone screamed stop him, he did, the man turned out to be the home owner. His wife just wanted her car keys back before he left, but her shrieking made it sound like he was a thief running out the door after stealing her jewelry. Well, it wasn't a bad break. There was a fine line between using Martial Arts on a person or just scaring the hell out of them. If someone wanted to fight with him he had no problem dropping the gun and obliging him but sometimes physical attention caused more harm than good.

He removed his shoes and made his way slowly through the house carrying the weapon in his right hand down by his side, finally returning it to its cradle after clearing the first floor. He was sure there was nobody in the house so he continued amazing himself with all the beautiful things he was seeing. He was more amazed by the inside of the house than the out side, and that was beyond beautiful.

Topping the winding staircase he listened for any possible movement on the top floor, there was none. On the second floor there were four large bedrooms each with complete bath and walk in closet, and every one of these rooms were beautiful. The walk in linen closet was loaded with expensive sheets, blankets, and bedspreads, but nothing looked like it had been touched in a long time, there was dust along the fronts of all the shelves.

"This man went all out, and for what?" Shawn questioned, while he continued on checking every room. Before going down into the basement he went out to the attached two-car garage. Here he became ecstatic, there was a red and white 1985 Mustang convertible with white leather upholstery and he immediately knew it had to be Beth's, it had an automatic transmission. The other car was a 1969 metallic blue Pontiac firebird. This car was also a convertible and it had a white top with white interior, but it had four on the floor with the name Forest written all over it. Shawn became instantly jealous, he wanted to find the keys and spend the rest of the day driving them all over Detroit. And somewhere there was an heir that would inherit the both of them he pouted. He returned to the house so he could check out the basement and what he found there continued the jealous streak that suddenly tugged at his insides. He found a large room with a pool table and several fancy pinball machines along with a fully stocked bar. There was more pop in the bar fridge than anything else and while he pouted some more he automatically counted everything in it locking the numbers into his subconscious.

"Beth must have drunk a lot of pop." He said aloud. Then there it was. He heard a door lock click, and the soft mild sound of a door being opened. Was that a key, he mumbled to himself as he quickly ran to the stairs taking them three at a time and was at the door he thought he heard open within seconds. No one was there. He opened the door and charged outside, going around the east side of the house first, he was sure he'd see somebody leaving the yard going towards the back garage, but there was no one out there. He made a complete circle around the house, and then returned back inside.

"Do you really like this silly game your playing?" he yelled out loud. He realized whomever it was they came into the house and seeing the garage and basement doors open they didn't leave, they just disappeared, but to where? There was no way any one could disappear that quickly. Then he realized his right foot was damp from stepping into something wet outside the door and noticed a damp footprint on the floor going towards the end of the hallway. It wasn't his footprint. He looked out the window of the door and noticed a leaking spigot leaving a wet area just at the right side of the door when entering, whomever came in the door also stepped into the wet spot. The person knew he was there, they had removed their shoes just as he had to keep down the noise, but he or she removed them outside the door and was now in the same fix he was in, a freaking wet right sock. Shawn smiled looking at the wet footprints going from the door to the corner. They weren't complete prints, just the front like the person walked on their tiptoes right to the corner of the hall, and there were no prints coming back from that corner.

This person must have walked right through the wall he thought. He began tapping lightly on the wall along the hallway adjacent to the side door; it all seemed solid until he came to the last two foot along the wall at the corner. He tapped on the other side wall going in the opposite direction, the first two foot sounded just as hollow as the last two. "You've got to be kidding me," he said looking at the corner his smile getting bigger all the time. "My mystery client is hiding right behind this fucking wall, it's his Goddamn girlfriend. Suddenly he heard the front door open and close and that shot his theory about her being behind the wall. "Somebody wants me to think this place is haunted," he said, feeling around the trim and pushing hear and there against the wall. He was intruding where someone didn't want him and he wasn't about to stop.

The front door activity was intended to pull him away from what he was searching for; it hadn't worked. Some how the corner of this wall opens up, Shawn told himself. Still feeling around every inch of door trim and flooring he was sure there was a button there somewhere to release a secret panel. He was looking for something, a lever a button, something that would trigger the corner wall to open. That part of the wall definitely sounded different for some reason and there was trim in both corners. Somehow the end of that hallway had to pull away and open an entrance to somewhere.

After a good few minutes of searching the hallway, he returned to the basement and began searching along below the hallway wall. From there he determined if there was a secret area it could only be about three foot wide. About the size of a stairway he concluded. "So how in the hell do I get in there?"

He kept looking and looking, along the trim, above doors, everywhere, then he decided to get a pop from the fridge and take a seat. He could think better sitting down. He helped himself to a bottle of pop then he sat down and tried enjoying it. He wondered if he sat there long enough his ghost might step out from where it was hiding. And as he enjoyed his drink he visually searched every inch of every wall, every piece of trim, and every nook and cranny. Then he noticed the wall behind one of the pinball machines had an area covered with smudges, fingerprints. Found it he mumbled. He reached behind the machine running his fingers along the wall and over the trim. He pulled on the trim and tried to twist it out of place but it wasn't moving. Then he pushed against it hard and a four inch long piece at the base of the chair rail popped out about an inch and pivoted to the right exposing a small button behind it, and it sprang back into place when he let it go. Pushing hard on it again it opened and he quickly pushed on the hidden button beneath it. Suddenly a two and a half foot panel along a smooth wall opened exposing a narrow staircase and the trim piece snapped back into place. The staircase was properly lit and when he looked inside there were lights showing the way right up to the top floor.

"Well will you look at that, I'll be damned, no matter where the girlfriend was she could slip past Beth and get the hell out of the house without getting caught, that scoundrel." He entered the stairway and the door automatically closed behind him. But the light stayed on showing him the way. He stopped at the first floor tripping a viewable door handle that allowed the corner to pull away, but only a fraction of an inch. Probably so the safety of leaving could be checked first, he thought as he pulled it completely open and stepped into the hallway. Leaving it open he continued on up to the second floor where he found another door like the one on the first landing and a similar handle, opening it he found himself in the closet of one of the bedrooms.

He shut the door from the room side, than tried to re-enter. After about five minutes hunting for the bedroom release button, he gave up. "This guy was amazing," he said shaking his head. He returned to the first floor expecting to find that door still open, only to find it shut and completely hidden again. "OH YES, this guy was very smart. How the hell did he get himself killed?" Shawn wondered while he continued looking for the door release. A half hour later he was still looking for the secret release somewhere along the hallway, and finding nothing. There was no smudged wall to lead the way but he knew the trick was there somewhere, but where.

There was an eight-unit apartment house one block to the west of the Foust Estate, which was where Helen Carter lived. His client suggested he speak with her, why, he didn't know. It was 11:00 a.m. and being a bit confused about what he'd found at the house he thought maybe someone there could shed some light on his puzzle.

Helen lived in apartment five which was on the second floor and as Shawn made his way up the stairs a ladies voice from the first floor stopped him at the second floor landing.

"Are you looking for Helen?" she yelled.

"Sure am, how'd you guess?" Shawn asked as he continued up the next flight of stairs.

"Because she's the only one living up there, but she's not home," the lady continued in the same disgusting loud tone.

Shawn figured the lady probably had the biggest nose in the place and would be worth talking to. Besides, he had to walk back past her to leave.

Before starting back down the stairs he noticed a pile of newspapers in front of unit number five and determined this lady was probably correct, no one was home. When he returned to the first floor the big nosed lady was leaning against the doorjamb of apartment one, but she had a very small nose.

She looked to be in her mid twenties, about five foot seven, maybe a hundred and thirty lbs. She had long blond hair down to her waist and she was slowly pulling a brush through it over and over. She was dressed in a very thin, very loose bathrobe and Shawn found himself glad she stuck her nose into his business. The word cute didn't do her any justice. As he walked up to her a little black kitten scampered out from her apartment door and she quickly bent down to pick it up. When she did Shawn could see everything she was covering with the robe she had on, right down to the left over beads of water still lingering from the shower she'd came from. The loose fitting robe hid nothing from where he was standing.

Shelly, you've got to get your fanny home, he said to himself as he softly bit his tongue. "Who says black cats are bad luck?" he mumbled reaching out and petting the cat's head as she stood back up.

"Mine's not bad luck," she replied, in a now soft and sexy voice. He wondered if this was really the same nosey lady that was yelling at him before? This lady had a cute blank look on her face and no way could that irritating loud voice belong to her. From the look on her face he could tell she was still trying to figure out what he was referring to about the cat. Evidently her mother had never told her to be careful bending over in front of men. Especially tall men.

Shawn was tall and very handsome, everything she liked in a man; she told herself. She was hoping he'd continue petting her kitten and talk awhile. The loose fitting robe never crossed her mind, or had it?

"Do you need to talk with Helen?"

"I was hoping she could tell me something about Forest Foust."

"What do you want to know?"

"Anything, I'd like to know what he was like, how he acted. Why he built such an elaborate home in this neighborhood?"

"Well, if you plan on getting any answers from her you'll be waiting a long time, she's up north for the summer. And what's wrong with our neighborhood?" she asked twisting her pretty face back into that frown.

"Probably nothing, but this isn't the place for a half million dollar home; this neighborhood doesn't support a house valued that high. Usually when someone builds a house they expect it to appreciate along with the neighborhood." He wondered if anything he was saying made sense to her. "I could understand if he'd bought more land around here and built more large homes, give a face lift to the whole area. Ninety percent of the homes around here can be purchased for less than fifty thousand."

"He didn't spend that much to build that house, I mean, he didn't spend any half million dollars building it. Who told you he did that?" She asked, giving him a quizzical look.

"Honey, I know real estate. That house is worth at least a half mill."

She laughed at him as though she wanted to say you're full of shit; but she was too polite to come right out and say so.

"He doesn't have over a hundred thousand into that place," she said laughing and lightly shaking her head.

"And how the hell do you know that?" Shawn was beginning to think maybe she knew Forest pretty well.

"Do you know, there wasn't one pay check written for the labor on that house, all of his friends pitched in and built it for him."

"Well I wish I had friends like that." Shawn replied, "But it doesn't matter what you pay to build something. It's based on an appraisal and what someone would be willing to pay for it. And there are plenty of doctors and lawyers who'd be willing to give a half million for it, believe me."

"It is?" she asked, her frown showing up with total disbelief.

"Yes." Shawn said taking his turn to laugh.

"I'm sorry, I thought you couldn't sell a house for much more than you put into it."

Shawn knew now she was a true blond. If Shelly weren't in his life he'd sure like to try teaching this little lady a thing or two for a while, he thought. Some women just don't need any brains at all to be exciting, he told himself, and she was one of them type of ladies. It could be a lot of fun teaching her things.

"Have you ever been in the house?" he asked, turning his laughter off and becoming serious again. The second she said she was sorry, he knew continued laughter could hurt her feelings and that wasn't his intent.

"I was in it shortly after it was built, but Beth was such a bitch, I just stayed away from there." She turned and pushed the cat back into the apartment, pulling the door shut.

"Who the fuck's out there?" some man yelled after she shut the door, "hurry up and get your ass back in here," he demanded.

"Why don't you come back later, we can talk some more. I can tell you a lot about those two." She replied with a beginning look of fear in her pretty green eyes, and then she pulled the robe extra tight around her body.

"Your boy friend?" Shawn asked, noticing a bare ring finger on her left hand.

"He's not my boy friend, he just thinks he is." She said waving a quick good-by. If the black pickup is gone it's safe to stop," she whispered.

"Wait" Shawn asked quickly. "I didn't get your name, will you be ok, He won't hurt you will he?"

"Sherin" she said with a whisper, but she didn't answer his other question, she just quickly re-entered the apartment. As she closed the door Shawn's eyes momentarily locked with the man's eyes doing all the yelling. He looked to be in his late twenties; about five foot ten, 180 lbs. He had a shaved head, and wore a long thick silver chain around his neck. He was very muscular looking; and for a split second he thought the man was attempting to tell him something with that look of his, and then the door clicked shut. He reminded Shawn of one of the men he ran into at a bar a few years back when he and Tony rescued a runaway teen.

Shawn listened a while after the door was closed while the man bitched up a storm doing every thing but hitting her. When things calmed down and he was sure they were smoothing out ruffled feathers he figured she'd be all right, so he left and went back to his office. He didn't feel right about leaving her there with the nut case, but she let him into her life and maybe he was just one of those loud mouth jealous types.

When he returned to the office there was another cream-colored envelope waiting for him in his new mailbox, he put the rest of the mail on his desk and opened his client's letter first. But there was no letter this time, just ten more one hundred dollar bills wrapped up in two pieces of that same expensive paper. He tucked it into his secret drawer along with the rest and scooped up the New York Times News Paper. After about ten minutes of being nose deep in the front section and President Reagan's views about the worlds terrorists he turned to the financial section. Jotting down a few stocks he made a call to his broker and purchased some stocks to cover others he'd sold short, and sold a few others short. "The best way to use the market," he said talking to the air. He sat awhile playing with figures on a note pad. Oh I love the stock market he said wadding up the piece of paper and tossing it into a waste basket about ten foot away.

He spent the next hour or so going over the material Starkway had given him covering the investigation. He cringed again when he looked at the pictures of Beth lying on the floor severely beaten. Then there was a picture of Forest laying on a day bed, he was dressed in clean clothes and it looked like he was sleeping, the only thing weird about the picture was the huge bump on the side of his head. He couldn't believe it. It looked like Forest had stepped into the path of one of Babe Ruth's pile driving home run swings. Shawn couldn't imagine ever doing that to another human being. And especially the counter attack such as this to a lady you've made love to.

"I guess it takes all kinds." He said talking again to that invisible member of his office staff. He began to make coffee, than changed his mind. Picking up his phone he called the restaurant across the street and ordered a sandwich with a large hot chocolate. Minutes later Angela walked through his office door delivering his lunch.

"Ding Ding; dinner's here she said sitting it on his desk. Suddenly she made a disgusting noise, her eyes were glued to the photographs on his desk he'd been looking at, her face twisted like he'd never seen.

"EEEEOOOOO WHO'S THAT?"

Shawn quickly covered the pictures with the newspaper he'd been reading.

"You don't want to look at those," he said handing her a ten-dollar bill to cover his lunch.

"Who is that?" she asked again as she slid the paper back off the pictures and took another look.

"That's the late Mrs. Foust," he said, allowing her to look through the few pictures lying there.

As she looked from one to another her face made various changes, all of which revealed horror from what she was seeing.

"I told you not to look," he said taking a bite of his sandwich and chasing it with drink of hot chocolate.

"How can you eat after seeing these?" she asked making another horrible face he'd never seen on her before.

"I guess I'm used to it. I'm also hungry," he said going through the same biting process again and showing his delight devouring the food she'd brought.

"That's Beth Foust?" she asked sliding the newspaper back over the pictures. I've seen her looking a lot better.

Settling back into his large leather chair he brushed a napkin across his lips.

"Did you know her?" he asked, relaxing.

"She taught aerobics. I took a few classes from her a couple years back, but I hadn't seen her since. We always joked about her husband being with the Mafia."

"We?"

"Us girls."

"What made you bring up the Mafia?"

"There was a blond bimbo in one of the classes, she said he'd built this huge house down from her, and he didn't even work."

"Was her name Sherin?"

"YEAH, how'd you know?"

She tucked the ten down the top of her blouse and took a seat in front of his desk, "an old girl friend?" she questioned, her eyes widening with a wrinkled forehead.

"NO, I just met her today for the first time, and she does live down from that house. She might have been right about the Mafia. Why'd you call her a Bimbo?"

"She's a Blond Airhead," Angela replied as if she had cornered the market on looks and brains.

"Did you ever try to get to know her?" The look she shot at him immediately told him no. As if she was too good to try being friends. He was sure it was because Sherin presented competition. Women, he thought to himself.

"I've got to go" she said, giving him that soft sexy smile, "let me know if you want to talk any more," she winked at him over her shoulder as she left his office.

Yeah, he thought, as long as I don't mention Sherin.

"The Mafia?" he questioned taking another bite of his sandwich. It had been a long time since anything to do with the Mafia entered his mind. He was surprised the thought hadn't sprung to his head before this. That would explain the house being built with free labor; probably most of the materials were free too. Stolen no doubt. He was curious about the building permit. How much did it cost; did it reflect the proper square footage. Had Forest been given any special deals on the property, or building process? A trip to the county offices was definitely in his immediate future he decided, "as soon as I finish my lunch."

CHAPTER FIVE

Shawn stared at the record somewhat confused at what he'd found; not only had Forest paid full price for all of his permits, he was charged a thousand dollars for a variance. A variance, why, because he was building and using the whole block? Shawn kept questioning everything he was finding in the permit ledger. What the hell would have made his permit cost him another grand, Shawn wondered? That's bullshit he told himself while he searched the records for other construction permits granted during that same time frame. Out of twenty others showing the same value and more, there was not one variance paid. "How quaint," he mumbled.

"Sir, did you need something?" Shawn had waited over two hours for this lady to get back from lunch, an hour lunch that lasted a little over two. He wondered if that was her usual thing? There's probably more money being ripped off in lost hours by these employees than anything else, he told himself allowing his thoughts to bicker. He really didn't want to talk to her.

"Have you worked here long?" He wondered aloud suddenly realizing he'd spoken and was no longer just thinking his disgust.

"I've been here for about fifteen years, been in charge for the last nine," she hotly replied. Is there anything I can help you with?" Her tone immediately pissed him off. He quickly clamped his lips making sure only the words he wanted getting out were getting out. His thoughts screamed and Tony's words charged through his mind again, "pick your words carefully Shawn don't piss people off." Yeah, what's with this two-hour lunch he blurted in his mind; but then he forced himself to hold his tongue as he heard Tony's words echoing "be polite you'll get farther ahead."

"Yeah, a variance. Why would one contractor have to pay it and others not?"

"You all pay it if it's over a certain amount." She stared at him over her horned rim glasses giving him a "get lost" expression, then her face took on a "what are you talking about" look. Not like she didn't know, but sort of a "how the hell did he know" look.

"So you're saying, if one guy pays it; and five straight permits are all in the hundred and fifty thousand dollar range, then all five permits were charged the variance."

"Yes! That's what I just said there's reasons for it, I don't make up the rules I just record them."

"Then where's the record showing it? I found one variance paid out of twenty one permits in the same price range…?" Before he could finish his words she spun the book around on the counter as if to look at it herself, then she quickly slammed it shut.

"Are you done here?" she asked jerking the book away from him.

"I guess I am," he said softly shaking his head, "thank you for your help." He left the office with more questions on his mind than answers, but he was sure he already knew what those answers were going to be. If you had the money to start a large project you were going to fork over a few bucks extra to the county, or somebody in it. She'd said the extra charges had been paid on all the permits; only they were never recorded. More than likely they were finding their way into some ones pocket and the one recorded was the mistake. I suppose if I was building something and wanted my permits as soon as possible I'd pay an extra grand too if that was what it took to get things started he told himself as he left the zoning office.

He remembered there was a huge new McDonalds going up on the corner of Michigan and Zephyr Street and he wondered if the contractor had been charged extra for his permits. When he pulled up to the building sight a tall elderly gentleman wearing a white hard hat was just coming out of the office trailer so he figured this was a good place to start.

"Don't park there," the man ordered hastily, pointing to a parking area across the street he added "All employees park over there."

Shawn was wearing Wrangler jeans with a light blue button up sport shirt; it was too hot to be wearing a jacket. He wondered if nail pounder's dressed like that, or if a new hire had been late and he was being mistaken for him. He quickly introduced himself.

"Hi, I'm Shawn Cassidy and I'm new to this area. I've got a client I just tried to purchase a building permit for and I just got the shock of my life. Like I said I'm kind of new at this," he was trying to show himself being vulnerable and a little stupid to the building trade. "I was asked to pay a grand over and above the permit fee. What the hell's that all about?"

"Did you pay it?"

"Hell no."

"What's the total of your project?"

"Close to a quarter of a million."

"Well you won't get your permit, not without a lot of bullshit," the man replied with a chuckle and a smile. He leaned up against a pickup truck and removed a pack of cigarettes from his shirt pocket offering one to Shawn, which was quickly refused, then he put one in his mouth and lit it.

"Why not?" Shawn shot back sounding like a stupid newbee to the construction business.

"If you want to get your project going, pay'em the grand," he said clicking his lighter shut. "I wish I'd have gotten off that cheap."

"So you had to pay a fee plus the permit?" Shawn asked trying to act more than shocked.

"Look," he said, taking Shawn for a short walk where no one else could hear. "If you want to do business around here pay'em their God damn kick back, tag it on to your client's bill. This building here is costing over a million bucks to build," he said gesturing to the McDonalds building sight. "The five grand they scammed me out of isn't crap! I'd still be waiting for my permits! Shit, I'll build four of these while the dumb shit refusing to grease their palms waits for his fucking permits," he continued as his tone dropped down to a whisper. "Who's the smart one? C'mon you tell me. You can't fight these bastards if you want to work in Detroit. If you fuck with them on this they'll give you your permit in about a month or so, then they'll find fault with every damn thing you do. They'll shut you down and screw with everything you do, and I mean everything. They'll make you wish you'd have paid their damn variance when they asked for it, because you'll end up paying a hell of a lot more before you get your project finished. Look." His eyes went wide and his forehead wrinkled. "Back a few years ago I fought with them, it cost me a lot of time and money in fines. Then I quit fighting, I pay'em what they want and there's no more bullshit." The look he gave Shawn said the rest for him. "Either pay up or go to another county to build. I don't know what's going on anywhere else, but I know I'm getting things done here." Jutting out his hand Shawn took it knowing the conversation was over, they shook and the man quickly walked off towards his building.

Now he was more pissed than when he left the zoning office. This contractor knew what was going on and settled for it, passing the loss on to his clients. And for sure there were many other contractors doing the same thing. He knew there had been county officials scoring kickbacks but this was bigger than free coffee or a free dinner, this was extortion and someone was getting rich from it. If there was one person he could trust to do something about kickbacks being scored, it was Judge Collin Therman. Judge Therman had become his mentor over the years, plus, he'd saved his ass literally more than once. It was the middle of the afternoon and he knew exactly where he'd find the Judge, nowadays he spent most of his waking hours at Harper's playing euchre.

Harper's was a men's club located in down town Detroit about three blocks from the courthouse. It was established in the late fifties by one of Detroit's toughest judges ever, District Court Judge Harland J. Harper. The J. stood for Jeffery, and if he ever heard you say it he'd do his best to hold you in contempt of court, no matter where he was when he heard you say it. Tale had it he'd put a young attorney in jail for two weeks on contempt just for calling him Jeffery. This was back some twenty-five or thirty years ago. Only nobody could come up with the attorney's name. Probably a hoax, rumor or not no one had the guts to call him Jeffery to check it out.

It was said Harland used to take walks through out the day, sometimes he'd recess court just to take the three-block walk to and from the club, he said it fit his agenda perfectly.

No matter what the weather was, pouring rain or snow piled up to your crotch, you could find him walking to the club for dinner and back to the courthouse every day if court was in session. If he recessed court for any reason, you'd see him walk to the club puffing on a cigar and return shortly after. Some said he left to get fresh air and settle his mind; others said he left to get a stiff drink, but he never returned smelling of booze, and he always returned with his mind sharp as a tack. There were times he left mad as hell, but he always returned calm and collected. He claimed the walk did him good, "you should try it," he'd say whenever some one asked him about it.

When the club was first established it was off limits to all police officers, no matter what rank you were. If a judge or the Mayor hadn't invited you in, you'd damn well better stay the hell out. Women weren't allowed in either unless they were judges or attorneys, but back then you very seldom found a lady attorney. The club was a haven, a place where the masters of the court could relax after a long days work. Kick back and bitch about their bad day if they wanted to. Attorneys could talk with judges without making appointments. They could discuss anything they wanted. If someone had a grudge to settle, Judge Harper made sure it was settled.

The governor once asked Harland if he'd take a seat on the Michigan Supreme Court, but Harland refused. He said he was the supreme justice of the city of Detroit and that was good enough for him, and he was. On the Supreme Court he'd have to work with other judges, share the podium so to speak, he wouldn't be in complete charge. In Detroit he was the boss. Even the Mayor asked him for instructions, the Mayer wouldn't admit it but he did.

In the late seventies many of the club rules began to be over looked, Harland was close to dieing from cancer and unable to hold people accountable to his rules. He died in late 1977 and the rules died with him, well most of them anyway. Keeping the name of the club the same was the only memory proving he'd even been there.

Judge Therman was just finishing his dinner when Shawn poked his head through the door of the main dining room, a wave from the Judge told Shawn he was more than welcome to join him at his table.

Judge Therman had retired from the bench some five years prior at the age of seventy; now most every day was spent at the club playing chess, euchre, or his fondest game poker when he could get someone willing to throw away his or her money. If you were playing poker and he was in the game you were certain to loose your shirt, and most every one knew it. But Detroit was a big city and there were always new lawyers for him to fleece, so he was happy.

Collin didn't believe in breaking the law, there was never any money found on his poker table or any poker table at the club, one of the rules installed since day one, and it remained. A very trusting butler and his staff controlled the chips and everyone knew if Jerome or any of his staff were asked to handle the chips the game was for real. All exchanges were recorded in the mind, never on paper. That was one of the rules Harland had created and it stayed.

"Shawn," the judge blurted, proudly taking him into his arms and giving him a big hug along with the firm handshake, it shocked the hell out of Shawn. "Sit down son let me buy you some dinner."

"No thank you Sir. I've had my lunch." Shawn was a bit shocked at the way he'd been greeted especially in the middle of this huge dining room with so many important people around it embarrassed him a little.

"I've asked you time and again to call me Collin," the judge said scolding Shawn for calling him Sir.

"It's just"…his eyes searched the other tables before finishing his words. He noticed other judges and a couple of

U.S. Senators sitting in this huge dining room all staring in his direction. Probably wondering who the hell was he to be getting such a greeting from such an important man such as Collin Therman.

"OH PISS ON THESE GUYS!" Collin ordered loudly waving his arms towards them. "You're like a son to me," he said loud enough for all to hear. I don't give a shit what any of these ass holes think," he continued. Heads quickly jerked back to their own plates and those that hadn't been looking were now suddenly staring at them wondering why the judge had raised his voice in disgust.

Shawn wanted to slide under the table, he'd never heard words like these come from the Judge's mouth, it made him feel good but it also embarrassed the hell out of him. He could feel his face getting warm and he knew he was blushing, before this he would have sworn nothing could make him blush.

Collin had helped him out of a few scrapes in the past; it was no secret. What Shawn didn't know was the judge bragged about him almost all the time to some people as if he was his son. He wondered if the judge was feeling ill or if he'd been drinking, his actions were a total surprise.

"What can we talk about?" Collin asked tapping him lightly on the back of his hand.

Shawn began with a whisper. "I was just over at county records and I think that lady over there let something slip she wasn't supposed to. Or more like I saw something I wasn't supposed to." Collin took a cigar from his shirt pocket and as he listened intently he prepared it for lighting, Shawn could see the wheels turning in his mind and he instantly knew the judge hadn't been drinking.

"C'mon lets go where we can talk in private," the judge said rising from his seat and dropping the paper from the cigar onto the table. He placed his hand on Shawn's shoulder as they walked. They headed down a hall with various doors Shawn assumed were offices and stopping in front of the last door on the right Collin gave it a few light taps, when there was no answer he opened it motioning Shawn inside.

Shawn had only been in the club a few times, and that had been quite a few years back. Back when the bullshit hit him the hardest and he decided to change his career. He'd listened to the words of various judges and lawyers and decided it was a place he wanted to stay away from, so he never officially joined the club of the elite. Another one of those reasons he figuered he'd received the shitty treatment in the courtroom he'd been getting back then. They all thought he felt as though he was too good to associate time with them, and they were right. That wasn't a good thing to impress on other members of their profession, not in Detroit. The club was where you came to air your differences and improve on your friendships, but Shawn wouldn't join. They figured he thought he was too good to join and mingle with them, and again they were right. They all looked down on him. The fact that his rich father had kicked him out on his ass seemed to make most of them think they could treat him like garbage. That gave them plenty to laugh at. Now he was rich and he felt better keeping it to himself. He'd never been in any of the private offices and didn't care to. And today he still wouldn't join the club.

This was a large office, about twenty-five by thirty feet. A huge mahogany desk sat close to the far wall near another door leading out to where, he didn't know. There was a small lamp on one corner of this desk, which made about three of his. He was jealous. In the center there was one of those large desk protectors with a tablet for doodling, at least that's what he used his for. Behind the desk sat a very old brown leather chair, probably kept because of its comfort and not its looks. It showed extreme signs of ware but its plush cushions still offered a haven for relaxation. He was sure it had belonged to Harland and he pictured him dozing off in it from time to time. The other furniture in the office looked very new. There was a long brown over stuffed leather couch with two large matching chairs and beautiful glass top maple end tables along side each of the chairs completing the ensemble.

His eyes lingered a few seconds on a large picture of an elderly gentleman hanging on the wall behind the desk and he knew that was Judge Harper, he'd seen pictures of him many times before. The room looked more like a den than an office he thought to himself. Collin noticed Shawn's eyes settle on the picture and as he gestured for him to take a seat in one of the over stuffed chairs he began talking about the picture while he reached into his pocket for his lighter.

"That's the great Harland J. Harper right there," he said, his cigar holding hand out as if presenting the man. "You never met him I take it?"

"No, I was still in law school when he died."

"Well, you missed meeting one hell of a man," Collin said relaxing into the chair next to him. He lit his cigar and began taking deep puffs sending smoke bellowing into the air. He knew Shawn didn't smoke unless they were playing cards, so he held back offering him one of his fine Cuban cigars. "His wife left that to me in her will. I thought about hanging it on the front door so these piss ant attorney's could see the man that started this joint," he added, taking a break from his cigar.

"Why don't you?"

"It would just giv'em something else to spit on," he replied, making a face like he'd just bit into something sour. "This place is nothing like it used to be when Harland was alive. These jerks would be pissing in there shoes at the sound of his voice."

"Do you know about heavy kickbacks getting scored somewhere in the zoning office?" Shawn asked, hoping the sour look would aid him in rating out some one.

"Another thing unheard of when Harland was around. I know there's always someone getting some type of kickback, but they usually don't amount to a hill of beans." His reply was followed by a questioned look, as though he wondered about the words coming from his own mouth.

"What?" Shawn asked questioning the look on his face, Shawn was sure someone's name had just flashed through that sharp mind of his.

"I guess I should have told you about this a few years back Shawn, I'm sorry I didn't. When Hinkley tried railroading you I had an investigation done on him, I wanted to find something he was doing wrong so I could force him to get off your back. I found out someone was charging variance fees on permits and the money wasn't going where it was supposed to go. And there was a rumor about people receiving kickbacks for doing favors. Oh, if it was him he wasn't scamming much, a few dollars here a few dollars there, dinners at the best restaurants. I didn't have proof at the time, I couldn't pin anything on him, but I told him I could. He dropped what he was pulling on you, and because he's a judge I left him alone, as long as he left you alone." Shawn wondered why Collin thought of Hinkley so quickly now.

"The lady over at zoning said all permits were charged the same amounts, well the fees have changed. I found one where the guy was charged a thousand dollars over and above the regular permit fee. She said every one pulling a permit around that value paid the same. I found twenty others with no variance charges. She was adamant about the charges, then took the book away from me and asked me to leave. I think she thought I was a contractor at first, then she wised up."

"A thousand dollars a pop? He must be putting away quite a lot of dough now, at that rate. She probably thought you were a contractor until you started asking questions. One of their helpers must have logged something she wasn't supposed to, and you saw it.

"Well he's probably been getting away with it for so long he thinks he's beyond reproach. That's not all, I talked to the contractor building that new McDonalds up on Michigan and he said he paid five grand extra. "Collins eyes lit up in surprise. "What makes you think Hinkley is doing it?" Shawn questioned.

"Oh, it's him all right, I'll bet my new box of Cuban cigars on it," he said tapping ashes into an ashtray beside his chair. "Actually I was going to get a hold of you, because this isn't the first time I've heard about this. Now I'm shocked about the dollar amount and how many he's hitting. I was going to have you do some investigating for me but it looks like you've already started. My old secretary has a grandson that started his own construction co. He complained to her about the charges he's been paying for his permits, so she called me. That's when the first bell went off this time. Back when he was after you he told me he was not involved, but he'd get to the bottom of it and get it stopped. You changed your career direction and I was so damn busy I had to drop it." He let his words filter through Shawn's mind, while he took a few more puffs on his cigar. "I didn't hear any more about it until just lately. Usually by the time the second bell goes off my thoughts are one hundred percent correct," he said sinking back into his chair and taking another deep puff on his cigar as if in deep thought, Shawn searched his own thoughts while he waited for Collin to continue. "Would you look more in to this, we need to see if it is him for sure."

"Sure", Shawn replied as Collin went silent again.

Collin didn't look to be in his seventies, more like his early sixty's. He took very good care of himself, always watching his diet, and very light on drinking. He was a large man, weighing around 260lbs. but his six foot four framework had that weight very well proportioned. He wore a full-faced beard, always well trimmed to about an inch long. He smoked Cuban cigars and only Cuban cigars. Offer him anything else he'd refuse it with a bitter look.

"There are things going on in Hinkley's life that don't add up," Collin continued. "I found out he's ripping off process servers by having his court officer's post their alternate services. More money for the county he says. So these poor suckers run their asse's off burning up their gas, making there attempts at service and he has his court officers post the papers. That's robbery. I wonder if he's putting some of that into his pocket too?" He took another puff of his cigar and as Shawn watched his face and listened he felt the conversation going somewhere the judge hadn't hit on yet. They sat in silence again for a while, neither of them speaking.

"I've got to ask you something Shawn," he said in a very low tone, so low that Shawn had to force himself to listen closely, he didn't want to ask him to repeat himself. "You can tell me it's none of my business if you want to, and I'll understand. But I'd like to know. And I wish I had asked you before, but I didn't, and that's my fault."

Shawn's mind began running wild. He wants to know where I'm hiding my money. WHY? I'm paying the taxes on it. NO, he wants to know why I'm not married yet, why I haven't made an honest lady out of Shelly. NO, he wants to borrow some money. NO, he's got lots of his own money...

"Would you please tell me what happened back in 82, what the hell did Hinkley have on you?"

Shawn was really shocked at his question. He'd tried putting that behind him. He actually had managed to let it escape his mind for a few months. The hatred he'd developed for certain people had actually faded to loathing, harboring on despicable, and he'd managed to move on hoping to create a future with Shelly and forget about all that bullshit. Would I tell him? Shawn asked himself. This man I call my mentor, the man that drove me to become something so I wouldn't end up behind bars. The man that could have put me in prison almost fifteen years ago, he just told me I was like a son to him. Shawn began to speak but he started to choke.

"That's ok, you don't need to tell me."

"No, It isn't that," Shawn said standing up and going to the only window in the room. He removed a handkerchief from his back pocket and pretended to blow his nose while he wiped the tears from his eyes. He thought this was all behind him. He had kicked himself many times for not pushing it farther, but he would probably have wound up in prison himself. He swallowed his pride and left the court system. They had won. But he also kept a man from going to prison. He was sure he could start all over somewhere else, but Shelly wouldn't leave. His love for her wouldn't allow him to proceed with his new plans. So he opened his own Law Office, and became a Private Investigator to boot. He liked what he was doing now, and his investments helped him stay above water, way above water lately. When he finally had his emotions under control, he turned back to Collin.

"I sold myself out," he said looking Collin straight in the eyes. Collin gave him a questioning look, but stayed quiet waiting for the rest. He could tell his request had opened a door Shawn would have rather left closed.

"I was defending a young black man Chapell Evans, he was…Collin broke in.

"Yeah, B&E third offence," he said finishing Shawn's sentence.

Shawn was impressed. He probably remembers every case that ever passed through Detroit's court system, Shawn thought. "Chapell was innocent," Shawn continued. "His first two offences were bullshit, one when he was fourteen years old; the other was when he was fifteen. He took his ten dollars pay out of the till at the store where he'd just froze his ass off shoveling ice and snow away from the man's door so customers could get in. The jackass that hired him told him he didn't have money to pay him. After Chapell just spent the last hour freezing his butt off. Can you believe that? The son-of-a-bitch wouldn't pay the kid after he just froze his ass off for him! He wanted to pay the kid with cigarettes! The boy didn't smoke. He was trying to earn money to buy his mother a Christmas gift. He got a year at the county farm for that. The third offence and the one that counted was a mistake. He was home sleeping at the time. The only witness saw the Perpetrator from about seventy-five foot away. He swore it was Chapell, after Forge convinced him it was. Hinkley was going to put him away for ten years and he was innocent. All he and Forge wanted was to nail the lid shut on another case, no matter what!"

Collin could see the hurt in Shawn's face as he unloaded the burden he'd carried so long. Randall Forge had been the District Attorney at that time, and had been for about ten years. He was working his way towards the governor's office with as many convictions as he could get. He didn't care weather you were guilty or not. There had been a rumor Forge would plea bargain if you could pay his, "I'll let you go fee," which varied between five and ten thousand dollars, depending on the severity of the charges and the amount of prison time those charges could bring. If you couldn't pay, your ass was grass. If you could pay, the arraignments were made through the Defense Attorney and channeled through the system ending up in Forge's pocket.

"I had sworn testimony from at least ten different people that Chapell was nowhere's near that store when it was robbed. You know what Forge said?" he quickly continued without giving Collin a second to give an answer. "He said, and I quote, "you know what that means," and he put out his hand. I hit that fucker so hard he slammed into Hinkley, knocking them both flat on their Asses!"

Shawn was afraid Collin would scold him for hitting the District Attorney; you don't ever allow yourself to do such a thing.

With a sudden slap to his knee Collin burst into laughter "I wish I could have seen that!" he blurted. Shawn couldn't believe his ears. He thought for sure Collin would give him a chewing out for doing such a stupid thing.

"I agreed to quit the Public Defenders Office if Hinkley would let Chapell go and not prosecute me for knocking them both on their asses. Because of the eyewitness they said they had, Hinkley gave him five years probation so they both could have another star on their foreheads. But in reality they gave in because of your threat, didn't they?" Shawn concluded.

"I wish we would have gotten together then, I feel I've dealt you a grave injustice as well as the people of Wayne County. I thought he was a hard judge, I was wrong, he's a crooked judge and it's time he was dealt with. Maybe Hinkley would have been sitting in Jackson Prison by now and you'd have his job. Shawn made a funny face, really listening to Collins words, and taking it as a joke. "I know you're not aware of this, but you could have his Judgeship if you wanted it." His eyes were wide open, his forehead wrinkled.

Shawn took his seat again looking flabbergasted. "What do you mean?" His face went white with shock.

"Don't say anything to anyone yet but there's already an investigation in the works, an investigation of Hinkley's actions now and in the past. If he's found guilty, prosecuted for anything, or if he leaves office, resigns to avoid prosecution, his office will need to be filled immediately. There'll be hundreds of judgments needing to be reviewed. I've been asked to recommend the best person for the spot and I know that's you. My request will be followed," he said with great certainty. "You're one of the most honest people I know, and you know more about the law than any one else in the state. When this goes down we'll need someone like you for the public to connect with."

Shawn sat staring in disbelief. He would have liked nothing more than to shove Hinkley's face into that Headline, along with Stan's. But suddenly he wondered if he was dreaming. Collin puffed on his cigar smiling. He hoped he'd here a "hell yes" from Shawn, but Shawn wasn't saying anything. Shawn didn't want to be a judge, but he knew some one that did. To him Shelly would have been the better choice. He had heard Collin could pull off the unusual so he had no doubt Hinkley's judgeship could be his for the remainder of Hinkley's term, providing Hinkley was removed. At this time in his life just seeing Hinkley go down would be enough justice for him. But if he took over Hinkley's judgeship, that would make Hinkley's years in prison excruciating. A smile slowly covered his lips but he remained quiet.

"I can see the wheels are beginning to turn," Collin said with a smile. "Keep this under your hat. This could take months, but I know he's doing illegal operations and he'll be out within ninety days, I'm sure of it. Especially with anything more you can give me. You do some investigating for me, and if you turn up what I think you're going to, plus the other stuff I'm collecting I'm sure he'll be on his way out. You don't have to let me know now. I know you've got reasons for staying away from the system, but come back and help change the system. We want someone we can swear in the moment he's discharged. Don't sit out there and allow this shit to continue, do something about it. From what you just said, Forge will probably be on his way out too. This investigation will go all the way. Do a good job and you're a shoe in come election time and for years to come."

Forge had wormed his way into the attorney generals office and hoped some day to become the next LT. Governor, and future Governor. Shawn wished he could see the look on his face when this shit hit the fan. He was in total shock from Collin's request and the look on his face told Collin there would be no answer today.

"I've got a Euchre game at four," Collin said looking at the clock. He wanted to give Shawn time to think about what he'd asked; he wasn't about to pressure him into an answer right away. "I know this is a lot to put on you but I also know you can handle it. Give it some thought. C'mon," he said placing his hand on Shawn's shoulder, "I'll buy you a beer. Hell yes, anything for the man that knocked those two on their asses." As he walked with Shawn to the bar he placed one of his Cuban Cigars into Shawn's shirt pocket. "This game is one you're going to win young man," he said proudly with a smile.

CHAPTER SIX

Shawn left the club his mind sifting through the request and information Collin had given him. He felt grateful to be thought of in such high esteem from a man considered to be one of the best judges ever in the state of Michigan.

Judge Therman had been requested many times as the presiding judge over various special cases through out the state, and he was a personal friend of the governor. At any given time you could find him having drinks or dinner with a state senator or one of the Supreme Court Justices. His request for Hinkley's replacement would be followed, Shawn was sure of that.

Obviously not too many people knew about the wrong doings Forge had been involved in, or the man hoping to have him as his LT. Governor didn't care. Right now he was on the attorney generals staff and thought his ass was protected from all that was behind him. How wrong he was.

"I don't want to be near that much politics," Shawn told himself as he drove back to Beckwith Street. "Besides I like what I'm doing." He was carrying on this conversation with his invisible assistant as he drove along. He hadn't found anything at county records showing Forest had been given preferential treatment. On the contrary, he was taken advantage of, and possibly by a judge. That in itself told him Forest had no involvement with any Mafia Group. Things would have been quite different, like no payment at all, or lower than usual. But that wasn't the case.

"Forest probably had more money than he needed, and another thousand meant nothing to him. Or he knew all about the rip off and knew he wouldn't get the permits if he didn't pay," Shawn said, still talking to his silent partner. "So where'd he get all the free help?" Shawn questioned pulling back into the parking lot of the building where Sherin lived. He knocked on the door to apartment one, hoping she'd be home. She was.

"Come on in," she said smiling, "I didn't think you'd come back so soon."

"I'm hoping you can give me a little more information about Mr. Foust. What happened to your face?" he asked softly, taking hold of her chin and turning it to the left so he could see better. The bruises were barely visible through the makeup she'd plastered on to try and hide them, but he'd seen it before. When you see a goddess fresh from the shower with skin needing nothing to beautify it, then you find her with makeup plastered all over her face, it's usually hiding something. He picked up a damp cloth lying on her table and began removing the makeup. She didn't refuse his wanting to see, but she closed her eyes and cringed waiting for his reaction at seeing what she was hiding. "Did that son-of-a-bitch do this to you?" The disgust he was feeling echoed deep within the sharpness of his voice as he viewed Ray's handy work.

"No, I fell against the door."

"Bullshit!" he said throwing the cloth back onto the table.

"It's my fault," she said trying to hide the bruise with her hand.

"And just why do you say that?" he asked, his voice still showing his anger.

"Because I was trying to get him to leave. First I asked him then I told him. Then I really goofed up," she said, her voice dropping to a whisper.

"What, then you did what? Speak up so I can hear you."

"I said then I really goofed up, I told him you were my new boyfriend," she squeaked, turning her eyes to the floor.

Shawn's mouth dropped as he tipped her chin back to look into her eyes. He was smiling now as he asked in a low whisper, "Why the hell did you tell him something like that?"

"I wanted him to go, get the hell out of here. I wanted him gone." Tears from her pretty green eyes began sliding down her cheeks. Shawn took her softly into his arms as she clutched tightly to his chest. She couldn't help but cry and his shoulders were more than willing to cradle her.

"C'mon, your going to ruin that pretty makeup you've got on," he said, with a soft forgiving tone and laughter.

"You've already wiped most of that off," she said mixing her blubbering with laughter while trying to wipe her tears.

Shawn began wiping her tears away with his thumbs, then seeing a box of tissues close by he took one and finished drying them until she took it from him.

"I thought maybe with you being so much bigger than him he'd get scared and just leave," she said trying to explain. "That's what William did."

"Who's William?"

"William Reynolds, he's a boy from Pontiac I was seeing before Ray. Ray scared him off about a month ago."

"Scared him off, did you ask him to?"

"No, Ray was bragging that William didn't have the guts to fight for me and he did. William just wouldn't come back. I called and left messages for him but I guess Ray was right, because he never called back. Then Ray started getting too demanding so I asked him to go. That was this morning before you came by."

Shawn was curious, and before checking his train of thought, his mouth spoke without allowing his brain to take control.

"Have you ever...?

"No I haven't! Not with anyone! I'm still a virgin!" she said pushing him away from her. "Although, If you don't stay away from here that could change," she added, finally producing another smile.

As much as she liked to flirt, she had this belief her virginity was to be captured by the man she would allow to steal her heart, but not until after marriage. Her beauty was actually ignored by her. She thought she was just another young lady trying to get by until she did find that one hunk of a man she'd be willing to loose her heart to. After all she'd been looking at that same face in the mirror for years, it didn't impress her at all. She didn't waste time putting on a lot of makeup. So many times she'd looked at her face in the mirror and wondered why she was born with that stupid little nose, her chin didn't look right, and why that stupid blond hair? She had threatened to dye it black, or maybe red, she had toyed with that notion various times. She did like her hair long though, so she kept it that way, just the way Shawn liked to see it on a lady.

Long hair well taken care of turned him on faster than any other attribute, as long as it was on a woman. To him, a woman with long hair could be flat chested; he'd look past that if she took good care of her hair. But Sherin wasn't flat chested, she was beautiful and voluptuous. When he looked at her he imagined seeing that beautiful long blond hair draped over those large breasts with her nipples peaking through. She didn't need any makeup to make herself look pretty, maybe a hint of it here and there would enhance her beauty, but it wasn't necessary. His theory was, if a lady looks great fresh out of the shower wet hair and all, you'd better hold on to her. Shelly fit that description, and until now he hadn't met any other lady that impressed him that much. Well, there was that day he was sitting in Tony's living room and Correen walked through fresh from the shower, she had no idea he was sitting there. She got a big laugh from it; he froze and was unable to speak for a while. Mainly because, seeing a beautiful black goddess stark naked with hair down to her waist was breath taking. She also needed no makeup for beautification. He hadn't seen that many ladies fresh out of the shower wet and naked, not in that order. A woman fresh out of the shower, wearing a robe, which hid nothing when she bent over in front of him, hadn't met him at the door before either. Well, what he saw could put his relationship with Shelly in jeopardy, if he allowed it, but he wouldn't. Not passed his thoughts anyway.

He remembered back in high school they had a name for girls that paraded around half dressed reveling what they had and warning the boys not to touch, (Prick Teaser) came to mind as he tried placing himself in Ray's shoes. It would be pretty hard watching this little lady parade through the house and not be able to touch her. Maybe Ray just took all he could, probably once he realizes what he's done, he'll come back and apologies, Shawn thought.

Well, so much for Angela's Bimbo theory, Shawn told himself. Shelly, you just don't know the sacrifices I go through for you, he told himself as he met Sherin's smile with his own.

"Young lady, I'm sort of trying to become attached. I'd be attached if I could get my girlfriend to marry me. Besides, I'm old enough to be your big brother."

"I'm over twenty one," she said sounding very adult like. "I can do what ever I want. You tell that girl friend of your's to do or give it up." Until now she had put up with boys in high school pinching her breasts and slapping her on the rear. Boring boy friends wanting to get into her pants, or being duds. This was the first time she'd looked into the eyes of a man, a real man, she told herself.

"I guess that's what Ray thought too", she said walking to her kitchen table and taking a seat. She motioned for him to take the chair next to her, but he refused. "I mean, that I was available to be laid." He was a little shocked by her reply, and he was thinking of the best way to change the subject. Their conversation was cut short by the sound of loud pipes coming from a vehicle outside.

"Oh shit he's back." She gasped, her hand quickly covering her mouth. She grabbed Shawn's arm with a grip he could sense showed the fear now seen in her beautiful green eyes.

"Stay in here," he ordered.

"Don't let him hurt you," she warned.

"You just stay back," He said leaving the apartment.

"Is this the asshole?" Ray yelled as Shawn walked down off the porch.

"You get off slapping ladies around?" Shawn asked keeping his distance. He quickly dismissed his thought of Ray coming back to apologies.

Ray had been sitting in his truck revving the engine, hoping Shawn would come out of the apartment, now that he had, Ray got out of his truck. In his right hand he held a wooden ball bat which he began swinging slowly over his head.

"Why don't you get the hell out of here!" Sherin yelled. She thought Shawn would be ok in a fair fight but she didn't know about the ball bat, now she was afraid he was in serious trouble. The tears Shawn had helped her control now quickly returned and were sliding down her cheeks.

Shawn walked towards the street hoping Ray would follow him and stay away from Sherin. As Ray walked towards him he swung the bat faster and faster above his head suddenly letting it go flying and twisting through the air it shot towards Shawn's head like a rocket out of control certain to cause damage when it hit. Sherin's eyes opened wide with surprise as she screamed for him to look out. Like a great dancer performing the steps to a well-known tune Shawn dipped at the knees reaching out into the air snatching the bat like a Baton twirler retrieving the baton after tossing it into the air. The look on Ray's face quickly changed from delight to fear as he watched something he'd never seen happened in the dozens of fights he'd started in the past. The bat seemed to perch for only a second on Shawn's fingertips when it was sent back towards him spinning twice as fast. When Ray saw Shawn catch the bat instantly he knew he was in trouble, he quickly scrambled back into his truck as the bat made a very loud crashing sound smashing against the outside of his driver side door. Ray quickly slammed the truck into reverse backing into the street almost crashing into a passing motorist. That car veered off into a neighbor's yard coming to a sudden stop after tearing out the chain link fence. The bat shattered into pieces as it caved in the outer panel of Ray's driver side door and breaking the window Ray had rolled down. His tires were smoking and tossing gravel everywhere as he fish tailed from one side of the street to the other making his hasty getaway.

With Shawn's haste to assist the lady Ray almost hit, he neglected to get the plate number off Ray's truck, something he wished he'd done.

"How'd you do that?" Sherin questioned excitedly with tears still running down her cheeks. "I thought it was going to knock your head off."

"Just a little trick I've learnt, I don't think he'll be back."

"At least not while you're here," she said throwing her arms around his neck and giving him a big kiss on the lips.

"Do you have a bag I can use?" he asked gathering the pieces of the bat.

"Are you sure you wouldn't like to stay for a while?" She asked hoping he'd say yes, she was very afraid Ray wasn't finished but she'd only known him a few short weeks and maybe this little episode would make him stay away for good.

For the first time in her life she was wondering if she could throw away her values and allow Shawn to stay over night. He definitely wouldn't be sleeping on the sofa if he did agree to stay. She wanted him against her body, held tightly in his arms, naked. She could feel his strength as he held her now and she didn't want him to let go. She had never felt this way being held by any other man.

"I'll stay long enough to make sure he's not coming back, besides, I still want to hear what more you know about Forest. A bag. Preferably a large one if possible," he asked again giving her a smile.

He had stood up now and she realized she was hanging from his neck at least a foot from the ground. His hands were around her waist and he held her as if she was a rag doll. She slowly let go of his neck as he lowered her to the ground, still looking into her eyes.

"The bag," he whispered, looking into her beautiful green eyes and wanting to kiss her.

"Why do you want that old thing, its all busted?" She asked whispering without really hearing his words, she was talking but she wasn't thinking about what he'd asked. She was hoping he'd lean down and touch his lips to hers. She wet her lips with her tongue, not knowing she was driving him crazy. They were both thinking about Shelly too, Shawn was wishing she were home and in his arms so he could follow through with the wanting his body was craving, and Sherin was wishing he'd forget all about her.

"Maybe I can glue it back together," he said being sarcastic, he knew he had to put some distance between them, even if it was only a couple of feet. He wouldn't allow himself to act on the feelings his body was begging him to, not now. Maybe if Shelly ever told him to get lost he would, but not until. He knew he could be a playboy if he wanted to, and Shelly would never know what he had done, but he'd know. That was something he couldn't work with. Not when he loved her so much. He knew she dated, but she swore she wasn't sleeping with anyone but him and he believed her. He knew the dates she had with other men were always something to do with her work, either to climb higher up the proverbial latter to a judgeship, or discuss a case she was working on. There was never any romance on her part, so she said. And he believed that too.

Shaking her head Sherin walked away to her apartment, quickly returning with a medium sized grocery bag.

"He had gloves on, or hadn't you noticed."

"I noticed, but that doesn't mean his prints aren't on it. That doesn't mean he's never touched it without gloves on some time or another. That just means he didn't want to bruise his pretty little hands on me."

She loved his answer. It was quick and witty, and he was probably right, she smiled thinking about him. How could his girlfriend refuse his proposal of marriage? Was there something about him she knew and was afraid of, something if she herself knew she'd tell him to just go home?

They walked back to her apartment where the next few hour's were spent discussing everything she could remember about Beth and Forest. Company logos on any of the vehicles she could remember seeing while the construction was going on. What time of day Forest would be home alone. What hours of the day Beth was usually home. He pried everything he could from her memory weather it was important or not, but he never made any moves towards her.

"She owned a Health Studio in Detroit. You know, where people go to try and loose weight." She said, furnishing information she was sure Shawn wasn't aware of.

Shawn gave her a blank stare, "I know what a Health Studio is," he assured her. He couldn't tell if it was her blond hair, or just an attempt at being a smart ass. The smirking look she shot back, told him she had a good sense of humor.

Being blond had nothing to do with it; that just made her look cuter.

"Did you ever try it out?"

"I tried a three month exercise program once, but those Detroit ladies are too hard to get along with. One lady thought for sure I was a stripper, and she wasted no time letting me know she thought so.

"Maybe she meant it as a compliment."

Now Shawn received the blank stare. He said no more about the subject, but he was sure he knew who that lady was.

"There was the vamp that hung around over there whenever Beth was gone," she added.

"Why do you call her a Vamp?"

"Because I think she is. I've seen her leaving that house at all hours of the night. She would never use the front door. She'd always use the side door of the house, and sometimes I'd see her sneaking around the place at all hours of the night, she's creepy."

"How old does she look to be?"

"I've never seen her up close. She looks to be sixteen or seventeen she could be older. She's tall, she looks taller than me."

"Have you seen her since the murder?"

"No."

"You don't think Forest was doing anything with her, do you?"

"I don't know," she said turning away. "What's she hanging around there for, if not for money? Sex for money, you know the old traders union."

Shawn smiled shaking his head. Some of the things Sherin said shocked him.

"Well, looks can always be deceiving. Did they have dogs?"

"Yeah, they had two beautiful German Shepards."

"I wonder if that's who's been playing games with me," Shawn mumbled.

"The dogs?" She asked with a sudden burst of laughter.

"NO, your vamp! Or the lady you call a vamp," he said giving her a confused look. "When I was there earlier someone was there, but wouldn't show themselves. Do you know where this girl lives?"

"I used to see her all over this neighborhood, but I haven't seen her lately, no idea where she lives," she replied still smiling over the dog reply.

"Have you ever called the cops on her."

"C'mon, she's a teenager. What would you have done to someone calling the cops on you when you were a Teen?" She questioned with a twisted look. "She hasn't broken any laws, she's just creepy," Sherin said shrugging her shoulders with a shiver. "I call the cops, than I really have trouble."

That would fit, Shawn thought. The goings on at the Foust home was certainly a bit creepy.

"So are you going to tell me?"

"Tell you what?" Shawn asked with a twist of his head.

"Well, you know my name and more things about me than any boy I've ever met, but you haven't bothered telling me anything about yourself. You're investigating a dead man, so you could be a cop but probably not. I'd say F.B.I. or maybe C.I.A., K.G.B. what was Forest into, or what do you think he was into?"

She was making crazy funny faces at him as she asked him these questions and he knew it was only fair for her to know the answers. He wondered if she'd realized she had no secrets after bending over and picking up her kitten?

"I'm sorry, my name's Shawn Cassidy", he said apologetically, and I'm nothing important like that, I'm just a P.I.V C."

"What's that?" she asked wrinkling her pretty little face into a child like scrunch. He could see she was trying very hard to put the letters into words .

"Private Investigator Very Confused." It was intended to lighten the mood, and it did. Sherin burst out laughing at his reply; even the bruise on her face couldn't hide the pleasure she was having with him being there. She hadn't felt laughter like this in a long time and she liked him more and more every minute. "The K.G.B. is Russian F.B.I. he said with a smile, I'm not Russian," her laughter continued.

"I know, I had to put that in for fun," she said still giggling. "You sound more like a lawyer the way you've been grilling me."

He gave her a funny look but didn't reply, which made her quickly realize she'd just hit the nail on the head.

"Don't tell me," she continued with a surprised look, "you're an attorney too."

He nodded his head yes while her feelings towards him increased ten fold. She wondered how a girl could refuse his attention. He was tall and handsome, a lot of fun to talk with, and an attorney to boot. She knew he was quite strong, when he was holding her in the air earlier he looked as though he'd been holding a small baby; her one hundred and twenty pounds hadn't fazed him a bit. And yes, he was very handsome she continued saying in her thoughts as she dreamed about sliding her fingers through his jet-black hair while looking into his soft blue eyes and kissing those soft lips of his. There must be something wrong with him she wasn't yet aware of she questioned, and she was more than willing to find out what it could be. He did set her straight right away about having a steady girl. Most men would have taken the chance with her and never told the truth. The problem has to be with the girl friend; she told herself as she looked at his smiling face and forced herself to quit dreaming, it has to be she thought. That girlfriend has to be very stupid.

"So what are you trying to find out?" she questioned slowly wetting her soft pink lips and wishing she could be kissing his.

"You know what? I really don't know. Every step of this case has been confusing. Some one thinks he was a victim along with Beth but I haven't found anything pointing in that direction, there's nothing but confusion every where I turn."

"Isn't that what's supposed to make your job so interesting?"

She was right, that was supposed to be the theory, only most cases weren't supposed to draw you into the criminal wrong doings of a District Court Judge. Interesting? You bet.

"Are you going to be alright, I mean do you think that jerk will come back?"

She wanted to say, "I'm scared as hell please stay with me," but she didn't. She knew if she did it would be a lie, a lie to keep him there against his will. Then what? She knew if he were going to dump his girlfriend he'd have done it by now. The best she could do was come right out and let him know where she stood.

"I'll be ok. Just think about this though, tell that girlfriend of yours to do or give it up."

Shawn smiled, he knew what she was offering and he knew it would be a permanent thing if the right man took her up on it. If Shelly weren't in his life he'd definitely think about spending serious time with her, if he could just convince himself to forget about the age difference.

It was time for him to meet up with Tony so he told Sherin to lock her door and he'd stop by the following morning. Driving to Tony's house would give him time to sift through the information Sherin had given him so he could kick it around while they had their workout. He left the parking lot of the apartment house deep in thought then suddenly as if smelling smoke where there shouldn't be any he sensed there was someone on the floor of his back seat. He'd checked out his surroundings before getting into his car and hadn't noticed Ray's pickup anywhere close by, he knew that didn't mean he hadn't hid the truck someplace and was still watching the apartment though. But for some reason he was sure it wasn't Ray, he figured Ray wasn't that type. Ray would make himself known right away, or would he?

When he was directly under the nearest streetlight, he slammed on the brakes reaching quickly back over the seat to the floorboard grabbing the person hiding there. The second he lifted the culprit from the floor he knew it wasn't Ray, the body was too light. As he pulled the person up and over the seat he held his left fist ready to smash it into the culprit's face, but the face was that of a young female, so with a push he quickly let her fall back to the floor.

"Don't hit me!" her voice screamed just before he gave her that shove. There was no mistaking the high-pitched scream as coming from a child, a female child. Turning on his dome light he saw the face of a young lady peaking through the spread fingers of her shaking hands trying very hard to hide her face and look at him at the same time, he quickly pusher her back onto the floorboard again.

"What the hell are you doing back there?" He questioned. She quickly scrambled her long legs over the seat plopping into the passenger seat beside him, the big smile on her face telling him she hadn't been the least bit scared. The vamp no doubt, he told himself. Shifting into reverse he began backing up towards the apartment house faster then he'd left, he was going to return her to where he thought she'd came from.

"NO! Go straight! I mean forward! That way!" she screamed almost hysterical, pointing straight ahead. Her actions told him she definitely didn't want to go back there.

"I hope that's in the direction of your home! I've got places to go! Who are you anyway and what the hell are you doing hiding in my car?"

She wouldn't say another word as he drove down the street and after two blocks her silence totally pissed him off so he angrily pulled over to the curb and stopped the car.

"Look! You either start talking or I'll take you straight to the police station!"

She turned to him with a very disgusted look on her face and the dim light from the street lamps revealed a very young lady of no more than thirteen or fourteen years old. This can't be the girl Sherin was talking about he thought; she's too young.

"How old are you, about ten?" he asked, hoping to piss her off.

"I'm thirteen!" she shot back. "Well almost! In another month, before I go back to school" she continued, her voice getting more quiet with each phrase. You probably just turned twelve, he mumbled. She had no bosom to speak of, and her face looked like the pacifier had recently fallen from her mouth. Her height was the deceiving factor though, he was sure she was pushing towards six foot or damn close to it.

"So you're almost thirteen, what's your name?"

"Brook."

"Well Brook, Brook what, no last name to go with that first one?"

"Just Brook"

"Well, Just Brook, can I give you a lift some where. I really do have some place I've got to be," he said, trying his best to be rude. "At this hour I'd say you should be on your way home any way; do you live in that big house back there?"

"Yeah right!" She snapped being sarcastic. "Just drop me off right here!" Before he could stop her, she was out of the car heading across the city block and off hidden by the darkness of night.

"Yeah, that's the girl Sherin was talking about I'll bet. I really need all this shit," he said getting out and waiting beside his car. What the hell did she want? He stood there a couple of minutes wondering if she'd come back; when she didn't he drove around the block hoping to find her walking along but she was no where in sight. Finally after a half hour of driving around the neighborhood looking for her he gave up and headed for Tony's place.

Tony was warming up getting ready for his workout when Shawn arrived, a bit later than was planned but he made it.

"I thought you might have changed your mind."

"It's this new case I'm working." Shawn busied himself getting dressed into his workout garb and also warming up while sharing the events of his day. "I've got two crazy women I can't get simple answers from. One's really making me wish Shelly would get her fanny home, real quick."

"That good."

"She could make a preacher horny."

Tony laughed while he braced himself for the attack Shawn was about to throw into his workout. They traded off holding cushion pads for one another during the light portion of their workout and when Shawn finished telling how his fun day had been, Tony brought Shawn up to date on what he'd been doing.

He had a new Academy opening up in Sterling Heights, and there were already fifty new students for him to start training. Four of his close friends and long time students had just returned from Europe where they had participated in the World Martial Arts Competition. They brought home

Second, Fourth, and Fifth place Awards which made him awfully proud.

"Why didn't you go?"

"Been there done that. Now it's their turn. Besides, I'm not going too far from home with Correen being pregnant. Her mother lost her first two with miscarriages."

"I'm sorry I didn't know. After all these years you've never told me that."

"Shit that's ok, I don't expect you to know everything about us. Just the promise you'll be there is great." He gave Shawn a hard look. "You are still coming aren't you?"

"Wild horses couldn't keep me away."

Tony let out a big sigh of relief, "I'm just scared, and you know you're the closest thing I've got to family."

"You're going to be fine." Shawn swept a spin kick to Tony's right hand pad followed by a nasty kick to his right temple, which he stopped within an inch of Tony's ear.

"Whoa." Tony blurted feeling the breeze from Shawn's foot, he had the strike blocked which Shawn knew he would but the force still could have knocked him for a loop if it had connected, the control Shawn had at stopping the strike was what really impressed him. "Damn you're getting good, whose been training you?" He asked, knowing what the answer would be.

"When you've been trained by the best." Shawn replied following that complement with a quick bow to him. Then he removed his pads placing them on a table. Tony was getting a little too sentimental and Shawn didn't want to go there. Tossing him headgear and gloves they both prepared for an hour or so of hard sparring. They proceeded with that portion of their workout while Shawn related every move he'd made so far with his investigation.

"What kind of vehicle does this Ray Drive?"

"A black 83 Chevy Scottsdale, it has a big dent in the middle of the drivers door now."

"Your work I take it?"

"Yeah, he wanted to split my noggin with a ball bat."

"You think he'll go back?'

"If you met Sherin and you were single, you'd have a hard time staying away. I just hope our first encounter scared him off for good. Maybe knowing I'll boot his ass if he comes around will coax him to return to Pontiac and stay there.

"Well, you know I'm here if you need me. Your work is so much more exciting than mine," he said laughing.

"Yeah, you can help me get into that teenagers head; she's the one messing around that house, I'm almost sure of it."

"You need Shelly for something like that, you know she's damn good at working with kids."

"She's gonna be gone for at least another week, and I'd like to clean this up before she gets back. What do you think Forest could have been into? This guy's got money and friends up the ying-yang. The electrician that worked on the house came from Dayton. Now, why would an electrician come all the way from Ohio to…?" his voice slowed and the look on his face went blank, then as if a light went on in his head his face beamed. His actions surprised Tony.

"What?"

"He went out of town because of all the hidden shit."

"What hidden shit?"

"The hidden passage going to all three floors. If an electrician from around here installed the electronics for those secret doors they'd tell someone, and no more secret. I'll bet Beth had no idea they were there."

"Maybe she finally found'em and confronted him, that could have started the fight."

"I think she found out something that pissed her off and she either caught him sleeping or she snuck up behind him. That's the only way she could have got the best of him. This guy would never have gotten hit without some deception."

"Maybe he was a bookie, that's why he never worked." Tony quipped. Maybe that's how he made his money."

"That's not a bad idea, I really didn't think about that," Shawn replied pushing back thoughts he'd been toying with.

"How many phone lines are there going into the house?"

"I know there were two," Shawn said wiping sweat from his face; "I'll check with the phone co. tomorrow."

"I'll do some checking too," Tony offered. "If he was into any of the rackets some one around here is going to know about it. More than likely he was, he didn't get his money from her. He certainly had lots of it to spend. I remember when I started my school just down the block from her Health club; the realtor was telling me she got her start with her husband's money, but after that she became quite wealthy on her own and her money was hers and his was his. He's the same realtor that sold Forest that city block. There were five houses removed to clean that area up," Tony explained. "They were badly run down, needed more to remodel than they were worth. He just leveled the whole block and started over."

Shawn knew Tony had more contacts with the investment people around Detroit than he did. He had bought and sold acres and acres of real estate in the Detroit area during the last ten years. Real estate brokers usually know who's got the money or where it came from, and weather it's new or old. Bankers around Detroit would call Tony whenever they thought they could push a deal his way, because they knew he had money and connections.

After their workout they ate a late supper of chicken stir-fry, one of Tony's specialties, while they made plans for Tony to follow up on his theories. Tony loved helping Shawn with his investigations. Lately he hadn't had much time to give, but with his four best instructors coming back home, he was sure he could offer Shawn more of his time.

"You know, Correen is going to be mad she missed you, her mother was feeling sick, and you know Correen, the family nurse."

"How's she feeling?"

"Four months into this and I still don't know; the morning sickness seems to be bothering her less. You're going to be there aren't you?"

"I told you I would! Damn, I'm beginning to think you're more nervous than she is."

"I'll probably need you to hold my hand. She wants me in the room with her when she gives birth; I've heard guys have fainted doing that." Shawn just laughed hearing his words.

"I can see the Head Line now. Great Martial Arts expert faints seeing baby born," How am I going to hold your hand in there?"

"Just knowing you're there will be enough."

"Tell her I said HI, and give her a kiss for me," Shawn said still laughing as he headed out the door. "I'll see you guys tomorrow," he called over his shoulder.

Wednesday morning Shawn returned to the Foust Estate. He was hoping to find out just who was haunting that house and for some reason he wondered if the girl hiding in his car the night before could answer that question. If he could find her again that is. After securing a large hot chocolate, along with his favorite bakery item a chocolate covered cream filled long john, he located a spot across from the Foust Estate where he could view the front and east side of the house. From there he could view anyone entering the property from either the front or rear drives. He figured he was wasting his time but time was something he had lots of. It was still dark, being 5:30 am. He hoped to catch whatever went on early in the neighborhood and it worked.

Soon the noise of a city garbage truck broke the silence while men emptied garbage cans tossing them back onto the lawns not caring where they landed or on whose lawn they ended upon. A lady walking her Rottweiler passed the workers tugging back on the leash while the dog tried its best to sink it's teeth into one of them. The men shrugged it off as if it were a normal every day occurrence. A mailman stopped at the corner to retrieve the out going mail from a large Mail Box, and as he stuffed the mail into his bag he swatted away mosquitoes attacking him from the grass. Shawn watched as a couple of people walked out onto their porches to retrieve their morning newspapers as the Paper Boy wildly tossed them from his bicycle. A small white fluffy dog ran out from one house and tried its best to yank the paperboy from his bike until the boy smacked it with the next paper to be thrown.

Half way through his snack Shawn saw the flash of a light inside the Foust home. From where he sat he could only see the front door of the house and no one had used that entrance. He hadn't been able to locate a place to park where he could view both the front and side doors and still remain hidden. He quickly finished his snack and quietly removed himself from his car, making sure to lock the door this time. He didn't want any surprise visitors when he returned this morning.

After a short walk he took up a position beside the rear of the back garage next to the dog kennels. From this position he could see the side door and the rear patio sliding doors. Who ever was inside the house either entered by one of these two doors or stayed all night he figured. There were no service vehicles in the drive, which ruled out any cleaning or maintenance people. He watched the house for another few minutes seeing nothing out of the ordinary happen. Suddenly he heard something hit the floor inside the house.

"What's the matter can't you see in the dark?" he questioned quietly to himself as he sprinted to the front of the house. He wished he'd been given the key for the side door as he quickly unlocked the front and slipped inside. Loosing no time he headed for the side door hallway, the beam from his flashlight lit up the hallway corner as the secret door just locked back into place. "Damn right sweetheart I'm right behind you." He stood at the corner listening, then he decided she was headed for the lower level so he took off for the basement, he was sure it was Brook. As he ran he quickly kicked off his shoes hoping to decrease the amount of noise he'd make running through the house trying to catch her. Using his gun was not an option at this point, so he made sure it was secure in its holster he didn't want to lose it running through the house. When he reached the basement he quickly tripped the button to that secret door and as soon as it opened he wasted no time entering as he heard footsteps going to the upstairs level. Someone was running up the stairs and the second he was in the stairwell he saw someone duck into the upstairs bedroom. He quickly sprinted to the top floor but when he burst into the bedroom there was no one there. He stood in the room listening and now he could hear someone on the first floor, so he ducked back into the stairwell and returned to the corner door in the first floor hallway. There he opened the door slowly listening but he could no longer hear anyone so he quickly jumped into the hall. Nobody was there. Listening, he felt a sudden rush of air come from the staircase, telling him the upper door just closed causing the down draft.

"She's fucking with me," he growled. Then, on second thought, maybe it's not her. "No matter, who ever it is they're having fun making an ass out of me." He took up a seat in a large soft leather chair in the living room and turned it so he could watch the hall and the door to the basement, pistol in hand he waited. It's like trying to catch a rat, he told himself, and sooner or later the rat will come looking for food. If you're real quiet it will reveal itself. He sat there playing a game, the hunter and the hunted he said, looking down the sight of his pistol and scanning around the room. Boom, boom, he said in his mind as he pointed at things in the dawning light and imagined blowing it to hell. He knew if he'd have ran up the stairs that whom ever was there would have ducked out through the bedroom, and he'd be running in circles. It's better to just sit still and let the fox come to the hound. He sat there for so long he just about fell asleep when suddenly he heard what sounded like someone on the roof.

"You've got to be shitting me," holstering his weapon, he slowly went to the door and returned outside taking a look across the roof of the house. "I'm sure this is what I'm supposed to do," he mumbled taking up a spot where he could see the side door. Seconds later the door opened, a hooded figure emerged and dashed around the back of the house, being well out of sight by the time he made it to a point he could watch from.

"Well, he was tall, or she, and quite skinny; the hood was a smart play. If that was Brook, she's been trained very well. I can't believe she'd go to such lengths to hide the fact she's been in the house."

He returned inside to get his shoes and noticed a large stand up ashtray lying on the floor near a window facing the direction his car was setting.

"That's great, I think I'm watching her and she's watching me. Who's the PI here?" he asked with a chuckle.

He took a seat by the front door and brushed the dirt from his socks so he could replace his shoes, then he walked through the house looking for anything that might give him an answer to some of his questions. When he was satisfied he couldn't find one thing pointing to Brook or anyone else for that matter he decided to return home. He was about half way to his car when he heard someone yelling his name and when he looked to see who was doing the yelling he saw a person running towards him coming from the direction of Sherin's apartment house. It was Brook.

" Shawn help!" She screamed as she ran frantically towards him, she wasn't wearing a hooded sweatshirt and she was dressed in shorts and a t-shirt. She couldn't have been the one playing games with him, no way Shawn thought, he quickly ran towards her wondering what was the problem.

"Shawn, Sherin's been beaten up, she's almost dead, she has a pulse but it's awfully weak." He was surprised she knew how to take a pulse he thought as he ran along with her to the apartment and he knew immediately Ray had returned. When he reached her side the sight of her blood covered naked body lying on the floor shocked him, he couldn't believe she was still alive. The pretty little blond he'd left the night before was lying naked on her kitchen floor in such a pool of blood he couldn't believe she had any left in her. He was in total shock. He knew instantly what had been used to make the hundreds of slices into the flesh of this once beautiful young lady, and he knew who made them. Now he wished he would have tightened that chain around Ray's neck the day before and this would never have happened.

"Can you drive?" he questioned Brook.

"What?"

"Can-you-drive?" he asked again in a low tone, looking her straight in the eyes.

"Yes"

"Go get my car, quickly." He said handing her his keys. "Pull it as close to the porch as you can." As she ran out the door he pulled a sheet from Sherin's bed and wrapped her lifeless body with it. Taking ice from her freezer he wrapped it into a dampened cloth and carefully began dabbing it to her face. There was no reaction what so ever to the cold against her flesh, she might as well have been dead, but her heart kept pumping blood from the cuts covering her body. He removed an ice cube and slid it over her lips and cheeks; still there was no reaction. She was covered from head to toe with blood, but most of it was coming from her head. He was so pissed at himself for leaving her there. He told himself over and over he should have known better. Now she needed medical attention as soon as possible and to wait for an ambulance could mean her death. When Brook pulled up she'd already released the top and had it down so Shawn could lay Sherin in the back seat with little difficulty. He wrapped the sheet a bit more snug, and placed her carefully into the back seat of his car. Without being told Brook jumped to the back seat floorboard and began caring for Sherin with the ice and wet cloth Shawn had brought. Wrapping her in the sheet reopened some of the wounds on her body and she began bleeding more but Brook worked diligently to stop it.

"Hold on to her tight. I hope she doesn't have any broken bones." He knew it would take at least a half hour or more to get her to the hospital by ambulance, and that would be to damn long. Also, he was feeling very guilty for leaving her there so Ray could return and do such a thing; he needed to help save her life.

It took Shawn about ten minutes to reach ST. Mary's Hospital on the west side and have Sherin in the emergency room receiving medical attention. You would have thought Brook was her closest relative; she wouldn't leave her side.

Sherin had been severely beaten and probably raped, and Shawn knew it was his fault. He was sure Ray committed the assault, but they needed proof. There was no telling how long she'd be unconscious or if she'd even live, his first call went out to Captain Starkway.

After introducing himself to the Amazon he quickly asked if Starkway was in, Pam recognized his voice and immediately put him through and in seconds he was briefing Starkway on the situation.

"What's up Shawn?"

"I just brought a young lady up to ST. Mary's. She's been beaten unconscious. She lives in that apartment house down from the Foust Estate. I'd appreciate it if you could put your best on this. You might want to put out an APB, on Ray Thorp. He drives a black 83 Chevy pickup. It has a large dent on the driver's door. I don't have the plate."

"I'll have someone up to take a report," he said without giving one ounce of back talk.

"You might want to give a quick call to Pontiac. She told me yesterday he hung out around there some times. I think he raped her too. Were still waiting for the doctor to tell us just how bad things are."

"OK Shawn, I'll get back with you. Is there anything else you can tell me?"

"Not right now, but if I get anything I'll let you know." Shawn was surprised but thankful at the way Starkway was acting. A lot of police officers could care less when talking with a PI. No matter how important the incident was. He'd wait and see if Starkway's concern was for real.

His next call went out to Tony. He knew Sherin would need around the clock protection for a few days any way, at least until Ray was caught. But Tony was unable to be found. Shawn left a message for him to call him on either his home phone or car phone, than he returned to Sherin's room.

He found Brook still holding her hand, and she was still unconscious. There were nurses and doctors dashing back and forth doing their best to clean her up and examine her wounds and make her ready for surgery. Suddenly a nurse ordered them both out of the room and seconds later she was wheeled out and taken to the operating room. Now all they could do was wait.

They'd been sitting speechless in the hall both of them wanting to say something and ignoring the erg to do so when he saw Starkway walk up to the nurse's station so he went to meet him.

"You asked for the best," Starkway said extending his hand. Shawn excepted it as he made a mental note, I need to reassess my faith in this police officer he told himself as he led him to an area where they could speak in private.

"Can I talk with her?"

"They just took her into the operating room. They have to stop the bleeding. Shit, I can't believe she has any blood left."

"Have they said weather she's been raped?" His concern seemed genuine to Shawn and gradually he reveled the process of events, which brought them to this point.

"Would you like me to leave an officer outside until you can set up protection for her?"

"Thanks, but I'm going to stick around until I can get some help from Tony. He has a couple of guys I've used before."

Starkway took all the information he could get from Shawn before leaving to search the apartment, on his way there he requested additional manpower to search and gather evidence.

Sherin's door had been kicked in and was still partially open when Brook had entered the building. She thought it was weird when she saw the door open and decided to investigate. That's when she found Sherin lying on the floor and Brook thought she was dead. As soon as she felt a pulse she rushed out and called Shawn for help, knowing Sherin needed immediate medical attention.

Ray hadn't been in any trouble around Warren and there were no outstanding warrant's for him, they'd never heard of him before. His description and vehicle were to be placed on an (all points bulletin) with Detroit and the City of Pontiac police departments, plus the Michigan State Police.

The investigation of Sherin's apartment indicated Ray had begun beating on her in the bedroom and continued through every room of the house. There was light blood splatter on the bed, which became heavier throughout the rooms, ending up very heavy by the apartment door.

"They kicked me out too," Brook said taking a seat beside Shawn. They have to sew up some of the cuts on her body, they're pretty deep and they have to stop the bleeding. She's cut all over. Shawn, they have to shave her head. What did he hit her with?" Brook asked, wearing a frightened look.

Shawn put his arms around her pulling her close. "Honey, I think he used that chain he was wearing around his neck. She's lucky you stopped over, she would have bled to death if you hadn't have found her."

Tears were sliding down Brooks cheeks, but she refused to cry. Shawn was beginning to worry about her now.

"I knew he was trouble the first time I saw him, she said. He's a bum, nothing but a bum. She was clinging to Shawn like a frightened child to its mother's side.

"Is there a Shawn Cassidy here?" A nurse asked after answering the phone.

Shawn took the call, finding a shocked Tony on the other end of the line, wondering what had happened.

"The lady I told you about last night?"

"Yeah."

"Well I really fucked up this time, the asshole came back and damn near killed her."

"Nooooo." Tony replied in shock.

"I don't know but I think I've got everything screwed up on this one. Thanks to me this little lady could die and the one I thought was screwing with me probably saved her life. Maybe I should go back to chasing after lost animals." There wasn't any laughter on Tony's end of the line this time; he knew Shawn was in pain.

CHAPTER SEVEN

Tony insisted on filling in as Sherin's guard so Shawn could continue his investigation on the Foust murders. Throughout his years of teaching Martial Arts Tony had developed a very close relationship with four of his students and he lost no time contacting them requesting their help setting up twenty four hour protection for her. Hearing Tony's request for help was reason enough for them to come running, knowing the details that caused his request ignited a fire inside each of them; A fire that would only be stopped by the capture of this rapist.

When Shawn left the hospital Tony had things well under control with two-hour shifts set up for each of his crew. The students themselves agreed to work four hour shifts, two men on duty at all times, and they had more men coming.

"You tell them I'll pay'em well," Shawn promised.

"You'll have to tell'em yourself, they've already refused any money from me. They'll go out and hunt this ass hole down for free." The look on Tony's face told him he wasn't the only one wanting Ray stuffed into an early grave.

"I don't think he'd be stupid enough to come up here, but you never know. Tell them he could be carrying more than just a ball bat this time. Is Terry one of your volunteers?"

"That's ok isn't it?"

"Sure it is I really like Terry, he's one of your best. I mean they're all great guys it's just he's a little better." Shawn had entertained thoughts about somehow getting Sherin and Terry together when he first met her, but that was before this happened. Now he put it behind him. Sherin would be a long time recuperating and romance was completely out of the picture. Tony knew immediately the thought going through Shawn's mind and he silently agreed with a nod. So many times he and Shawn would develop the same train of thought with only a look or a few simple words. Tony knew Terry could use the friendship of a lady in his life, especially one as fine as Shawn had told him about the night before. But there was nothing beautiful about her now. She looked as if she'd been dragged face down and naked by a horse across rough terrain, the way he'd seen done in the old western movies. Only, those guys's were always well clothed. The possibility she could loose her life was very evident, and the thought of mixing her with Terry would have to be put aside for now.

"Look, she's going to pull through, that's all we can pray for," Tony said taking him by the shoulder. "I know you're beating yourself up, but it's not your fault."

"I should have known he'd come back."

"Right, and I should have kicked Holland's ass the first time he pushed me."

Shawn thought it was pretty funny Tony brought him up after all these years since neither of them had seen or spoken of him since high school.

"He won't get another chance to hurt her, were all behind you. Even if we have to find him ourselves we'll stop him."

"Do you think of him often, Holland I mean?"

"No, I don't know what made me think of him now, I just know all of that happened for a reason and so did this. She's going to make it, and were going to make sure he never touches her or any one else ever again."

"Thanks," Shawn said as he prepared to leave. He was actually hoping Ray would stop by, he knew Tony or any one of his students would fill one of the slabs in the morgue with his body if they had the chance. "I'm going home and clean up, than I'll take this little lady home if she'll tell me where she lives."

Brook gave him a quick burning glance, and then turned back to look out the window she'd been staring out for the last ten minutes or so. He could tell she was putting up her shield again. Women, he thought to himself. Why is it they can't verbally express themselves and get it over with?

"Will you at least bring me back up here later? I'd like to sit with her, at least until she wakes up."

"Let's see what your mother has to say." Hearing those words she did a quick about face and headed towards the elevator, her body language told him he'd probably have hell to pay once he went back outside. He was sure by the way she turned away her rotten attitude had just kicked in again. But while Tony and Shawn worked on setting up their guard roster, she borrowed cleaning materials from a nurse so she could clean the blood from Shawn's back seat. When Shawn finally made his way to the parking lot he cringed as he approached his car, until now he hadn't thought about the mess on his seat, now he did. Glancing into the back as he opened his car door a shocked look crossed his face. The white leather seat he remembered being covered with blood was as white as could be, no longer covered with the mess he'd seen there when he carried Sherin into the hospital. The look on Brook's face told him who had cleaned it and now his plans became scrambled. He'd been toying with the idea of taking her to the Warren Police Station if she wouldn't tell him where she lived, now he'd have to give her a few hours more to see if she'd start being honest with him. If she hadn't have been such an important part of saving Sherin's life he could have shown more anger and forced her into being straight with him, but the circumstances wouldn't allow him to do that now. And showing him she could pitch in and do something without being asked made him rethink the whole police idea.

"You cleaned my seat?" he whispered nodding his head in complete approval.

"Yes."

"Well thank you."

"You're welcome," she said in a pleasant tone. "Please don't make me go home?"

He was surprised her tone had changed back to the nice Brook he'd been talking with earlier in the day. He checked the anger building up inside himself and tried the polite approach again.

"I need to know where home is before I can do that, and you need cleaning up as bad as I do." They were both covered with Sherin's blood and until now neither of them had really thought about that.

"I can shower at your place."

"And change into what, my clothes? Honey they won't fit," he said with a jovial reply.

"Don't you have a washer and dryer? I can clean'em at your place while you're showering."

"And sit around my house naked until they're dry? I don't think so. Sweetheart I'm a lawyer. That means I'm an officer of the court. Do you know the trouble that could cause me? Besides, I have a girl friend I don't need to be explaining things to, especially about a twelve year old girl in my place running around naked."

"Thirteen."

"If you say so."

"Who's going to know?"

"I will!"

"So what do you plan on doing with me while you're showering?" She had a smirk on her face as she questioned him; she thought it was funny making him squirm.

"I'll drop you off at the restaurant across the street you must be hungry, aren't you?"

"I don't want to eat alone. Besides, I have blood all over my clothes too. They'll throw me out, or call the police on me," gesturing at her clothes she continued, "Christ, I look like I sliced some one's throat."

She was right; she wasn't any more presentable than he was. She needed clean clothing as bad as he did and he couldn't blame her.

"Let me take you home."

"No!

"Well then, you sit in the car until I get finished and then we'll get you taken care of." His main idea for being difficult was so she'd tell him where she lived, but it wasn't working.

"OK." She seemed to have no problem with that solution, but she still didn't know where she'd get clean clothing. She figured she'd let Shawn work that out. But when they reached Shawn's place all plans went moot. Shelly's car was sitting in his driveway.

"C'mon, I've got company and I think she might be able to help us." His whole demeanor took on a sudden cheerful tone and Brook instantly put up her shield again. She was enjoying her private time with him and she wasn't about to let it become crowded.

"Good! Now I won't have to sit out here and fry!" she shot at him as they got out of the car.

When they entered the house Shelly was sitting on the floor in front of his coffee table, shoes off legs crossed Indian style with her nose buried in a brief. She had paper work strewn about along with various law books lying here and there. Jumping up she went to greet Shawn with a kiss but seeing his blood covered clothing a frightened look engulfed her face. The fact he was walking kept her from screaming but her hand quickly covered her mouth as she tried to muffle her fright.

"Oh my God you've been shot!"

"No, I'm ok, it's not my blood." The shocked look didn't disappear while her thoughts scrambled around in her head wondering what had happened.

"You've killed some one, haven't you?"

"No, we've been at the hospital it's a long story. What are you doing here?" He wanted to take her in his arms and kiss her but the situation wasn't quite right at the moment. "I thought you were tied up for at least another week?"

I'll bet you did, her thoughts conceived. "I've got my own long story, I'll tell you later. Who's this?" The look on her face finally changed to a quizzical one, as she explored the blood-covered clothing Brook was wearing.

"It's not my blood either," Brook said, as if she was bored with the whole thing already. She was looking at Shelly as if she was a serpent after her man. Her nose flared and her face went cold as her eyes surveyed Shelly's well-formed bust nudging its way out of the thin white blouse she was wearing. She thought about her little breasts and wished they looked like that as she stood up straight and tried pushing out what she did have as far as possible. The expensive slacks Shelly wore hugged her small behind and Brook instantly hated her.

"What have you two been up to, and why the hell are you both covered with blood?"

"Could you possibly come up with some clothes Brook can change in to?" Shelly could tell Shawn was in no mood for explanations, so she stopped her questioning. As long as he hadn't been shot and it wasn't his blood she figured she could wait to hear the reason why. Brook huh, first name basis too, who the hell is this chick she wondered?

"My bags are still in my car, I'm sure I can come up with something for her." Shelly brought in the luggage and coaxed Brook to look through it until she found clothes to wear. She had done some shopping while she was in Chicago so she offered the new clothes along with the old. Brook chose the new. "They might be a little to big but you're not that much smaller than I am, except in the..."

"Thank you!" Brook shot cutting her off. She took the clothes and plopped down in a chair a few feet away giving Shelly the impression she didn't want to hear any more. She wasn't the least bit happy about having to borrow clothes from Shawn's girlfriend, but being able to take new items

Shelly hadn't worn yet made the decision a lot easier. She liked Shelly's taste in expensive clothing, all the way down to the frilly panties she chose. And she hoped Shelly hated herself for offering because she wouldn't get them back.

Shelly was dying to know what was going on but she wouldn't ask Brook about it. If Brook wanted to talk she was more than ready to listen, but she was waiting for Shawn to bring her up to date. Brook sat quietly in the chair while Shawn took his shower. The questions, who the hell is this chick and had she been there before kept running through Shelly's mind.

"You know you can use the other bathroom if you'd like," Shelly told her.

"You mean there's two?"

Shelly led her to Shawn's guest room and showed her where everything was, and then left her to clean up. As she shut the door she was quite satisfied in her mind that Brook hadn't been in the apartment before this. Minutes later Shawn returned to the living room half dressed still toweling his wet hair. Shelly's eyes glowed while she took in the sight of his tanned muscular upper body. He had put on a clean pair of tight fitting jeans but no shirt. She hadn't seen him bare-chested in a long while and it amazed her how well he took care of himself. She had no idea how much he worked out, but she knew from his tight well-defined muscles that he still took pride in his looks. She pulled the towel slowly from his hands and resumed drying his hair after giving him a long tender kiss. Her hands glided across his shoulders to the back of his neck, her whole body wanting his solid muscles against her, preferably the bottom half as naked as the top.

"I was hoping to have you to myself the minute you walked through the door," she whispered running her fingers through his hair.

"You've got to go away more often," he said taking her face in his hands and giving her a slow kiss while burying his tongue between her lips.

He didn't know what sparked this moment of passion in her but he was all for it. Something had happened, good or bad he didn't care. Instantly she was becoming disappointed they weren't alone. Reluctantly her thoughts snapped back to Brook.

"Don't forget you've got company," she said pulling away just far enough to escape his hot thrusting tongue. "You'll have to hold that move until later." After your little girlfriend leaves, she added in her thoughts.

"Shit, see what you do to me, I completely forgot about her." His actions told her what she wanted to know, there was a budding romance there but it was definitely one sided,

Brook's. She wanted to ask him just how old Brook was and where she fit into his life, but she was sure she'd learn that soon enough.

He pulled back with an unhappy look on his face, "Shit." Then he spent the next few minutes giving her a quick explanation of why he was covered with blood, and where Brook fit into the picture. He was happy she came home early so he dropped the subject of her seminar, leaving it up to her if she wanted to say anything more about that. He couldn't care less about what had brought her home, he was just glad to see her. Feeling her body next to his every muscular fiber tensed solid with blood cells eager to enjoy her every move. The mixed fragrance of her body and her hair wouldn't let him release his hold as he felt her breasts firmly poking against his bare chest.

"Do you think you could talk to Brook and maybe get her to confide in you? I'm sure she's the one messing around in that house, I could be wrong though. Did you talk with her at all?"

"No, I didn't want to step on your toes. I knew you'd fill me in when you were ready. She is a pretty young lady though isn't she?"

"The operative word there my dear is young, She's only twelve years old." He was still holding her close, trying to keep her talking while he secretly allowed his body to feel every inch of warmth she held against him when the question of how had Brook known his name that morning tugged at his thoughts.

"Thirteen!" Brooks voice pierced the air startling them and they both quickly turned in her direction. "I'm almost thirteen!" Neither of them had heard her approach and her tone told them she wasn't at all happy with their conversation, or was it what they were doing. Shawn quickly released Shelly from the imprisoned clinch his arms were refusing to give up.

"See," he whispered with his eyes getting wider. He had that deer in the headlights look and Shelly wanted to laugh but she was just as startled as he was, he quickly turned away from them trying to hide the effects of Shelly's closeness. But Brook had already been annoyed at what she'd seen. Shelly's firm breasts were now fighting to escape the confines of the silk blouse she was wearing and Brook couldn't believe it was possible for them to grow that much bigger. Now they were pointing upright like sharks ready to chew their way through the fabric of her blouse. Brook was really becoming furious.

Shelly knew what he meant without any explanation, Brook moved quietly like a cat. She was actually scary. Shelly new right away Shawn was probably right. Brook had the ability to be sneaky and stealth like, he was probably right about her being in that house she agreed. I might as well get started she thought as she began gathering ideas to begin her approach.

"Can I run you home before going back to the hospital, I mean, is there anything you need from there?" Brook stared at her as if trying to burn holes through her head. Shelly wanted her to know the effect Shawn had on her, and express the rule that he belonged to her. She knew she'd become very excited feeling Shawn's body tight against her, and she knew Brook could see it too. She felt a little bit foolish but it had to be done. It had been a long time since she'd pulled this kind of subtle attack on a member of the same sex, and this was a child. But she knew this child had a crush on her property and it was best to let her know right now that Shawn wanted a woman and didn't need a child. The clothes fit her very well and if she'd had a bust it too would probably be fighting its way out of her blouse. Shelly realized Brook was even taller than her, and when she finally did mature she'd be driving every male crazy old enough to notice her.

"I thought I was going with Shawn? I don't know you!" Brook said being short. She hated seeing the effect Shawn had brought on Shelly, the thought of them two being so physically close to each other shot disgust through her whole body.

"I'm sorry Brook." Shawn apologized. "Shelly, this is a new friend of mine, her name is Just Brook. Just Brook, this is my girlfriend Shelly Barnes. She's the best lawyer in the state. Wait a minute," he said holding up a finger as if a light suddenly went on in his head, turning away he quickly left the room and returned seconds later with a dollar bill in his hand. "Here," he said handing it to Brook. "Give this to Shelly." Brook gave him a confusing look and just stood there, she was totally perplexed. The last thing she wanted to do was look back at Shelly, she was enjoying looking at him, even though Shelly had caused the effects still prominently exposed in the front of his jeans.

"Go ahead give it to her!"

Under duress, she took three steps towards Shelly, jutting out her arm, shoving the dollar bill into her face. "Here."

"Are you giving this to me?"

"Yes!" Brook said, giving Shawn a dirty look as if to ask, "What fucking game are we playing here?"

"You have just given an attorney a retainer," Shawn explained. "No matter what you tell her or show her now, she cannot tell to anyone. You can confide in her your inner most secrets and they are safe. Please, let her take you home. She can't reveal to me where you live."

Shelly knew what Shawn was up to when he handed Brook the money, now they waited for her response.

"Is that true?" she asked looking straight at Shelly.

"Yes, It's true."

"Can a person have more than one attorney?"

Now Shelly gave Shawn a confused look. "Yes, some people have a team of lawyers," she replied.

Reaching into her pocket Brook removed some crumpled bills and taking a dollar from the mess she walked over to Shawn handing it to him. "Will you be my lawyer too?"

Taking the money Brook handed him Shawn gave Shelly a despondent look, "yes" he replied shrugging his shoulders. Maybe now she'll start giving me some answers he thought.

"That's neat," she said turning and heading for the door. "Two attorneys for two bucks, I really feel important now. "Lets get back to the hospital!" she yelled over her shoulder as she went out the back door. She didn't want to leave Shelly alone with Shawn but she knew sooner or later she'd have to.

They stood looking at each other dumbfounded; things were not working out the way they'd hoped. "Well, at least she's out side," Shelly said wrapping her arms around his neck again. She couldn't believe he hadn't caught on to Brook's jealous streak. She put that thought aside and began kissing him when suddenly the blast of a car horn filled the air. "Isn't that your car's horn?" she asked pulling back from his lips with a puzzled look while still combing her fingers through his thick black chest hairs. Shawn tipped his head as if trying to assess the situation.

"That little scamp, I aught to strangle her."

"Not before I do," Shelly replied quickly heading for the door, the horn still blasting away. Shawn grabbed a clean shirt putting it on as he ran out the door after her.

"The thing just stuck?" He heard Brook saying to Shelly as he approached his car.

"Are you two ladies ready to go?" He was hoping to stop any conflict starting to brew, and he couldn't understand why there was such an amount of tension between them. Like two cats, he thought as he buttoned and tucked in his shirt.

"I've got a call I need to answer, I'll be right back," Shelly said heading towards her car. She had her car set up to blink the parking lights every few minutes when there was a missed call on the car phone, and they were blinking now. Shawn and Brook sat giving each other dirty looks while they waited in silence for her to return. Brook sat gloating over pulling them from the house the way she had. She was also fantasizing about herself being hugged tightly against Shawn's bare chest, with her being as naked as he was. Her breasts were as full as Shelly's and she was enjoying every inch of Shawn's hairy chest pushing against her. After a few minutes of a heated discussion Shelly made her way back to Shawn's car snapping Brook back to reality and popping her balloon. Both Brook and Shawn had heard enough of her conversation to know she was very upset with someone about something.

"I've got to stop at the courthouse before I do anything else," she said sounding disgusted. "I'll meet you at the hospital as soon as I can," she said giving him a quick kiss. She looked very agitated now and Shawn wondered why, in all the years he'd known her he'd never seen her like this. There was a look in her eyes, which to him looked like fear where only moments ago there was passion and he was sure she'd wiped away tears before returning to his car. He knew the phone call and not Brook had brought on this sudden change, at least he hoped so. It had to be something to do with the reason she'd came home early and he was sure of that too.

"Are you going to be ok?"

"Yeah, I'll be along in a while."

"Shelly?"

"Everything's all right, please don't ask me any more questions, not now." She was too afraid she'd be in tears if she allowed herself to tell him. If it was only Shawn there she would have let go now, but she wasn't about to fall apart in front of Brook, no way. "I'll be up there in a little while," she said giving him another quick kiss, then she shot a quick glance at Brook before returning to the house for her shoes and brief case.

On the way to the hospital Shawn beat his brains out wondering what had happened. The seminar she said she'd be at for at least another ten days had been quickly cut short after two, why? That phone call upset her to a point he'd never seen before. What the hell's going on he wondered?

"So you're not going to talk to me now? It really did stick."

"I wasn't thinking about that, I'm sorry, I had something else on my mind."

"You mean, what kind of trouble is your girl friend in?"

"Who says she's in trouble?"

"I'm not stupid, that look on her face said it."

"She's an attorney, she has lots of court cases she's working on. That call could have been about any one of them. What is it all of a sudden you're an expert on peoples looks?"

"She went from, (happy to see you) to (frightened), in five minutes. I know that and I'm only thirteen." Brook was emphasizing every word with jutting hand gestures Shawn hadn't seen before.

"Twelve, you're twelve!" He didn't know if it was the joyful smirk on her face while she related her thoughts to him about Shelly's sudden change of emotion, or her ability to asses the situation so quickly, that was pissing him off.

"Ok! I'm twelve, but I can read peoples expressions."

"Very perceptive of you, but I'm perceptive too. And I believe you're keeping me from your house because you know if your parents knew what you did with your free time they'd be pissed off!" He was hoping changing the subject would get both their minds off Shelly's problem.

Brook didn't say another word until Shawn parked the car in the hospital parking lot. As she was getting out of the car she turned to him.

"I don't have parents, I have a mother and she couldn't care less what I do!" She didn't wait for a response; she just turned and hurriedly ran off for Sherin's room.

"Brook, Brook!" He called after her, but she kept running. He wasn't sure, but he thought she was wiping her eyes as she disappeared through the main entrance. He couldn't believe he'd caused any reason for tears. For a tough young lady she sure sheds tears fast, he told himself as he made his way through the hospital following her. "She sure as hell doesn't mind causing friction when she can," he blurted to the air while the people around him wondered if he was nuts.

When he got off the elevator he noticed Tony and Brook sitting in chairs at the end of the hallway across from Sherin's room. He figured at least one of them would have been sitting in with her, something must be up he told himself as he walked passed the nurses station. Then he wondered if maybe she was out for x-rays or something, so he turned back to the nurse's station to enquire about her progress.

"Mr. Cassidy?"

"Yes.

"Your friend in room 304 has requested no visitors, except you. And she'd like to see you, ASAP. The only thing is, she doesn't need you in there bothering her either," the six foot tall over weight nurse scolded as she waved her finger at him. "So you have two minutes!"

"How is she doing, has she been awake long?"

"Are you a member of her family?"

"No."

"Then I'm unable to tell you a thing, other than she's in critical condition, she shouldn't be seeing anyone; you have two minutes Mr. Cassidy! Two!" She shot, holding up two fingers and shaking them like an old schoolmarm. "This young lady is not out of the woods yet, she could go down hill fast." Now her voice dropped to a snotty overbearing whisper. "I've seen burned victims relapse and even die because of the trauma their body goes through trying to recover from the shock and abuse. This little lady has had almost the same abuse as a burned victim. The amount of cuts on her body are ridiculous."

Shawn decided it was time for him to leave before he lost his temper. To listen to this bitch another second could become fatal, she acted as if he was responsible for Sherin's condition and he was fighting hard enough with himself trying to believe he wasn't. As he walked away he figured he'd just met the head nurse, or warden, now he knew why Tony and Brook were sitting in the hall.

"That bitch won't let anyone in to see her!" Brook blurted as Shawn approached them.

"I heard," he answered calmly. The nurse had explained to him Sherin requested no visitors, and in her weakened state she wasn't to be bothered. Shawn wondered why the request for no visitors?

"The... nurse said I could have two minutes, so why don't you two go get something to drink, or grab a snack," he said looking at Tony. "I'll be here for a while."

Sherin was sleeping when he approached her bed so he quietly took a seat and scrutinized Ray's handy work. She had multiple stitches closing various cuts that were visible on her face and neck, and he knew there were twice as many across the top of her head. Her pretty blond hair had been hacked away and completely shaved in certain areas. He reached up to move some of the hair she had left so he could look at the wounds when she slowly opened her eyes. He softly brushed her forehead with his lips kissing between stitches. Now the feeling of being totally responsible for her being there hit him like a rock. He knew the rest of her body was covered with stitches too, probably hundreds from the amount of cuts he remembered seeing before he rapped her in the sheet.

"Thank you for the body-guard," she whispered.

"I'm very sorry he did this to you, I should never have left you there alone," he whispered, a tear sliding down his cheek. Tears didn't come easy from Shawn's eyes, but looking at her and knowing how close to deaths door she was, hurt him very much. It was his fault; at least he claimed it was. He should have moved her to a safe place, or at least suggested it. No, he should have stayed there on her couch if she refused to leave he told himself as he looked at her. He saw how Ray acted. This man was prepared to split his head wide open. He had left Sherin in harms way and he couldn't forgive himself for that. With all the fights he'd been in, and the entire tough guy bullshit he'd been through, now he felt like crying because he knew it was his fault. The nurse was right. Sherin could have been killed. Ray had definitely planned on leaving her that way. She could still end up dieing if her body went into shock or serious infection from all the cuts. He sat there looking at her while fighting back the tears. Sherin reached up and tried wiping the tears from his cheeks as she looked into his sad blue eyes.

"It's not your fault," she said fighting back her own tears.

"I'm still feeling very guilty about this mess. That's why I'm making sure you have a guard at all times; At least until he's caught. Please let me do this much for you?"

"Thank you, but I don't deserve your help. I've probably put you in serious trouble too. I'm sorry I told him you were my new boy friend, he said he'd kill you too." She was talking in a very low whisper and Shawn pulled himself close to the bed so he could hear her. Taking her hand he gave it a careful squeeze.

"Don't worry about me, you concentrate on getting better, Tony and I will keep you safe." To wish Ray had only beaten her was unthinkable, he wanted to know if she'd been raped but he was too afraid to ask.

Her eyes made a weird gesture as she said thank you, it made him wonder if she had a problem or at least a question she wasn't asking.

There was a knock on the door and a very disgusted looking "warden…" nurse interrupted their conversation. "I said two minutes!" she said in a heated whisper.

"Get the fuck out of here!" Shawn commanded in a low growl and a look to match. Turning back to Sherin he whispered, where were we? Oh yes, is there a problem with me giving you a guard?"

"Could you ask him to stay out side?"

"Why? He's good company he likes to play checkers. And he'll even read to you if you ask him to."

She stayed quiet for a while, too long for Shawn. "C'mon, what's the real problem?"

"He's Black, I'm scared of him," she whispered.

A big smile came across Shawn's face as he thought about the best way to tell her how close he and Tony were, and just how safe she was. He moved his chair as close to the bed as possible and took both her hands softly into his.

"You know, I never noticed, that's probably why he never goes to the tanner with me."

She started to laugh, than scolded him.

"Please don't make me laugh, it hurts so bad."

"I want to tell you a story about my friend out there if you're up to listening."

"Yes," she whispered giving him the best part of a smile she could develop.

"If I bore you you'll have to promise me you'll tell me to leave so you can get some sleep." She squeezed his hands softly and gave him as much attention as she could. She liked having him in the room and anything to get him to stay was acceptable.

"I first met Tony when I was a freshman in high school. He was a new kid in school, one of those lucky one's pushed into forced bussing. He hated it. To add to his problems we had a big bully in the neighborhood. I'd grown up with Rick, his name was Rick Holland, he and I had our falling out during grade school, hated each other, mainly because I could kick his ass and his big bully act wasn't working, I was bigger. So freshman year rolls around and Rick has a lot of new people to push around, one of them is Tony. Tony wouldn't, or what

I thought, couldn't fight back. Shit, he only stood about five three, maybe a hundred and twenty pounds. Rick was five eight a hundred and seventy, mostly all fat." Sherin giggled a little and reset the squeeze on Shawn's hands.

"Rick started in on him from day one. The first time I witnessed Rick's bullshit, I told him to lay off. So naturally I became " the nigger lover." I smacked Rick against the lockers a few times and he made sure I never heard those words from his mouth again. Oh, he didn't quit saying it; he just made sure I didn't hear it. Tony told me in various terms to stay out of his business, so I figured I stuck my nose in and my head out when I shouldn't have. This sort of crap continued for the next three years. A dozen or so times I broke things up between them, telling Rick I'd kick his ass if he didn't stop, and Tony would tell me to mind my own damn business. I don't know how many times Rick pushed him around when I didn't catch him, but I'm sure it was plenty. I think it was in our junior year when Tony started asking, instead of telling me to stay out of his business. He'd say, "Would you just mind your own business?" But I knew he was starting to like me because that's when he began asking me with a smile. The first month of our senior year, Tony now stands about five eight, weighs around one fifty, one sixty. Rick stands six two, tips the scales at one ninety. He's solid as a rock, captain of the football team. It was a Friday and everyone was excited because it's our first football game, and Rick had eaten the entire box of wheaties or cheerios for breakfast I guess, I don't know." She giggled again still giving him her complete attention. "But he was full of piss and vinegar and figured he had to knock Tony on his ass for the first time that year. I guess Tony told him no, it's not going to happen. He told Rick to leave him alone but Rick wouldn't do it. When I reached the third floor of the schoolhouse after sprinting all the way from the welding department, some five hundred foot away then up those three flights of stairs because I'd heard some kids whispering about how Holland is planning to kick Tony's ass and I thought Tony was in trouble. I froze in shock when I hit the third floor. Tony was in the process of kicking Rick's ass from one end of the hall to the other, and back again. When I arrived I saw moves from him I couldn't believe. I knew right then he'd been training in some form of Martial Arts, not just the last year, but for years. He could have kicked Rick's ass that first time in our freshman year. I walked up to him and asked why? He just looked into the crowd of kids and said, "because I told him not today, not this year. I'm a senior too and you're not going to do it any more."

"I told him no, I want to know why you didn't do this the first damn time instead of putting up with his bull shit the last three years? He looked at me and replied."

"I've kicked the shit out of him dozens of times, I've got his name printed across the front of my heavy bag at home."

"A quick look into the crowd where he was looking told me why he wasn't letting Rick have his way. I saw one of the prettiest black young ladies I'd ever seen and her eyes were glued to him. She was looking very disgusted at what he'd just done, but he wasn't going to get pushed around in front of her. All that was over. Well today that little lady is his wife, and in about five months they're going to have their first child; and I'm going to be a God Father. I just wish he'd go to the tanner with me once in a while," he added with a questioning look. "Now I know why he won't," Shawn finished with a big smile.

Sherin now had tears running down her cheeks, but they weren't from the pain she was feeling. She started to laugh at his last few words as Shawn took a tissue and began drying her tears.

"He'll guard you with his life, and he'll treat you like a queen. He's a better man than I am, he's smarter and he would die before allowing himself to screw any one over. And if you tell him I said any of those things I'll plead insanity."

"I'm sorry, I didn't know he was such a close friend. Ray has made me so afraid of all strangers; I'm so scared now.

Would you ask him if he'd play checkers with me later?"
she said still choking back tears. "Please don't tell him I said
anything."

"I won't, I just want you to know you have nothing to
be afraid of from him." There was a long pause in their
conversation and he figured she'd dosed off so he started
to leave but she stopped him. Then he turned with a funny
look on his face and added, "something else, that little lady
you call a vamp?"

"Yes."

"If it wasn't for her, you'd probably still be laying on your
apartment floor. She's the one that saved your life. If she
hadn't have found you it's no telling where you'd be right
now. She and I brought you here and she's been waiting ever
since to get in to see you. Oh, and by the way," he continued
as he softly squeezed her hand again, "her name is Brook."

"Oh my God," she said in disbelief. "I've been so wrong,
will they ever forgive me?"

"They won't even know."

"Would you ask them to come in please?"

"Sure," Shawn said giving her another soft kiss. "I'll be
back in later, but you need to get lots of rest. Everything will
be taken care of. You don't have anything to worry about but

getting better, ok. That goes for your rent and any bills you have, don't worry about a thing."

"Shawn."

He had just turned to leave again but she hadn't released his hand yet so he turned back to her as she pulled him softly back to her lips.

"He might be your equal, but he's not better than you." She gave him a soft kiss on his lips and thanked him again. He sat beside her a few more minutes until she dosed off, then he slipped back out of the room. He delivered the message to Brook and Tony and made sure the nurses knew it was all right for them to be in her room. Shelly had finally arrived but seemed still in her agitated state.

"Can we go to dinner or some where private? I've got something I need to tell you."

"Tony, we'll be back after a while, take care of Brook for me too, will you?"

Both Tony and Brook gave him a dirty look, as he and Shelly walked away smiling. Brook hated hearing Shawn say she needed taken care of as if she needed a baby sitter, and as Shawn looked back over his shoulder he caught her quickly pulling her tongue back into her mouth. Tony gave him a frightened look of thanks for nothing.

CHAPTER EIGHT

There was a large family restaurant across from the hospital so Shawn suggested they go there, he wanted to stay as close to the hospital as possible. They took the short walk in silence, Shelly rehearsing what she wanted to say, and Shawn fearing he was going to hear the worst.

They took a booth in a secluded corner and ordered coffee, when it was served Shawn asked the waitress to leave them alone, they'd let her know when they were ready to eat. There was nothing he hated more than a waitress bugging him every minute when he was trying to have a serious conversation unless the waitress was Angela.

"Ok, what's been bothering you?" He finally questioned. He was afraid what he was about to hear was going to hurt. He'd heard of women trying to make the final break giving one last love making session, than saying it's not working, I've got to move on. Maybe she met someone at that damn seminar, he wondered? Or maybe her boss Stan finally got to her? He knew Stan had been after her ever since he'd left the Public Defenders office. The fear of what he was about to hear darted through his mind, he wanted to just sit there with her but he knew they had to get it over with. That argument was probably with the new boyfriend wondering why she hadn't broken it off with me yet, he pondered.

Shelly reached across the table taking his hands into hers holding them extra snug expressing her love and wishing they were someplace she could be holding him in her arms. She gave him a soft smile and he knew she was having difficulty beginning, but she finally managed. "I want you to promise me you will not run off half cocked and hurt someone or get yourself put in jail when I tell you what I have to say?"

Here it comes he thought, she's going to tell me who, and she's afraid I'll go kick his ass. "When have I ever ran off half cocked and done something wrong?" he asked, feeling as though she was already showing a loss of faith in his character.

"Never." She replied, thinking about the many nights he'd spent in jail for contempt of court.

He gave her a quick smile and for or a second he thought she'd lost faith in him. It had been a long time. He'd asked her at least three times to marry him; maybe the ring didn't have a large enough diamond on it. She always said "not right now." No engagement, but no promise to marry in the future. A "maybe when my career is established," she'd say. He hated hearing that from her mouth. So we get together every once in a while, have great sex, and float until the next time, his thoughts were on overload.

"But I've never had to tell you something like this before" she continued. I know how much you love me, and this could cause severe problems."

Maybe I'll move to Florida, or maybe Texas, his thoughts continued on allowing his mind to progressively conger up danger as if a lost cause was being presented and he might as well consider new plans for his life. I guess it's about time I got my ass out of Detroit anyway. That's the only way I'll be able to get through this. Maybe Sherin would like to leave Detroit too, he wondered? He was sure this news was going to end their relationship, or at least put an end to his future plans of marriage with her.

Shelly realized she was probably driving him crazy with delirious thoughts so she'd best get it over with. "Last night after hearing our last speaker I went back to my..."

"Wait, last night, this is something about last night?" The questions in his mind unraveled like a deck of cards being fluttered into the air. Must be this thing with Ray and the investigation he was doing, coupled with Sherin and the crap with Brook, all had his mind fearing the worst.

"Wait, start over again, what?" He asked, turning his head and shaking it as if it would help him process the words she was speaking; his face was all scrunched with delirious question.

"If you'd listen I could tell you."

"Ok I'm listening," he said putting both hands up in a stop motion, "you were saying last night?" she took a hold of his hands again needing somehow to feel him against her touching her as she told him.

"Last night I came back to my room after listening to the last speaker, I had planned on going over some of the material I'd picked up and maybe watch a little TV." She took a deep breath and continued, which told him whatever she hadn't said yet was tearing her up inside. "I took a shower and as I was toweling my hair dry I walked into the bedroom, I was looking down the way I always do until I get the towel wrapped around my hair and I heard someone clear their throat, it startled the shit out of me."

Shawn's attention suddenly peaked, waiting for the answer of who had cleared their throat, he quickly thought of Ray raping Sherin and was sure this wasn't what she was about to say, that she'd been raped. No, he thought, she'd be a hell of a lot more worked up if she had been. Unless she had been having an affair with someone, and that someone sprang a surprise visit on her. He realized his thoughts were running wild again and it would be best to wait for her to finish. Then he could get pissed off.

"It was Judge Hinkley." The look on her face showed complete disgust quickly reflected by his.

"Hinkley! Shawn felt like he'd been smacked in the head by Ray's bat. "What the fuck was he doing there? And you were standing there stark naked, right?"

"You promised!" Her words shot out in a gruff whisper, fear gripping the look on her face. She looked around to see if people were staring in their direction, and they were.

"That fucking son-of-a-bitch." Shawn was suddenly happy and pissed off at the same time. He wasn't hearing what he feared he was about to; but the words he was hearing still made him disgustingly mad. Then he wondered if she'd ever given him a reason to think he could be there?

"You promised," she replied squeezing his hands as tight as she could. "People are watching."

"I didn't say yes."

"Please?" She picked up his hands clutching them in hers shaking them, tears were slowly sliding down her cheeks. "I need you to stay calm and back me up. I won't be able to get through this with out you." He didn't want to cause her any more anguish, he removed his hands from her grip and took her face in them softly wiping her tears with his thumbs. The happiness he was feeling took over as he leaned over to kiss her and she quickly responded. He wanted her in his arms, and nothing else mattered.

"OK, go ahead, I'll keep my mouth shut," he said, taking her hands back again and holding them softly.

"He was sitting on my bed in his robe drinking champagne."

Shawn started to say something then he put up a hand in that stop motion again, so she continued.

"He thought maybe I'd have sex with him seeing how he was in town for the evening."

The end of the list of tortures Shawn was thinking about couldn't be found, while he kept his mouth shut listening to her words in his mind he was stringing Hinkley up by his balls. She was trying her best not to burst out crying but it wasn't working. She sat quiet for a few seconds just looking at him; she was unable to find another word to explain.

"Well, aren't you going to say anything?"

He wanted to say, "you told me to be quiet," only because he was too pissed to say anything but he didn't.

"So what happened next?"

"I covered myself with my towel and kicked his ass out of my room. Then I packed and came home." As she finished she began wiping tears away with her fingers. No, she hadn't ever given him a reason to think he could be there; Shawn was satisfied without even asking the question.

He was happy, pissed, madder than hell, and disgusted with himself for thinking the wrong things. She came straight to him, and asked him to please stay cool when she was exploding inside. She needed to be held and from where he was he wasn't doing her any good. He quickly moved to her side of the booth taking her into his arms. They hugged and kissed until she noticed everyone in the place was still watching them.

"Lets leave," she suggested.

He dropped a five on the table for the coffee, delivered and never drank, and then taking her by the hand he pulled her from the booth crying and giggling. She followed as he guided her between the dining room tables. Outside he pulled her against him as though they were running through the rain trying to stay dry. When they reached the car he pulled her into his arms again, giving her a warm wet kiss.

"Let's go to my place," she said pushing her body tight against him. "It's closer." Smiling, he followed her request as fast as possible. Traffic hindered his movements, but he didn't care. He drove swiftly holding her against him. There was no more discussion of what had happened in Chicago, not now.

They made love like they had during those first few months when their affair was fresh and they were full of lust. They couldn't seem to get enough of each other. After running out of steam, they showered and started all over. He loved it. He didn't know weather fear from what had happened caused this sudden change in her or what, but he wanted to thank Hinkley very much before kicking his ass. He caught himself wondering how much time he'd have to spend in jail for beating up a judge. Probably the best thing would be to catch him in the dark, pulverize the shit out of him and see if the cops could pin it on him. As much as he'd like Hinkley to see who was beating on him, it would be better to keep it a mystery at least from most people. Hinkley would know exactly who had done it though.

He lay holding her tight to his chest after the third round, knowing this was what he wanted for the rest of his life.

Why won't she marry me? He asked himself.

"Do you want to know what else happened?" she asked breaking the silence.

No, he told himself. I just want to lie here for the rest of my life with you in my arms. No other worries, no questions.

Just making love every time the urge strikes us. She pushed herself up on his chest looking into his eyes. He couldn't help himself, his lips searched down her neck to her shoulder and past, to her beautiful voluptuous breast, kissing one and than the other.

"Honey?" She pushed back looking into his eyes. There was a glow of happiness there; she thought she'd satisfied everything for the moment, but there was still something. "Am I missing something?" she asked smiling.

"It's just, I was afraid I was going to hear something from you I didn't want to hear. I mean, I didn't like hearing what you did tell me, but you scared the shit out of me working up to what you did say." Now I can't get enough of you."

"You thought I was going to say it's over between us, didn't you?"

There were times when he'd swear she could read his mind and this time she was right on. He fought it but couldn't hide the look of fear that suddenly entered his eyes after hearing her words.

Pulling herself tight against him she kissed him softly.

"That's not ever going to happen," she said in a soft whisper, "were an item. You don't ever have to worry about that. I know I haven't been giving you all of me lately, but that will change."

If she could just keep giving him the percentage she'd shared with him the last two hours he'd be happy. He couldn't help it; he had to merge into forbidden territory. "Then why won't you marry me?" He asked, holding her extra snug for fear she'd jump from the bed and BOLT from the room screaming. She was still looking into his eyes, and now her face took on a brighter smile.

"That's still in my plans, I haven't cancelled any of those thoughts."

He wanted to say, "you could have fooled me" but those words were all he needed to hear, for now. "It's in your hands, you let me know when you're ready." He drew her softly back to his chest tucking her tight against his whole body. "But my clock is ticking faster and faster." She gave him another loving pinch, but this one made him say ouch.

"Ok, what happened next?"

"I kicked his ass out of my room. He had the adjoining room and I never knew it. I had this funny feeling someone was in my room the night before, I woke up feeling like someone was watching me. Now I know damn well it was him."

Shawn knew she usually slept naked; at least she did when she was at his house. He felt her tears on his chest as she continued telling him about that evening.

"I packed and left right away. He said he'd ruin my career if I told anyone about this. He's going to send Lacy Carrigan to prison, if I don't let him lay me, I just know it."

"That fucking prick. Who's Lacy Carrigan ?"

"She's a girl I'm defending on child abuse charges, she says the baby sitter beat her child and I believe her. He's going to send her to prison. Now that I think of it, I'm afraid he's done this before, just to get at me. That's why I had to stop at the courthouse. He needed to tell me a few things."

"What do you mean?"

"Well, first off he told me not to tell you about this, he was very adamant about that. I said oh sure, he's the first one I'm telling, and I left his office. He was mumbling something about "I'd be sorry" but I just kept walking. I'm afraid he's going to ruin my career, or do his best trying." She wiped her tears with a corner of the bed sheet as she continued. "Two weeks ago I had a young man that pleaded guilty to B&E, the deal was, he'd do six months jail time and two years probation. I gave the case back over to Stan, thinking he'd finish things like was planned because I was swamped and he wasn't, I mean all the work was done all he had to do was get it on record and have it signed. Then I found out Hinkley gave him the max. Stan let him change things without challenging him on it."

"Stan's a suck ass. Haven't you caught on to why I left yet?"

"I know, but I still feel as though I can make a difference. I want to become a Judge. I know then I will be able to make that difference. You could have been a Judge. You'd have made a wonderful Judge."

"You think so?"

"Yes, You're the most honest man I've ever known. You would never screw over a defendant. You know more about the law than most Judges."

Shawn didn't know what to think. He had never heard Shelly talk so positive about him. It felt good to hear her talk this way.

"I'm liking you more every second sweetheart, go on," he said giving her rump a soft squeeze.

She pinched him back playfully on his side. "Well, we know that will never happen, don't we?"

"What?"

"You becoming a judge."

"You've got that right," he said thinking about Collin's offer. He could become a Judge; he wasn't going to say anything though, not just yet. But he did decide to ease her feelings as much as he could.

"Collin says Hinkley's under investigation, he might not be around to screw up your career.

"Judge Therman?" she quickly pushed herself back up on his chest so she could look into his eyes.

"Since when do you call him by his first name?" she asked with a concerning look.

"Since he insisted." He had never told her about how he became such close friends with Judge Therman.

The Judge had been the driving force behind Shawn's quest for his career in the judicial field. And it was a request from the Judge that he keep things between themselves. Only a few people knew the Judge kept him from going to prison; but they didn't quite know all the facts. Neither did Shawn. The main reason, hidden from Shawn, was Collin and Shawn's mother had been very close. It was highly probable that Collin was Shawn's biological father. It was considered very thankful that Shawn exploited most of his mother's traits, her looks, her hair and her eyes, and his father's height. Both his father and Collin were tall, which helped the secret stay between Collin and his mother.

Collin was sure if Delores had lived, she would have cleared up the mystery; then he worried that maybe her death was do to her infidelity, the infidelity he'd caused. She believed she had committed an unbearable sin when she gave herself to him, and would be punished by God some day. He blamed himself for that. He pursued her relentlessly until he managed to win her love, than he moved on. He realized way too late that he was in love with her, and if she had told him Shawn was his, he would have continued his quest for her total commitment. Her death not only ended his search for the truth but it also ended his womanizing way of life. He stuck to call girls and prostitutes after that. Less of a chance to fall in love that way, he told himself.

He had no idea Shawn had been treated the way he was growing up, because he put most of his time into his own career. Until Shawn was charged with murder, Collin had a chance to renew a long lost friendship with Delores' brother, Shawn's Uncle Tim, and very good friend. It wasn't until Shawn came before him charged with second-degree murder that Collin renewed his interest in Shawn's life. He made sure Shawn had the way and means to attend Law school, keep his tail out of trouble, and pay his debt to society.

After pleading guilty to minor charges, the second-degree murder charge was dropped. Collin was given praise for helping another Detroit youth grow to help society, instead of becoming a juvenile delinquent. Collin insisted the amount of his help be kept between him and Shawn.

Shawn never reveled their secret to anyone, but he did request that Tony be given the same help to keep him out of prison also. After all, they were both being held on the same charges. They both had been involved in a bar brawl in which two thugs lost their lives. Shawn and Tony were charged with second-degree murder because they had been trained in Martial Arts. No matter if the thugs started the fight. Collin made arrangements for Tony to receive the same minor charges as Shawn, and a loan to start his first Martial Arts Academy. This also had to be kept between him and Shawn. Both defendants were given community service to perform, with time served canceling any more jail time. They both pleaded guilty to misdemeanor charges, which were expunged after three years of good behavior.

Shawn never told Tony why things were cleared up so easy, they each cleaned up their acts and became improved members of society. The city of Detroit loved it. The chamber of commerce praised the judge on the front page of the Detroit Free Press, And Shawn's father told him to get out. Life goes on.

"I knew he was quite fond of you, why I don't know."
Now Shelly sat across his chest as though trying to hold him
down waiting for his answer. "What are they investigating?"
She questioned excitedly.

"He's got his claws into the county permits. Some how
he's tunneling fees into his own pocket."

"You're kidding me." Her chin almost touched his chest
as her mouth dropped open from the shocked look after
hearing those words, and her eyes lit up with excitement.
"You mean he could end up being removed? That would be
so cool. It sure doesn't say a lot for our court system though.
Do you know how many of his cases could be recalled? Oh
my God, this could be a blessing mixed with disaster," Like a
child she flopped off his chest back onto the bed beside him
rubbing her face pushing her hair back. "It doesn't matter
to me what way they find to remove him, I'll be so glad to
see him go." Suddenly she jumped back into his face almost
hitting him in the nose.

"This isn't something that's going to tilt is it? I mean,
that's all I need, hoping he's going down and he puts the
blame on some clerk. I would think someone besides me
could see the injustice he's serving from the bench."

"It's been noticed, no one wants to listen. I told you that
when I left."

"But he's a judge. Don't you think he's probably got all his angles covered? He's no dumb fool."

"He's not? What do you call what he pulled on you? I think he's dead in the water." He felt a slight cringe, he knew he shouldn't feel guilty keeping secrets from her but he did. He wanted to tell her everything but decided against it.

"God I want to believe that." The look on her face showed total delight but for only a second. "It would be great to find out he's off the bench. It would sure make doing appeals easier. I'd have about thirty to do immediately. Can you imagine the cases that would get reopened? Would you come back if Hinkley were removed from the bench?"

"I don't think so." A look of disappointment covered her face as she turned away hoping he hadn't seen it, but it radiated through out her whole body. "Does that bother you?"

"No."

"Honey, the temperature of your body changed when I said no, don't tell me it doesn't bother you." She sat up looking at him, the disappointment still showing on her face.

"You're an excellent litigator..."

"I like what I'm doing, besides I still do lawyer stuff."

"You became a lawyer so you could do lawyer stuff!" she asked, emphatically emphasizing the word stuff. Her mood was quickly changing as she got out of bed and headed for the shower again. She never blew up at him when she was mad, her eyes would roll as if trying to spin in their sockets, then she'd relax and regain her composure. She never really had any reason to be angry with him.

"So, if I became a judge, I'd make what, maybe fifty thou. A year?" He asked loudly talking to her from the bedroom. He didn't usually use his hands for expression when he talked, but they were in use now, only she couldn't see them.

"You'd probably make over a million before you retire," she replied while turning on the shower.

"So, if I made say, a million doing what I do now, would that change things?" he asked stepping in after her. There was a sudden burst of uncontrollable laughter from her as he pulled the shower door shut. He met her laughter with a big smile. He wanted to say, "what the hell, I've got twice that amount stashed" but he held his tongue. He allowed her the moment; she needed to have a good laugh even though it was at his expense. Besides, he loved hearing her laughter, and it was much better when she was stark naked. The dimples and smiling face on this beautiful naked angel was a vision to behold.

"Just keep laughing." He said smiling while he poured her favorite liquid soap over his shoulders. He loved her so much there wasn't anything she could do to erase what he'd heard from her lips the last couple of hours. He wondered if he told her about his stash if her mouth would drop and she'd be at a loss for words, or laughter. Maybe then she'd say let's get married, NOW! He really wanted to, but he told himself to wait. He was sure she wasn't after money, but for now he'd keep it to himself as he had all along. He decided to change the subject while he waited for her laughter to settle to her sexy little smile.

"What do you think of Brook? I asked her about her parents, she said all she has is a mother that couldn't care less."

"I think she has a crush on you," she replied as she began lathering the soap across his chest and shoulders.

"What!"

"I mean it. She's got a crush on you. For a moment when I saw her I thought maybe you had a new girl friend, until I saw how young she was. But she does have a thing for you" Shelly said sliding her hands along his sides and over his behind. "She is a very pretty young lady."

"You know! Just when I'm about to remind myself that you're one of the smartest people I know! You come up with one of the dumbest thoughts…!" Her look told him he might better stop right there.

"I'm a woman, believe me I can tell when a women is jealous. She has a crush. I see it in her eyes when she looks at you. She was jealous the second she saw me."

"She's a little girl."

"She's a young lady." Shelly replied softly. "And you're a very handsome hunk of a man. She looks at you the same way I do", she said stepping back from him still washing certain areas.

"Well thank you," he said giving her a pleasing smile. She wasn't sure if those words were for what she'd said or for where she was washing.

"Oh, pooh," she said stuffing a wet washcloth in his face. "Let's get back to the hospital so I can try making friends with your little scamp. But first, would you wash my..?" A half hour later they were finished with their shower and on their way back to the hospital.

CHAPTER NINE

After Shawn convinced Brook he'd be too busy to run her home, she agreed to let Shelly take her.

"I could take a cab."

"Yes, but Shelly has to go right by your house, she's running over to Warren on other legal matters, C'mon Brook cooperate a little."

That was all Shawn had to ask. Brook wanted to please him as best she could, but she didn't have to be happy about it. It surprised Shawn when she didn't even ask how he knew Shelly was going right by her house.

"I guess," she replied in her usual snotty tone. She laid her head on Shawn's chest a while as she gave him a long hug. Every one there locked eyes with him telling him exactly what Shelly had said and now he knew it, her crush was very evident.

Her house was located about six blocks north of Beckwith Street, in a crowded neighborhood of Warren. She lived in a small three-bedroom ranch style home with about nine hundred square feet of living space. In this area you were lucky if there were ten foot of space between houses. On her street every third or forth home was empty and boarded up, and half the homes were neglected as far as up keep and lawn care. Hers was no exception, the grass needed mowing.

I can see why she'd fall in love with the Foust Mansion, Shelly told herself as she pulled in the drive. The bedrooms here couldn't be much larger than ten foot by ten.

"Will you introduce me to your mother?"

"I don't think she's home!" Brook snapped.

"Isn't that her looking out the window? She's probably worried about you."

"Yeah right!" Brook said, her tone expressing noticeable doubt as she exited the car.

Shelly quickly followed as Brook headed for the house but being just a few steps behind her didn't matter, Brook with a little help allowed the screen door to slam shut right in her face. A second later a middle aged lady with a cigarette dangling from the corner of her mouth reopened the door apologizing. Smoke from the cigarette drifted into her eyes but she didn't remove it, she just squinted and began talking.

"I'm sorry, my daughter has forgotten her manners." Extending her hand she continued, "I'm Karen Shepard, is my girl in trouble again?"

"No Mrs. Shepard, she's not. On the contrary, she's to be commended, she helped save a lady's life today."

"She doesn't want to hear about that!" Brook yelled from an open bedroom, then that door slammed shut.

Shelly and Brook's mother looked at each other, neither of them liking her attitude. Her mother waved Shelly into the kitchen where they could have a little privacy.

"Is she always like this?"

"She seems to hate the world," Karen replied, wiping tired eyes. Shelly figured she must be about fifty years old, either that or she'd had one hell of a hard life. She could see where Brook got her height though, and if she followed after the rest of her mothers traits she'd be cuddling some very large breasts of her own some day soon. Karen stood about six foot tall and was quite top heavy supporting a very large set of breasts. "I'm at my wits end with that young lady, she's supposed to be mowing the grass today, I can't seem to do anything right with her. You said she saved a women's life?"

"Yes, she happened to be in the right place at the right time I guess, there was a young lady about six blocks from here beaten up this morning. Thanks to Brook she was taken to the hospital before she bled to death."

"At least her heart works for someone," her mother replied showing no emotion over what she'd heard. The pain she'd been having with Brook was pronounced heavily by the look on her face and the tone of her voice. Her voice was soft and kind, but lacking concern. Telling Shelly most of the problem was probably Brook herself, and her mother had been through it hundreds of times, maybe thousands. She wondered if the problem wasn't just teenage rebellion.

"Doe's her father have problems with her also?" The look Karen shot at her could have frozen boiling water.

"Her father? Karen turned and walked to the stove where she began pouring herself a cup of coffee, then she turned back towards Shelly expressing great strength of suppressing an explosive temper. Slowly she removed the cigarette from the corner of her mouth the ash falling to the floor where it mingled with others from lack of sweeping. Then, as if reading the words from paper she announced, "her father has been dead for years."

Shelly thought if she looked close she'd be able to see a hint of flames coming from her nostrils as she announced those words.

"I'm sorry to hear that."

"Don't be, he wasn't all that great of a man the cheap bastard." She flipped more ashes towards an ashtray on the table, which missed and she brushed them to the floor along with the rest. At the sound of her words Brook came running out of her room screaming.

"He was too! And he hasn't been dead for years either!" Then she gave a grunting shout before running out the front door and slamming it again. Shelly's face turned to shock but Karen's look never changed. It was as though she'd seen and heard it many times before. Shelly wondered if she'd placed herself in the middle of a hornet's nest. Someone was lying but she wasn't sure which one it was.

"This last year or so things have really gotten worse. When I think she's in her room, she's gone somewhere. I check her room at all hours of the night she's not there. I go into her room at three in the morning sometimes, and she's gone."

"Have you called the police?"

"You don't have any children, do you?" Without waiting for an answer she continued. "You don't call the police on your own kid. If they hate you they'll damn sure kill you some day. I can't do that; then she'll have problems with them all the time. I don't want her to hate me any more than she already does. The cops around here have a habit of slapping teenagers around; no I don't need that shit."

"But, you have to get her some help before she does something to hurt herself."

"What, suicide? She loves herself too damn much to do that. Sometimes I wish she'd just kill me and get it over with!"

"You don't really mean that."

"I don't know what I mean any more," she said setting down to the table. I have tried and tried, I can't keep this shit up. My whole life has been a fucking mess. You get pregnant by a man you love and you think he loves you, than he drops you like a rock. You spend the rest of your life raising a child that hates your guts."

Shelly listened while Brooks mother let go of feelings she'd probably been holding in for some time. She was beginning to feel sorry for her now, especially knowing Brooks attitude already. As she listened she allowed her eyes to drift through the house at the rooms and walls she could see. There were various pictures of Brook hanging here and there which told her Karen was a very proud mother and cared a lot for her daughter. She really had a lot of hatred built up towards Brooks father though, and there were no pictures of any man on either of the walls. Shelly thought she could understand. Karen didn't seem willing to elaborate on the real time of death of Mr. Shepard, and she decided to leave that alone.

"Will she be back soon?"

"Your guess is as good as mine. That rich son-of –a-bitch, he could have done a lot more for her that's for sure."

At that moment the front door opened and slammed shut again as Brook crossed back into her bedroom yelling, "You can stop talking about me now!" Karen just slowly shook her head.

"Can I talk with her? I mean if there's anything I can do to help I'd like to try."

Karen was so tired of Brooks attitude that she willingly accepted Shelly's help without asking where and how she came to be so much into Brooks life; Until Brook came stomping back into the kitchen.

"You're supposed to be my lawyer damn it! Quit telling my mother things about me! You don't even need to be here, you brought me home, now leave!"

Karen's face lit up as she crushed out her cigarette and lit another one. "Her lawyer?" Karen questioned. "You're an attorney?" Her face lit up with great surprise.

"I had to do that so she'd tell me where she lived. This way I can't reveal to anyone where she lives or any thing she tells me. Because it seems she doesn't want some people to know where she lives."

"She better ask you to straighten out her fathers estate, seeing how she's supposed to know so much about him," Karen blurted. Before her mother could say another word Brook grabbed Shelly by the hand quickly pulling her from the kitchen into her bedroom.

"You're supposed to be my attorney, why are you even talking with my mother and telling her things?" She questioned in a heated whisper.

"You're the one that left me alone with her, remember? And you don't have to be so damn rude." Shelly had had enough and was ready to let her have it back. "Look, you want to be treated like an adult, than start acting like one. Show some respect for your elders, especially your mother. I know you've got a crush on Shawn, but he hates disrespectful little twits like you!"

She may as well have struck Brook Across the face with a flailing hand because as those words struck Brook's ears tears began streaming down her face. Shelly knew her words were sharp, now she was afraid they might have came from a sudden streak of jealousy. She hadn't talked to anyone like that in a long time. Out of the courtroom anyway. She had no idea her words would cut into Brook this way, not after all the toughness she'd witnessed from her so far.

As soon as she saw what she'd done, she took Brook into her arms. She felt instantly sorry for her ridicules out burst, but it was the best thing she could have done. The hug Brook gave her back was one from a young lady in dire need of support from her mother or somebody older, maybe that was why she'd set her sights in Shawn's direction. Before Shelly could say she was sorry for her words, Brook was asking for forgiveness.

"I'm sorry," Brook sobbed squeezing Shelly so tight the past few hours of her rotten attitude were immediately forgiven. Shelly knew she was holding a young lady in need of someone to put her confidence in. Brook latched on to her and wasn't letting go. It was as though she'd needed to cry for a long time, and Shelly's ridicule had been the catalyst to break it loose. Maybe she was just what Brook needed and fate had sent her here to help get her life back in order, Shelly wondered? She believed the lord intervened when it was necessary; placing people in the right place at the right time was his doing. She'd quit asking herself why, and promised to give Brook all the help she could.

"How long has your father been gone?"

Brooks crying let up very little but her grip stayed the same. Shelly stood hugging her for some time, feeling her tears on her shoulder. It was a long while before Brook finally answered.

"About five months," she replied between sniffles. But momma doesn't know. Brook still wouldn't relinquish the hold she had around Shelly's waist. After a long period of standing, Shelly coaxed her to sit on the bed, but she kept her grip as tight as she could.

"What do you mean she doesn't know?"

"It's a long story," Brook mumbled.

"What did your mother mean about your fathers estate?"

"Nothing."

Shelly knew there was a lot she was missing, but this was no time to dig into it. She let Brook search her feelings while she let her eyes take in the surroundings of her room.

The bedroom of a teen-aged child could tell her a lot, especially this child. The room was about twelve foot by twelve. She, or her mother, kept it very neat and clean. She had a desk with writing paper and pens kept neatly arranged. The penholder was on the left side with envelopes and paper in a holder to the right. The walls had various pictures of Walt Disney characters hanging on them and she thought that was pretty peculiar for a girl her age. But then she noticed a set of colored pencils and paints on a shelf above the desk and wondered if Brook had painted the pictures herself?

"Did you paint these pictures?" That was the best question she could have asked, because it brought Brook out of her state of mind.

"Yes." She moved away only enough to turn her head towards the pictures Shelly was looking at. She stayed cuddled against Shelly like a hurt toddler clinging to its mother. Her crying was finally reduced to deep sniffles, but the tears were still running. Shelly pulled a few tissues from a near by box and proceeded to dry her eyes.

"I'm sorry for what I said," Shelly told her as she dabbed at her eyes.

"That's ok, you were right. My mother says I've been quite a bitch lately. Things have really been screwed up these last few months. She thinks my drawings are a waste of time."

"You draw and paint very well," Shelly said admiring her work. The pictures weren't paint by the number oil paintings either, they were free hand drawings done on white paper then Brook had painted them. Some were filled in with colored pencils, and they were all good. The expressions on the faces of the characters made them look almost life like. Shelly stood up to get a closer look at one on another wall and as she looked she noticed other pictures done in colored pencil lying in a stack on a shelf.

"May I", she asked, indicating she'd like to look at them. A nod from Brook told her to go ahead. She was very impressed by the detail Brook had captured and brought alive in each and every one of them. As she looked she found sketches of farms and animals not yet colored, but showing the promise of ending up as beautiful as the rest. A painting poked in behind a shelf caught her eye and she reached to pull it out, as Brook quickly said no. But she already had her hand on it so she pulled faster.

A sudden look of shock engulfed her face, because in her hand was a beautiful painting of Shawn. She had captured his wonderful blue eyes and handsome face as she'd seen it only hours ago when she had made love to him. It was as if she'd taken a photo than transferred it to her painting. Her surprise at seeing the picture left her momentarily speechless. It was as good as anything she'd seem from the best photo shops in town, and it was Shawn. She looked at Brook, then back at the painting.

"This is…beautiful…it's, it's Shawn." She wondered when and how Brook got the picture to work from. She stood staring at in awe. Brook had captured that glistening look in his pretty blue eyes, the one she had been looking at only a few hours earlier. That bright smile and dark hair which made his handsome face so kissable.

"Would you like to have it?"

"Could I pay you for it?" Shelly asked, unable to take her eyes from it.

"No, I've got more of them."

Shelly gave her a quick look. "Where, can I see them?" She was really hoping to see more pictures.

"No because they're still up here," Brook quickly stood pointing at her head.

"You painted this from memory?"

"Yeah."

Shelly looked back at the painting with more disbelief. It was more beautiful knowing she did it from memory, she was afraid to ask just which memories when Brook cleared up the question.

"I left the dog out." A quizzical look from Shelly told her she didn't know what Brook was talking about. "I saw him on the news when he found that champion poodle at the airport. I wanted someone to paint so I painted him."

Shelly was sure that was impossible. She had seen the picture on their television, no way could she have caught the sparkle of his blue eyes on that old thing. She knew Brook was still hiding things, things she would work very hard on finding out, but later she thought.

"You're not going to marry him are you?" Brook asked, giving her nose a good strong blow into a tissue. Now Shelly was really stunned at what she was hearing. She wanted to say yes, we just spent about three hours today making love, have you ever…

"Honey, you're only thirteen years old, Shawn's thirty five."

"Do you think he's to old for me?"

A big smile came across Shelly's face. Not too old she thought, but society might frown on it. She was becoming totally confused but she tried her best to explain.

"He's old enough to be your father. Look, you're going to meet hundreds of men your own age by the time you graduate college, handsome men. Men you'll want to paint hundreds of pictures of." Probably nude pictures she told herself.

Brook looked into Shelly's eyes as she dried her tears. "You are going to marry him aren't you?" she said in a melancholy tone.

"Yes sweetheart I am," Shelly answered softly, almost apologizing. She felt as though she was setting the law down, and she felt a bit ridiculous. She was sure Shawn had never touched Brook, but her mind kept playing tricks with her.

"Why have you waited so long?"

Shelly wondered how she knew anything about the length of time she and Shawn had been seeing each other, and their subject of marriage. She knew Shawn usually kept his personal information pretty tight to himself, so how did this little lady know so much?

"I've been too tied up in my own career for some time. But you know, this lawyer thing goes both ways."

"What do you mean?" Brook asked with a very questioning look.

"Anything we discuss cannot be told by you to anyone else, even if it's information about me," she said fibbing.

"I won't say anything, but if you love him so much, it seems like you'd marry him so you could make love to him every day of your life. If he were my boy friend I'd never get dressed."

Another wave of shock went through Shelly's body. Her mouth dropped, a young thirteen year old telling her how she would treat Shawn and she was right. She suddenly realized all the time she'd thrown away, the time she could have spent with him. Making love every day. Maybe staying naked for days, making love when ever the mood struck them. Why did it take a child to open my eyes, she wondered? I love my career but how could I put that ahead of Shawn? Why am I so worried about what he likes doing? I know how well he loves what he's doing. What he could be and what he wants to be is really up to him. We could get along on my paycheck, her thoughts touted.

"Are you going to be all right?" Shelly asked. "Because I think I should be going." She wanted to talk to Shawn before she settled down for the night.

"Will you pick me up tomorrow morning and take me back up to the hospital?"

"I think I can manage that. Would you like to give me your phone number?"

"Our phone is shut off, we can't afford to pay for it."

"I'm sorry to hear that. I'll be by about 8:15 ok."

"I'll be ready. Take the picture, you can have it," she said smiling.

Shelly thanked her and headed for her apartment, deep in thought about all that had happened through out the day. In a way she was glad Judge Hinkley had came into her room. If he hadn't, she'd still be in Chicago board as hell. This day was one of the most exciting and eye opening days she'd had in her life and she loved it. Now she had to clear things up in her mind. She didn't believe Brooks mother could have problems with the paintings Brook had done. Any mother would be proud of the work their child could do, and this work was wonderful. Brook probably misunderstood her mother; teens have a bad habit of mixing things up. She knew Brook had to have seen Shawn close up before being able to paint that picture. There was no way she could have captured that starry-eyed look in his beautiful blue eyes without looking into them at one certain moment. Impossible, she told herself shaking her head.

She stopped at a late night drug store and purchased a picture frame for Shawn's picture. When she got home she put the picture in the frame and stared at it while she tried getting him on the phone. There was no answer. She tried his car phone and the hospital with no luck. She even tried Tony's line, only to find it busy. Finally she gave up and went to bed.

CHAPTER TEN

Thursday morning couldn't have come sooner for Shelly. She had tried reaching Shawn before going to bed but his line was busy. She tried various times getting the same results. She also tried Tony's number, which too was ringing busy. She figured the two of them were gabbing about something important so she finally went to bed.

First thing this morning she wanted to see if she could get Lacy Carrigan's case changed to a different Judge, but she needed some help from her boss with that. Part of her restless night was caused from worrying about, so she decided that after dropping Brook off at the hospital she'd go to her office hoping to discuss the matter with Stan. If she could get him to help her before Judge Hinkley got to him, it just might work. She had toyed with different scenarios since she woke up from her restless night. Besides worrying about Lacy, her sleep had been disturbed by continuous nightmares about Shawn.

She dreamt about him making love to Brook. In one instance Brook was laughing at her, she was tied up in a chair in front of the bed while Brook was sitting on him in the bed having sex looking over her shoulder at her with glaring satisfaction. Naturally Brook was naked and those budding breasts were now triple D's. She closed her eyes and refused to watch. Another dream Shawn was leaving Detroit for good and when she pleaded with him to stay Brook popped up naked in the front seat of his car as he pulled away from her. In her dreams Brook's bust was bigger than hers. In another dream Judge Hinkley was sending her to prison for refusing his advances, she was sitting in the courtroom naked and Shawn was in a jail cell in the courtroom being forced to watch. He was reaching through the cell bars swearing he'd kill the judge. Every one in the room was laughing while Hinkley walked towards her removing his robe reveling his naked body, he was going to have sex with her right there in the courtroom and she'd been hand cuffed in the defendant's chair unable to run.

She didn't go back to sleep after that one, she watched an hour or so of a mini series on television featuring Gone With The Wind while consuming a fresh pot of coffee. She wished she had gone to Shawn's for the night after leaving Brooks house. At least there she could have slept in his arms and been free of bad dreams, there was no way bad dreams could have crept in while she was locked in his arms, she was sure of it.

She was starting to believe Brook was right. She knew she'd feel better every morning waking up next to him; and his massages were heavenly. She couldn't believe she'd been leading him on for so long and he hadn't found someone else to cuddle up with. For a few seconds when she'd first seen Brook she wondered, but only for a few seconds. Once she realized Brook was just a teenager she cancelled all those stupid thoughts. Now she decided she'd put him first, and her career second, with some serious thought to his marriage proposal.

She knew her stupid dreams were the results of her mind playing tricks on her after all the crap she'd been putting up with. Seeing Shawn with her just added to the confusion, he'd never have relations with a girl so young.

She wasn't at all prepared for what she ran into when she walked into her office; Stan was collecting all of her files.

"What are you doing?"

"The question is what the hell have you been doing?" Stan asked, without changing the speed of his movements.

She shook her head trying to make sure she wasn't still dreaming, instantly she was satisfied she wasn't.

"What's going on Stan?"

"You've been put on suspension till further notice. Clean out your desk, and get the hell out of this building before Hinkley sees you."

"I thought he was going back to Chicago?"

"What do you mean back, he didn't go any where. Why should he go there when he knows Hasting is there?"

"Senator Hasting, what the hell has that got to do with anything?"

"Oh, act like you weren't going to play the two of them against each other?"

"What the hell are you talking about?" At that moment a secretary tried to enter the room and Shelly ushered her right back out the door locking it behind her. She stood momentarily frozen. She hadn't thought about the lengths Hinkley would go to, but now she knew. Surely someone else must have seen him in Chicago, but if Stan didn't know he'd left Detroit, who did. He could drum up some charge and put her in prison if he wanted to. If this investigation into his wrong doings fell through, no one would doubt him. He could hang her with what he'd been doing and walk away laughing. No one except Shawn would believe her. For the first time in her career she was beginning to fall apart and she was getting very scared.

"I don't believe this bullshit," she said shaking her head. What has Hastings got to do with all of this?"

Stan stopped what he was doing and planted his rump on the edge of her desk. A half ass grin quickly developed across his lips and he began after folding his arms across his chest the way he always did when he was boasting about something.

"We all know you've been," he paused as if grasping for the proper words to say what he wanted to say, "having fun with the Senator. Judge Hinkley knew you wanted him to come to Chicago, but with Hastings there he knew you were trying to fuck with his job. What the hell are you doing?"

She couldn't believe it. The Judge was going to pin on her what ever it was he was being investigated for; she just knew it. Somehow he'd twist around everything Shawn had told her about, and Senator Hasting would be drawn into the mess. A US. Senator tied into her life while she scammed money from the zoning department would be headline news. She had gone out with him a few times but only for dinner and conversation. There had never been any request for more by him, or from her. She had let him know right off she was in love with a man here in Detroit and would probably marry him some day. The Senator would never have said the things Stan was talking about. It had to have come from the Judge.

"Where have you been getting your information from? No don't bother, I think I already know."

"Look, let me tell him you and I are getting together, he'll reinstate you and things will cool down."

He attempted to give her a hug, which she quickly pulled away from and he promptly took up his seat again on the edge of her desk. As he settled he put the smirky look back into place.

"Look, I'm not the one after you. You don't have to hate me over this."

"This! What the hell is "this" has Hinkley said? How in the hell can you let him tell you what to do?"

Stan's hands went up in the air in his usual; "hey don't ask me shrug" while his mouth went quiet. Shelly looked at him still shaking her head. It wasn't until now she realized he was a spineless bastard. Total disbelief shot through her mind. For years she'd admired him, and even toyed with the thought of marrying him at one time, but Shawn had always come out on top of those thoughts and now she knew why.

He sat there with a shit-eating grin on his face and it made her sick. She was done talking with him so she turned and began walking towards the door. She'd taken all she could handle from him and Hinkley both. Stan had to be on the Judge's side, if anybody knew where the Judge was at any given moment of the day it would be Stan. He knew exactly what the Judge had done. They probably had a good laugh about it after Hinkley told him what he'd done in her hotel room. The look on Stan's face told her he knew exactly what had happened, at least Hinkley's version. She was sure Stan had the impression she'd gone to bed with the judge, after all Hinkley wouldn't lie. Now she was feeling sick and wanted to be far away from both of them forever. This bad publicity would ruin Senator Hastings chances for reelection and probably ruin a friendship she valued dearly; her stomach was becoming very upset.

"You going to clean it out?" Stan asked sitting there looking smug waiting for her answer.

"I'll do it when I'm damn good and ready. Hinkley's going to get his."

"What the hell's that mean?"

"It means, it took too damn long for me to see what someone else saw years ago. I must be blind. Just don't let him put Lacy in prison, please. Find one ounce of good in your damn soul and do the right thing." She knew she'd lost any chance of helping Lacy stay out of prison. But she'd fight to get her out if Hinkley put her there. And if he had her disbarred, she knew Shawn would help her without even asking him. "You know what?" She asked as she unlocked the door and stood ready to turn the knob and leave.

" What?" he asked, still sporting his disgusting grin.

"It's great knowing who you can trust without having to ask."

"Well I'm behind you, you know that" He said cheerfully."

"Oh go fuck yourself Stan!" she half screamed as she opened the door and made her escape. She couldn't help it, when she was alone in the ladies room she broke down and cried. Years of the career she loved were being destroyed and the likelihood of her being able to save it or even rebuild it was unthinkable and Senator Hasting would be pulled into the mess with her. Hinkley would stop at nothing pulling the pressure off from himself; Hell was just beginning to churn. She needed to talk to Shawn, she needed his arms around her while she cried and tried putting some sort of reasoning into this whole mess. When she was able to dry her eyes she headed for his office, she didn't want anyone in the building knowing she'd been crying, that information would get to Hinkley faster than water running down hill. And he'd just gloat over it.

"Please Shawn be home," she begged out load, as she grabbed her car phone and tried calling him, but she had no dial tone, it had already been turned off. "That asshole didn't waste any time," she mumbled, referring to Hinkley. "God, I hope this investigation sends his ass to prison."

When she arrived at Shawn's office his car was nowhere to be seen. She had her key ready to unlock his office door but it wasn't locked. Her whole body felt a happiness that she'd never felt before, she knew he was there and she needed him badly. As she walked in he was sitting at his desk with his back to the door reading the newspaper. Hearing the door he slowly turned his chair in that direction towards the front of the desk. He was wearing a pair of reading glasses as he tried making out the fine print in the stock section and peering over the top of them his heart did a flip flop as the look on his face quickly formed a smile erasing the scowl he'd developed reading the stock market.

"Hi," she said softly. She wanted to jump right over the desk and have his arms wrapped around her immediately. She didn't even care if he said, "I told you so," she just needed his arms around her. "I didn't know you wore glasses." She said making small talk while forcing her tears back, but she wasn't hiding anything from him.

"I just picked'em up to read this damn small print, what's up?" he asked as he rose from his seat placing the glasses on the desk. Before taking one step she was in his arms tears falling like rain like he'd never seen before.

"I've been suspended," she managed to say between sobs.

He held her in his arms as she let go of the hurt she'd been trying to hide, he didn't say "I TOLD YOU SO", he just held her tight the way she knew he would. She was so glad he just held her without saying anything, telling her he knew exactly what she needed. As she cried she wondered how she could have stayed away from him for so long. Putting all her time into her own career she felt very stupid about now. She held on to him the way Brook held on to her the night before. She suddenly knew just how she must have been feeling. She didn't want him to let her go, and he knew it. They stood locked in each other's arms for a long time until the ringing of the phone interrupted them.

"Hello," Shawn said to the caller, "hold on I'm going to put you on the speaker." He pushed a button on the phone than replaced the receiver taking Shelly back into his arms. She cuddled tight against him loving him more for such a small gesture. As he wiped her tears Captain Starkway came on the line.

"The prints on that ball bat you gave me belong to a Raymond Thorp, a.k.a. Ray Little, a.k.a. Ron Lite. He's got a rap sheet as long as your arm. His latest was about six months ago for attempted murder and Judge Hinkley let him go on some technicality."

"Some how that doesn't surprise me." Shawn replied with a chuckle. "Hinkley probably put him on his payroll."

"Well, the all points are out on him, we'll catch him."

"We'll help if we can," Shawn assured him as he finished the conversation and turned his complete attention back to Shelly.

"Do you want to talk about it?"

She nodded her head no and snuggled back against him as he picked her up and carried her to a large leather love seat he kept in his office for his power naps. He sat down pulling her tight to his lap and held her there for some time before she finally told him she was afraid Judge Hinkley was out to destroy her and Senator Hastings.

"For a second I even thought about screwing him and being a lousy lay, maybe then he'd leave me alone."

Shawn took a hold of her chin turning her head so he could look into her eyes but she burst into tears again after realizing what she'd said. He knew she was falling apart inside and he didn't really know what to say or do except hold her. He wanted to tell her there was nothing to worry about, he'd make sure things went fine. But he knew her career meant everything to her. She was a strong lady but the thought of starting over had never entered into her game plan. Who'd think of having things brought to an end by a crooked judge?

After another long period of silence he turned her face to his again so he could look into her eyes. "I could use an assistant," he said softly.

"You couldn't afford me," she replied blubbering. Than she took his face into her hands and kissed him a long warm kiss. "I love you Shawn," she said cuddling back against his chest. His arms felt as if a warm blanket had been wrapped around her and she cuddled blissfully for quite some time before breaking the silence. "Do you really think this investigation will pull him from the bench?"

"Ninety percent sure."

"I was hoping you'd say one hundred percent sure. At least that way I'd have something to look forward to," she replied still sobbing.

"I could probably fix it so he quits breathing," Shawn offered.

She quickly looked him in the eyes and a cold stern look of steel gripped the face looking back at her, so serious she had never seen before. "Don't even think of it. I don't want you going to prison for me."

"Who said I'd go to prison?"

"You don't think they'd come looking for you, or me? Stan knows everything he knows. I'm beginning to think they're linked at the brain or something," she said sniffling while wiping her nose.

"Did Stan tell you he knew?"

"The look on his face told me."

Shawn remembered, even though he hadn't seen Stan in a long time, he remembered Stan gave a lot away with his expressions. Hinkley probably told him a lie about how he was invited to Shelly's room for sex he thought.

It was no different than when he was in high school Shawn remembered. The jocks would ruin the good girls reputations by bragging they'd had sex with them. It was a game with them. Either play the game and put out or we destroy you. Give in or get out, and they meant school. Some of the jocks would rather ruin a girl's reputation and drive her out of the school rather than admit they never even touched her. It was still here, and Hinkley was the worst jock of all. Shelly was probably right. Stan wouldn't stoop to Hinkley's ways, but he would play the "believing, gawking tell me more jackass," that always believed every word the jocks said, and was sure to spread the news.

"I didn't mean end his breathing, just cut it off long enough so he'd be using crayons for the rest of his life," Shawn mused.

"You're talking about a District Court Judge."

"I'm talking about a fucking back stabbing dog that would attack his own mother if it was beneficial to him." There was anger in Shawn's words with a tone Shelly had never heard come from him before. She felt good that his response was geared at protecting her, but she also felt afraid because it was bringing out a side of him that scared her a lot. Was he capable of doing something like that? She remembered one late night a couple of years back seeing him come home covered in blood and when she asked what had happened he said the less she knew the less she'd have to testify about. All she knew was it wasn't his blood and he immediately burnt all the clothing. It ended there. Nothing ever came of it. But until now it had been a long time since she'd even thought about it. Now it really scared her. She squeezed him extra tight afraid to look at him for fear she'd give away her feelings of that night.

"Ok, do something to take your mind away from it, and make them think you could care less what they think.

What would you do to settle your mind when a case is going bad?"

"I've never had one go this bad."

"Just think of it as your worst one ever. You're going to work on your brief in your mind while you shop. I know you've done it this way before. Just go out and do the extreme. Go nuts."

"I would go shopping."

"Then go shopping. Be seen spending lots of money. Laugh and have some fun. And make sure it gets back to them."

There was silence again for a few seconds until Shelly finally agreed. "I don't want to be seen spending lots of money though. What if his idea is to put some of his kickback crap on me?"

"Ok, spend a little money."

"Maybe Brook would like to go shopping?"

"There you go, take her shopping. She'll be starting school soon maybe you can help her get ready." Shawn was being a little sarcastic but he wasn't aware they'd become a lot closer the night before.

"I've got something I want to show you," she said getting up from his lap still wiping tears. "Wait right here," she ordered as she quickly ran out the door to her car. Seconds later she returned with the painting. He sat waiting patiently where she had left him, becoming very curious.

"Look," she said placing the picture in front of him.

He was almost as surprised as she had been when she first saw the painting. She was still wiping tears but finally starting to come out of her depressed mood.

"Did you do this?"

"Brook painted it, isn't it wonderful? I told you she had a crush on you." Shawn stared at the painting speechless. It was hard to believe such a little brat could have such talent he thought as he admired her work. "She's got a lot of paintings."

"Of me?"

"Well, there was one other one hanging on her bedroom wall which looked a lot like you, 'til I turned on her bedroom light."

"And?"

"It was one of Winnie The Pooh," she said laughing and still wiping tears from the corners of her eyes. But now some of them were from happiness. He grabbed her pulling her back to his lap and placed a warm kiss to her laughing lips. She was coming out of her bought of depression and her laughter sounded great.

"So how does this spell a crush?"

"Shawn," she replied with a tip of her head, and he knew she was probably right.

"You know if you'd come and work with me you'd laugh like this every day."

"I believe that would be payment enough," she said kissing him back, "You offer a very tempting pay rate."

He smiled thinking of where things could end up once this mess was finished and he wondered if it would be appropriate to send both Judge Hinkley and Stan thank you cards for driving her into his arms. All he could do was hope and that would have to do for now.

"Oh, I'm staying at your place tonight, and tomorrow night, and the next night and the…"he took her cheeks softly into his hands squeezing her lips and kissing them while she continued talking. "Possibly a long time, maybe forever she mumbled," finally shutting up and returning his kiss. She sounded like a little girl inviting herself to stay over, and he loved it.

YES, he shouted in his mind. Mental note, add candy to those thank you cards. Taking her into his arms he said, "You can stay forever if you want to."

CHAPTER ELEVEN

As Shelly drove Shawn's car across the county to ST. Mary's Hospital she was in a lot better spirits than when she'd arrived at his office. She agreed with him, doing some shopping would make her feel better, especially if she shopped for a new pair of shoes. Maybe even a new pantsuit would help raise my spirit she wondered, or maybe something to surprise Shawn and raise his blood pressure. It wouldn't take her mind completely off her problems, but it might cloud them up for a while at least.

At the hospital she spent a few minutes talking with Terry and Tony, then after telling Brook her plans for going shopping she waited to see if she'd ask to go along. Sherin was doing better, and Brook was getting board. After a few minutes listening to Shelly and Shawn talk she realized Shawn was staying at the hospital while Shelly went shopping so she offered to go along and Shelly quickly accepted the offer, not letting her know that was her intension all along. Brook was more than happy to accompany her during her sudden desire to shop and ignore the heavy work schedule she'd claimed she had earlier that morning.

Shawn was elated with Shelly's decision to stay at his house, and in his mind he began working on plans to keep her there. That was the reason he suggested she take his car, at least now he knew she'd have to come back and get him.

He didn't want her to stay out of fear. Oh, that was ok for getting her motivated to move in, but he didn't want that fear to be the reason she stayed. He hoped she'd realize she loved him too much to be away from him. He swore to himself he wouldn't bring up the word marriage again, that would be up to her from now on. He had tried various times in the past and each time she seemed to pull farther and farther away. He was very surprised she hadn't run out the door the day before when he'd said something, now he figured he'd better be quiet. Let her stay, and then he'd work on showing her why she should never leave he thought.

He knew he couldn't improve on his lovemaking; she always seemed quite satisfied in that respect. He always did what she liked and as many times as possible, if she'd stay longer she might find out he was more of an animal in that area. No he thought, maybe I'd better curb those ideas until I'm sure she'll marry me. I could chase her through the house and change her mind about thinking the bedroom was the only place for making love.

As much as he loved her, he felt there were times when she acted a bit old fashioned and prudish. She thought making love was a bedroom activity. The teenage years were gone, no more quickies in the back seat of the car, they were adults and that's what bedrooms are for. It was hard for her to show affection in public too, a quick peck on the cheek was about all he could give her if it was possible people were watching. Or unless they were on a dance floor in a dimly lit barroom. He was sure he could change her mind on many of her quirks, if he could only get her to marry him first. Right now it would take dynamite to get him off the cloud he was floating on, quirks be damned, he loved her and things were headed in the right direction.

He took Tony for coffee at the hospital cafeteria, leaving a very capable student of Tony's in charge of Sherin's safety. Terry said he needed coffee too so they all headed for the first floor where the cafeteria was located. He told Tony everything Shelly had been through, expressing the fear she had about her career being ruined.

"You're kidding me," was Tony's response after hearing Shawn's information. "Maybe we need to put some critical action practices in force?"

"That thought passed through my mind too; but you know we can't start that again."

"I didn't know we stopped," Tony replied giving Shawn an "I'm ready when you are," nod, "I thought we just took a hiatus."

Shawn gave him a satisfied look with his usual understanding smile, which told Tony they would both think over the best ways to make corrections to the problems at hand.

"What happened to your tire did it finally fall off," Tony questioned with a smile. But Shawn was paying more attention to Terry and wondering what he was up to so he didn't answer right away.

Terry had removed a picture from his shirt pocket, looked at it and placed it back. The three of them sat talking about Ray and if they thought the police were doing their best.

"I'm surprised Starkway is putting his own time into this," Shawn said, placing his coffee cup back on the table.

"I told you!" Tony shot back. "If you would just give an inch you'd be surprised, these guys are pretty nice people. I know a lot of them hate PI's, but you have to get them liking Shawn again. When did you take the tire off your back bumper," he questioned after seeing it missing.

Terry removed the picture again, gave it a quick look then replaced it back in his pocket. It was obvious he was waiting for one of them to question his actions.

"It had some surface rust on it so I took it off and dropped it by Haskins. I know, it looks funny without it on there doesn't it?" Haskins was a body shop He and Tony trusted to do any repairs they needed to their vehicles.

"Yeah, now it looks like any ordinary chrome covered ford," Tony replied, pointing at Terry and wondering what he was up to.

"OK, hand it over," Shawn said reaching out towards him.

"What" he asked with a big smile?

"C'mon," Shawn said, his fingers dancing in the air waiting for the picture, "give it up."

Terry handed him the picture and Shawn smiled when he looked at it. It was a picture of Sherin before Ray laid his grubby hands on her and carved her up close to death. Shawn could tell Terry was very impressed with it. She was wearing a bikini bathing suit and her beautiful blond hair was blowing in the wind, it showed how beautiful she was and hopefully would be again. She could have passed for a Play Boy Bunny she looked that good.

"Where did you get this?"

"Brook brought it to me. She wanted me to see the lady we're keeping watch over. She's a knockout," Terry said still smiling.

"I'm reading something more than body guard here," Shawn said with a smile.

"There's nothing wrong with that is there?" he asked still looking at the picture, than back at Tony and Shawn.

"Not at all," Shawn said, "but she's got a long haul ahead of her. At least you can see how pretty she'll be once she recovers." He was wondering how Brook managed to have this photo in her possession. I'll bet she uses a lock pick more than I do, he told himself as he handed the picture over to Tony.

"Don't forget I used to look like shit too," Terry said still smiling.

Shawn remembered that very well. Terry had come to train at Tony's first academy about ten years earlier. He had been suffering from various childhood allergies, at least that's what his doctor claimed his problems were, he'd be that way all of his life. He was a very skinny kid and he had very bad acne, and he seemed to have colds constantly. His mother enrolled him into Tony's Karate class program against his will, and it was the best thing she could have done.

Tony had taken Terry under his wing putting him on a special diet with various herbs included, and started him on a light exercise program. It Tony took over a year just to remove the damage caused by bad medications. Terry's doctor warned his mother telling her she'd made a very bad mistake and Terry would be on his deathbed within weeks if she allowed this change to continue. But today, Terry is in very good health, he stands five foot ten inches tall, weighs one hundred and ninety solid muscular pounds. He took second place in the World Martial Arts competition in Europe, and agrees that his mother made a very good decision introducing him to Tony.

As Shawn handed the picture to Tony, he thought about the last time he and Tony used their special skills to right a very bad wrong. There had been times in the past when a persuasive force was needed to coax certain people to do the proper thing and Shawn thought about a night a couple of years back when he and Tony were forced to rescued the son of a client. The teenager had joined a skinhead cult and when he realized he was in too deep the cult members would not allow him to get out. The boy's parents were furious. The young man had no idea what he'd placed himself into, until he tried getting out. The father begged Shawn to bring his son home to them, and Shawn couldn't refuse.

Late one night Tony and Shawn visited a hang out on Eight Mile road known to be the Club House of that particular group, and after a few minutes in the smoke filled dimly lit establishment, they removed, well kidnapped the client's son. There had been a few minutes of severe negotiation which left quite a few of their members needing immediate medical attention, and then Shawn and Tony walked away with the young man between them. Places like that rarely call the police for help; they're usually too embarrassed that someone walked in and trashed the place kicking their Asses. Both Shawn and Tony left covered in blood, none of it their own. Shawn gave the parents of the boy enough money to move out west and get the child some help, and from the letter he received from the boys parents about a year later the boy was doing fine and had decided to become a lawyer. The ten thousand dollar check that accompanied the letter more than reimbursed him for his faith in humanity.

"She could definitely use a new friend," Shawn said as Tony handed the picture back to Terry. Shawn was quite surprised that the idea he had about introducing Terry to Sherin was taking place even though he had dismissed it. Fate must have taken over as soon as I dropped the idea, he thought.

They returned to Sherin's room and spent the next two hours trying to raise her spirits. Her wounds had swollen much more and now she looked like the Pillsbury doughboy. Shawn and Tony traded silent looks of anger and words weren't needed to relay the way they were both feeling. They would get the chance to face Ray very soon, his life was hanging by a thread and they agreed with each other that thread would be cut if they had anything to do about it.

"You're going to be just as beautiful as you were before he touched you," Shawn assured her, while he held her hand and wiped her tears. Her pretty blond hair had been hacked to the scalp so they could stitch the many wounds Ray had left. Why didn't they just shave it all off he wondered? She evidently had a very thick skull, which helped her escape receiving multiple fractures.

The doctors were sure he had left her for dead, which meant as soon as he heard the news she was still alive, he'd probably be back after her sooner or later to finish the job so she wouldn't be able to testify against him for attempted murder. That was the charge against him. The doctors said she was lucky her blood clotted quickly, that helped keep her from bleeding to death; from the wounds she had they were totally surprised she hadn't. Brook showing up was the balance of the angels blessing. "Oh yes," Shawn told himself as he sat looking at her, "step back in front of me you bastard, just for a second." He looked at Tony and knew he too was thinking those same words.

Sherin slept most of the time when she wasn't crying, still afraid Ray would come back some day and kill her. She knew Shawn and Tony were doing their best but they couldn't be there every day, every minute of her life. She feared Ray was the type to wait until she was alone, weather it took a week, a month or even a year. He'd get to her some how. The fear couldn't be erased from her mind no matter how hard Shawn and Tony tried convincing her things would be ok. When she closed her eyes she could see Ray coming towards her wheeling that chain through the air. She kept having dreams about him beating her again. The drugs they gave her for pain were contributing to her delusional state of mind, but no one knew it. She had a right to feel the way she did, but the fear she was expressing was causing her more anxiety than she needed to be going through.

"She seems ten times worse than she was yesterday," Shawn said to Tony after they stepped out into the hall. "Do you know anything about the shit they have her on?"

"No, but we can take a look."

Shawn went to the nurse's station and drew their attention while Tony looked over her chart. He made a mental note of the medications she was on, and then signaled Shawn he had what he needed.

"Do you think some of your methods would help better than the stuff they have her on?"

"I'll do some checking on her medication and be right back, I'm pretty sure we can come up with something better than she's getting here."

While Shawn stayed to watch Sherin, Tony made a visit to the pharmacy across the street from the hospital. When he gave the pharmacist the medications she was on, his surprised look told Tony more in one second than their ten-minute conversation.

"You're sure she's taking both of these?" He asked pointing at two different items; his voice contained a hint of shock as he looked at the list of medications Tony had written down.

"That's what's on the chart."

"Well, they can be used together…"

"But?" Tony remarked, hoping for some honesty.

"Well, talk with her doctor. If you have concern about what she's taking get with her doctor immediately. If her actions are causing you to wonder about the medication…"

Tony had already made up his mind. The man was definitely afraid to tell him the problem, he was afraid whatever he said would get back to the doctor and end up causing him trouble.

Tony's father had been hospitalized with cancer before his death years earlier, Shawn told him to find something to ease his pain. Tony had a grandmother that believed only in herb medication; she was sort of the witch doctor of the black neighborhood they lived in. She taught Tony everything she could before she died at the age of one hundred and ten. She never went to a doctor a day in her life, so she claimed, but he knew she'd had all of her childhood vaccinations some time or another. And she did have her appendix removed. He gave her the respect and belief she required though, mainly because he knew she'd beat his ass if he ever showed one second of disrespect. He loved her and trusted her and that was more important.

She introduced him to herbs that would shield you from pain and misery, and she showed him herbs that would give you pain and lots of misery. She also introduced him to teas made from herbs that could help cure almost everything. In the case of his father's death, she helped him ease his pain and speed up the death he begged for. Terminal cancer was tearing him apart, and he wanted to die quickly, not rotting away in a home somewhere. His grandmother couldn't cure the cancer but she could help him with his wish. After many tears, Tony followed his father's wish, allowing him to die peacefully in his sleep. He actually had a smile on his face when the nurse discovered he'd died. His smile convinced Tony his mother and father were together again forever.

"Have her doctor check her; tell him what she's doing. I'm sure your sister will be better off without the second medication. He'll have to try something else."

That was all Tony needed. He knew talking with her doctor was a worthless idea. He made a second stop at a health food store where he purchased certain herbs he knew would cure Sherin's anxiety problem, and remove most of the pain she was having. Any time he or Shawn needed pain medication; he would brew it up. His concoction of ginger root and other herbs cured most of the ailments they incurred, he was sure it would be better than anything she was receiving in the hospital. It would also help her heal a lot faster.

When he returned to the hospital Shelly and Brook had also returned and were talking with Shawn in the hallway, as he approached he heard Shawn saying, "I can't believe it." He had slight fear that something else bad had happened from Shawn's tone and he was a little afraid to ask.

"You can't believe what?'

"Look at her," Shawn said pointing at Shelly. His face was beaming; there wasn't the frightened look Tony was expecting to see along with the frantic tone of his voice. He took a quick look at Shelly then he looked at Brook, her smiling face told him something was awry, he just didn't know what at the moment. Then, before anyone said another word Shawn pointed at the pants Shelly was wearing. "She's wearing Blue jeans." His shock rivaled the look of disbelief covering Shawn's face.

Shelly wouldn't wear denim. She thought women degraded themselves wearing it. Blue Jeans were definitely wrong for her wardrobe. She always wore skirts and dresses, or an occasional pantsuit, with jacket of course, or very expensive slacks.

"You don't approve?" Shelly asked, looking from Shawn to Tony, and back to Shawn again. She wanted to do something drastic so she let Brook talk her into purchasing a pair of Blue Jeans. She hadn't worn jeans since high school.

Both men spoke at the same time, "You look great," They said in unison.

"I told you they'd like'em," Brook said proudly. It was no secret who's idea it was for her to buy them, Brook was becoming a welcomed influence on Shelly; Shawn was happy and afraid at the same time. The thought of Brook becoming a member of their little family scared him, but she was sure helping Shelly out of her mold.

Shelly had replaced the slacks and jacket she'd been wearing, with Blue jeans and a tight white blouse. Her hair was down and flowing, instead of up in one of the usual pinned up fashions she wore it in, she looked very sexy.

"Do you really like'em?" she asked Shawn. "I needed to do something really ridiculous, and this is it. I feel like a hypocrite now. Brook is a bad influence on me.

"Oh no she's not," Shawn joyfully replied. "If this was her idea you might want to listen to her a little more often. Don't beat yourself up, listen, you look great. You need to keep doing ridiculous things. Your starting to grow out of that shell you've been in." He bit his lip as soon as he finished his words. The look on her face went cold, but only for a second.

"You really do like'em, I mean really?"

"YES I DO, I hope you bought more than one pair he said taking her in his arms and sliding his hands down over her behind. I love'em, and I love you."

She pushed tight into his embrace wondering why she hadn't let herself go long before this. For some reason everything Shawn said made her feel better, she wanted to be closer to him. Had she put too much of her time and energy into her career she wondered? She was locked in his arms and didn't want to let go. She was liking Brook more too. She didn't have a sister she could share her life with, and this little bit of time she'd shared with her so far made her want more. But she knew she'd have to break the crush Brook had on Shawn if their relationship was to endure.

"I want to tell you something," Shawn said, walking her down the hall. "When I see you my whole insides smile. It's like you turn on the sun in my life. I see your pretty face and I instantly want to hold you and kiss you. You could be flat chested, and I wouldn't care. You could be in rags and I'd still love you. You can be dressed in anything at all, or nothing at all, and I'd still want you forever."

"Can we go home soon?" she whispered into his ear at hearing his words, she wanted him naked in her arms. The reality of life was making her again ask herself why, why had she allowed herself to place her career in front of him. Money wasn't everything she told herself.

He knew what she had on her mind, and he was all for it. He wondered if his life had suddenly slipped into a dream, things were going fast in his favor and he couldn't believe it. If it was a dream, he never wanted to wake up.

"I'll make sure Tony has things in control here and we can go." She was still holding on to him with a grip she didn't want to release. She didn't know why but she was also feeling a bit scared. "Honey." He slowly pried her hands from his neck. "We'll go in a little bit," he said giving her a kiss. He wanted to escape with her and rip her new jeans off. His whole body was begging for her hands and lips to roam all over it, but he didn't want to leave Tony so quick.

"Ok," she said, giving him a soft kiss.

As he looked into her eyes he was seeing something he had never seen before; there was a vulnerable look. As though she was completely under his control, void of any move of her own. That look she usually had of "I'm in control" was missing.

"Honey, are you ok?"

"Yes, I'm fine," she replied softly.

If he hadn't known better, he'd say she was on something. Then he suddenly thought of Brook; could she have given her something while they were gone? He gave a quick glance to where she had been standing, but now she was gone. He'd been trying for so long to get Shelly hung up on him again that it didn't register; she was becoming high on him like she'd never been, and it over whelmed him.

"Tony, where did Brook go?"

"She went to get me some hot water so I can make some tea, why?"

Shelly still had her arm locked around his so it was impossible for him to say anything. "I just wondered."

Seconds later Brook returned with two coffee cups full of hot water. "I've got to go back and get the other two," she said with a giggle.

"That's Ok," Tony said smiling, "I'm only making one right now."

Both Shelly and Shawn knew what he was up to, but Brook looked quite confused.

"Just for you and me?" she asked looking at Tony. Tony walked her down the hall quietly explaining who and what the tea was for and when she let out a loud "OH!" they knew she'd finally caught on. She went into Sherin's room and helped him mix the herbs into a tea while Shawn watched out for any nurses that might come by and interrupt them. Minutes later she came out smiling.

"Sherin wants you," she said with a big shift of her shoulders. Shawn quickly took her by the shoulders for a moment looking into her eyes. They were shiny and her face sort of lit up like there was an excitement in her look, but there was nothing wrong with them. There was nothing weird about her pupils so Shawn shook his head and dismissed the thought he had about her being on something. She smiled at him, which made her look glow even more.

"What?" she asked cheerfully.

"Nothing." He slowly shook his head letting her go. Looking at Shelly he asked, "Would you like to meet the lady getting so much of our attention?" She was still wrapped around his arm and he didn't want to be rude, telling her to stay out would be dumb.

"Sure," she replied with a smile.

They spent most of an hour with Sherin; she was still quite worked up mentally, asking why Ray hadn't been caught yet. She carried on more and more about what was going to happen if they couldn't find him, how would she be able to go home she asked. Brook assured her she'd stay with her until he was found, but that only scared her more.

"I'm afraid he might hurt you too if you're there. No, I've got to move away, someplace where he can't find me," she cried.

They tried changing the subject, but every few minutes she'd ask them again to call the police and see if he'd been caught yet. Shawn promised he'd call before he left, but she picked up the room phone and asked him to do it now. When he finished his call, the news Ray was still at large brought her immediately to tears again. Brook and Shelly held her hands and tried their best to calm her down until she fell asleep. Ten minutes later she awoke again and asked who Shelly was. Brook introduced her and carried on as if it was the first time they met. She got them talking about Shelly's new Blue Jeans, and how she hadn't wore any in years. Before long Brook had them laughing like School Girl's.

"Please stop making me laugh, it hurts when I laugh," she told Brook. "Can I stay with you when I get to go home? Just until Shawn puts that ass hole in jail."

"Sure you can," Brook said taking up a seat beside her on the bed. Shelly sat down on the other side and the three of them began talking as if they'd been friends for years.

Tony gave Shawn a wink tipping his head towards the door, they both knew the tea was finally kicking in and time with Brook and Shelly would do her a lot of good. They walked out into the hall leaving the girls to them selves. There were no more questions about Ray, no more feeling sorry for herself, just a lot of girl talk.

"I think she's going to be fine, I'll make sure she's watched very close, you get back to your investigation," Tony suggested. "I'll make sure she doesn't take any more of that medication, she knows which one I'm talking about.

"You know, he's going to show up some where, he can't let her stay alive. I'm wondering about the boy he supposedly scared away. Some young man living in Pontiac. Talk to her later, see if you can get more information from her about him. Try not letting her know why though, Ray might have done something to him and we don't need her crying about that."

"So you two are looking like newly weds what's up? She's making a complete flip flop," Tony said smiling.

"Yeah, isn't it neat. She even said she's staying with me, staying. Sleeping with me every night. For how long I don't know, but I'm going to do my damnedest to keep her there. Do you think she's on something?" he asked Tony with a wrinkled look.

"Yeah, she's finally back being high on you, Good luck." Tony said smiling. Shawn knew there was a lot of doubt behind that smile.

After so many years of listening to Shawn's wishing Shelly would stay, wishing she'd marry him, Tony had serious reservations. He never tried to turn Shawn against her, never told him to forget her and try someone else but he felt she was just dangling him. He knew Shawn loved her and he'd do nothing to hurt either one of them. He was very fond of Shelly; he just couldn't figure her out. "Maybe this thing with Hinkley will drive her away from the Hill like it did you, maybe she's high on the combination of fear and the realization of what you really mean to her. Have you ever told her money's no object?"

"NO"

"Why not?"

"Because I want to know she wants me with the work I'm doing," Shawn's face suddenly had a huge smile.

"What's so funny?" Tony asked.

"Something that happened yesterday. We were getting into the shower and I made some silly comment about how I could make a decent living doing what I'm doing, she started laughing hysterically. Well, actually I asked her if I made a million doing what I'm doing now if that would do."

"Don't tell'er, don't tell her a damn thing until she says she'll marry you, than you laugh." Tony coaxed smiling.

"We can only hope," Shawn replied with a devious look.

Tony was worried Shelly would flip back to her old self after her problem at work was straightened out and the fear she was feeling had been removed. Now he could see the glow in her eyes every time she looked at him. That same glow used to be there when they worked together, he didn't want it to go away for Shawn's sake. When Shawn left the hill Tony noticed a depressed mood in him for quite some time, especially when the subject of dating came up. Now Shawn was back on cloud nine. That was good, but he was afraid if she did it to him again it would drive him deeper then before. He held his tongue out of respect for Shawn, but he was worried this could be a bad thing.

"You know Ray could pull some shit like putting on a doctors coat or something like that. He could come up here and mingle 'til he's sure the coast is clear then slip in and finish the job. Make sure all your guy's know exactly what he looks like," Shawn warned.

"I will, you take Shelly home and convince her to stay. I'll touch base with you tomorrow morning."

Shawn collected the girls and they quickly left the hospital. His plan was to drop Brook at home, and have a long night with Shelly. First he'd take her out for a nice hot meal, anything her little appetite desired. Then maybe dancing or a movie or maybe she'd just want to go back to his house and curl up with him on the couch. That would be just fine with him. He didn't have to have sex. Unless that was where she wanted to go. No matter what, he'd be sleeping against her naked body tonight and his whole being was tight with anticipation. Maybe I could replace her Birth Control pills with something else, he thought to himself while he walked behind her and Brook on their way to the car. At this point he didn't care, if her getting pregnant could get her to make up her mind, so be it. He watched as her tight little behind strutted along in her new Blue Jeans and how he was going to like helping her out of them later that night.

"Brook wants to know if she can stay with us tonight? I thought you might let her use your guest room. And if that's ok with you we'd order pizza from The Corner Deli'."

Shawn listened while his plans were systematically being shot down. Well what the hell, he'd still be jumping into bed with her later. Nothing should ruin that, he told himself, she even said she was staying it was her idea.

"Sure, but you better make sure it's ok with her mom. We don't need any trouble from her. I was thinking about taking you two to Stafford's, but pizza will be fine."

Both ladies gave a sharp rude verbal reply to his offer of going to Stafford's, followed by laughter. They were sounding more like sisters and his fear was building.

Stafford's was a restaurant located in downtown Detroit. If you were able to get away for less than a hundred dollars a meal, you must have just ordered water. Shawn had been there once, and only once. He swore he received better service at McDonalds. But it was the best come back he could think of while hiding the disappointment he had at his plans being ruined.

Shelly was hoping to get more information from Brook. Shawn had asked if she'd help him in that area, and after spending so much time with her it was possible the closeness would continue. Maybe she could get some answers for him about who was playing games with him in that house? She just might give answers that Shawn couldn't draw out. She began listing as many questions in her mind as she could, questions that would require only a yes or no answer. Hopefully all yes answers. One of the tricks she'd developed for questioning a witness on the stand. Especially one she wanted to trip up. Most of all, she hoped to catch her off guard and get the answer to one very important question.

She had a feeling Shawn was right about Brook being in the Foust Mansion. She had a plan of action and she couldn't wait to try it out. She wanted so bad to help Shawn solve his case. Maybe it was more fun to solve cases than offer her skills as an attorney she wondered? She knew she was feeling much better being around him, and for the life of her she couldn't understand why she hadn't realized it before. Maybe she owed Hinkley a great big thank you herself she wondered? She knew she'd never tell him that though, well, maybe not.

The Corner Deli' was quite busy, so Shawn ran out to another pizza place to retrieve their dinner. The next best place for pizza was a few miles away which gave Shelly about a half hour to grill Brook on a few things while he was gone, so she put her plan into action.

"So you'll be going into the eight grade this year?" she asked Brook as soon as Shawn left.

"No, I'm going to be a freshman."

"High School, God I can remember my first year of High School, I was so scared. Do you like the school you're going to?"

"It's ok."

"Do you have lots of friends?"

"A couple, a couple of good ones, ones I'm pretty close with anyway." The way she was fumbling with her thoughts Shelly figured she was probably hard for her to make and keep friends.

"Are you involved in any of the sports programs? I played softball when I was in high school," she said, hoping to hit up on something Brook would be interested in. Shelly tried to make her conversation seem like normal chitchat while they prepared the kitchen for supper. "Do you have a boy friend?" They were getting plates and silverware around for the pizza, as they talked. This question brought a stern look from Brook, which Shelly knew reflected back to Shawn.

"No, I think boys are jerks. I want a man for my lover," she said leaning her back against the counter and hugging the plates to her chest. Shelly's mouth dropped and her eyes opened wide. She wanted to laugh but allowed a quick smile and then she quickly wondered what all had Brook tried. No that's stupid. Just another question had popped into her mind. She knew some girls Brook's age had already become sexually active and in her mind she toyed with asking Brook if she had.

"Have you ever…" then she thought more about the question and said forget it.

"Have I ever what?" Brook asked, placing the plates on the table.

"Did you just meet Shawn this week? I mean, you seem to have an attachment I'm not connecting with."

"Actually we met about five years ago but he doesn't remember. I was quite a lot smaller then."

"Five years, you'd only have been seven years old how did you…?" Brook could see more of a question in Shelly's look and she wanted to clear things up quickly so she cut her off.

"He represented my mother in a law suit against my father. We were trying to get money from him because we couldn't afford to keep our house and car, we were about to loose everything and he wasn't paying any child support." She suddenly had a big smile on her face as she talked and Shelly wondered what brought that on.

"What's so funny?"

"I was just remembering that day," she replied with a childish giggle. "Shawn got himself in real trouble with the judge and he had to go to jail. I didn't think they could put your lawyer in jail when he was doing his job," she said showing disbelief. Shelly quit what she was doing and gave Brook her complete attention. The judge didn't seem to care that my father didn't show up, he said my father couldn't be found and it wasn't their job to make sure he came to court. Shawn said the order should be given to my mother and my father should be forced to pay something. Then he asked why my mother had been turned down for any help from the county. And the judge said that wasn't his problem either. Then the judge said he was giving my father another ninety days to show and Shawn got really mad. He raised his voice and said, "you don't feel bad about going home and drinking your liquor and smoking those expensive cigars do you, why should this lady have to wait for you to do your job. The judge slammed his gavel down so hard that it broke. My mother and I were taken out of the courtroom and some guy said for us to go home everything was over, like there wasn't anything we could do. My mother started crying and she dragged me out of there, she was so pissed. And my mother never tried suing my father again. But a few days later there was a new car delivered to our house and my mother didn't even have to pay for it, everything was straightened out. We had food in the house and my mom was happy. My mother was offered a job so we could start paying our bills and I think Shawn had something to do with all of it."

Shelly was rubbing her hands over her face. She knew Shawn had either paid for everything or somehow made sure it was taken care of. She wondered if that was the weekend she and Shawn had planned to go away and he ended up in jail. He'd spent quite a few nights in jail back then so she wasn't sure. She remembered being a little disappointed in him for it, but he never told her what he had done. There was so many times Shawn would be involved in something and never tell her anything about it. She'd usually find things out through the grapevine, which really made her mad but there wasn't anything she could do about it. Now she had more questions for him. The next question she hadn't planned on asking but it just jumped out, she had already said forget about asking it.

"Have you ever slept with a man?"

"Yes," she said without missing a beat in the conversation, "I've slept with my father."

Her answer was sharp and direct, as though Shelly wasn't supposed to be surprised. But she was. The sound of Shawn coming through the door put her thoughts on hold. She kept hearing Brooks answer over and over in her mind and she wanted to scream, "WHAT THE HELL DO YOU MEAN, HOW COULD YOU YOU'RE TOO DAMN YOUNG, DO YOU WANT TO END UP PREGNANT", but she didn't. "AND WITH YOUR FATHER?" Her mind was reeling with disgust, which was making her next question boil in her brain. I would not make it as a mother she told herself as she joined the conversation with her mind still deeply engraved in Brooks replies.

"Everyone ready to eat?" Shawn questioned after walking through the door and seeing the look on Shelly's face. Brook was beaming at the sight of him but Shelly had a look on her face like she'd just been told there was no Santa Clause.

They ate their pizza while they talked about Sherin, and weather Shawn thought Ray would be caught before she went home. The conversation was continuous, but Shawn sensed he had interrupted a major discussion between the two girls that wasn't finished. He caught certain looks between them which convinced him something was left on a hot burner.

"Did you talk with your mother?" he asked, steering the conversation into a new direction.

"I left a message with my neighbor, she's supposed to have my mother call as soon as she gets home."

"You don't have a phone?"

"No, my mom doesn't make enough money to pay the bill." If Shawn had of known Brook's last name he would have recognized her instantly and offered to help them out, but Brook had changed so much he didn't make the connection.

Her answer was followed by a quick look at Shelly, telling him there definitely was some unfinished business between them. He kept the conversation going about Sherin and the possibility of Brook helping her get back on her feet once she's was released from the hospital.

"I'd be glad to help her, if she'll let me. But you heard her say she'd probably move."

"Well, let's see how things go. That could have been her anxiety talking. I don't blame her for being scared, but you can't let garbage like that control your life." He was sure Ray would come after her once he found out she was still alive, unless he was too stupid to check. Maybe he couldn't read because the incident had been in the newspaper.

He finished his meal and excused himself, telling them he had a few things he needed to do in the office. After grabbing another piece of pizza to go he left them to work on their discussion.

When he got into the office he first checked his mail, there was another letter from his mystery client along with a handful of other letters. He tossed everything but that one onto his desk; using a ballpoint pen for a letter opener he removed the contents. There was more money than usual this time but he didn't count it, dropping the cash onto his desk he unfolded the letter hoping he'd learn more about his client. There were a few short words telling him to continue his good work, along with a thank you for taking such good care of the young lady that had been beaten up. There was extra money so he could put some towards the hospital bill.

"Who the hell is this?" He almost shouted, tossing the letter on the desk. Then he picked up the money and counted it, there were fifty one hundred dollar bills. "Five thousand dollars, you've got to be kidding me!" He tossed it all into the secret drawer in his desk and snatched up the newspaper as if it was trying to sneak away from him, then he opened it with a wicked slap as if that was a necessary movement for getting to its insides then he threw everything aside but the financial section. He looked that over circling certain stocks and jotting down notes now and then making a list of changes he'd call into his broker the following morning, then he sat back and without planning to he dosed off where he sometimes spent the night against his will, zonked out in his large leather chair.

Shelly was hoping Brook would elaborate on the subject of her sleeping with a man, and just whom that man was, but to learn that man had been her father, had she slept with other men? Was it her plan all along to sleep with Shawn? She was afraid to think of Brook as being a little tramp but that could be possible with the rotten home life she'd been living; Shelly shook her head in disgust. While Brook talked with her mother, Shelly worked on her next group of questions.

"Did your mother say it was ok?"

"Yeah, she just asked if I could be home by eight in the morning, she wants me there for something."

"She didn't say what?"

"I didn't wait for her to say why, I just hung up."

Shelly gave her a stern look of disapproval for her actions; Brook just shrugged her shoulders.

"Have you and your mother lived there long?"

"Yeah, ever since I was about five years old."

"Are you guy's buying the house?"

"Yeah, you'd think my mother would have it paid off by now, but it's not."

"Was Forest your father?" Shelly asked, as she put some dishes away. She hoped Brook would answer without thinking about the question.

"Eeeee, what?" Brook asked twisting her head.

Shelly knew she almost said yes. For her to answer so quickly on the question about her having sex and pause on this question, Shelly already knew the answer. Brook turned away; she wouldn't look at Shelly now, where before she was more than willing to talk face to face. Shelly took her by the shoulders turning her around so she could look into her eyes. "Look at me." But Brook wouldn't look her in the eyes. Shelly took a hold of her chin and softly tipped her head back. "Forest is your father isn't he, isn't he," she said again sternly?

"Was,"Brook said wiping tears now trickling from her eyes. "He's dead now. Beth killed him."

"Maybe she found out he'd been sleeping with you?" Brook's crying deeply increased and Shelly took her softly into her arms drawing her to her breast and letting her cry. Her plan had been to tuck Brook in and grab a shower after their conversation then take Shawn to bed, but she fell asleep along side of Brook while trying her best to comfort her.

It was about 3A.M. when Shawn woke; mad because he allowed himself to fall asleep and he was surprised Shelly hadn't came looking for him. He found her in the guest bedroom lying on the bed holding Brook in her arms. He figured they finished up what ever they'd been working on before he made it back with the pizza and it had ended up in a crying session 'til they fell asleep. He stood awhile watching them sleep, than he covered them both with a thin bedspread. As much as he wanted to have Shelly sleeping next to him he couldn't wake her. She was sleeping too peaceful. He knew she'd had a very bad night the night before so he decided not to bother her.

He took a quick shower with plans on getting into bed when the thought suddenly struck him, if it had been Brook in the Foust Mansion when he was there, she wouldn't be there now. He knew where she was, so now would be the perfect time to check things out again. He quickly dressed and headed for Beckwith Street.

CHAPTER TWELVE

Shawn pulled into the Mansion about 4:45 A.M. parking as close to the front door as he could. If there were anyone inside he wanted him or her to know he was there. He rang the bell constantly for about thirty seconds, then he unlocked the door letting himself in. Shutting the door with a loud slam he kicked off his shoes and ran up the stairs going from bedroom to bedroom checking to see if any of the beds were occupied, but they were all perfectly maid none had been slept in. As he ran through the house he turned on every light switch he passed leaving things totally lit up. The only way he could get into the secret hallway was from the basement entrance so he ran down there and triggered the door open. Before entering he carefully listened for footsteps on the stairs, there were none. He took the stairs to the first floor opened that door and listened, then he ran to the second floor opening that door and listening; there was no one in the house.

"Well, if there's no one here I can almost bet Brook was the one driving me crazy." He went back to the living room where he turned on the stereo loud enough to wake the dead, after about five minutes he turned it back off and began shutting off all the lights he'd left on. Walking through the house he had another idea, so he returned to the basement and played pinball for a while. When he was convinced he was definitely the only one in the house he finally decided to leave.

"I guess I should have dusted for prints," he said jokingly. And then another thought hit him. "Why not he told himself, she won't know. I'll just bluff her. She's a kid, and she won't know I'm lying, especially if she's been in here. Shit yes," he said putting his shoes back on. "I'll tell her I dusted the house for prints and found hers all over it." A big smile pursed his lips as he walked out the door, by tonight he was sure he'd have the answers to all of his questions, well most of them anyway he recanted.

He stopped at a restaurant for a quick breakfast but after waiting over twenty minutes to be served he left, he gave a wanting glance at the last long john sitting on the tray in the doughnut counter and forced himself to continue his way out the door. The place had become crowded shortly after he entered and he could tell being a regular was most beneficial because the newcomers were being put ahead of him. "I probably tip better than they do," he commented before pulling the door shut. But his words were ignored just as much as his presents taking up space in the second booth from the cash register had been. "I'll bet if I waved a ten in the air I would have been waited on," he said to his invisible partner.

Now there was a heavy mist in the air so he turned on the wipers as he pulled away from the restaurant, a block away he pulled into a gas station to purchased a coffee from an outside vending machine. His bad luck continued because the cup got stuck coming down and after most of the coffee had run out on to the ground the cup finally popped into place saving about one gulp. Cussing he drank that and tossed the empty cup into the nearest trashcan. On his way back home he pondered over the events of the week and wondered if it was possible Ray could have gotten into the Foust home and killed both of them. Maybe one or both of them knew him personally, after all Ray did like using a ball bat to get his point across. He managed to get back to the office around six thirty and being wide awake from the mouthful of coffee he'd drank he began reading the morning paper making changes to his notes for his broker. It was five minutes to seven when Shelly and Brook walked into the office calling for him.

"Did you ever go to bed?" Shelly asked giving him a big hug.

"I fell asleep out here," He replied with an apologetic look. He wanted to tell her what he'd been up to but he didn't want Brook to know, so he kept it to himself. Shelly wrapped her arms around him dismissing her questioning thoughts about where he'd been when she looked for him earlier, it wasn't important. He was here now and that's all that counted. The thin nightgown she was wearing was causing a very serious problem with him and he hoped she'd decide to take Brook home and hurry back. Her warm breasts seemed to get larger and larger with every breath she took, or maybe it just felt that way because she was taking deeper breaths. He wasn't sure but it still felt good. He slowly slid his hands along her soft backside hoping Brook wouldn't catch on to his predicament.

"Can I wear some of your clothes," Brook piped up, giving Shelly a pouting sisterly look. Shelly quickly replied yes and Brook was off to take her morning shower. Going through Shelly's clothes again would be fun she thought, so much fun she momentarily forgot about the two of them being alone.

They both had crucial information to tell each other, but their closeness had stirred up a sexual desire neither of them wanted to ignore and they both wanted to pursue. Surprisingly she pulled him to the love seat and began sliding her hand down the front of his trousers, she knew he wouldn't object. He slowly removed her gown and began kissing her breasts while clumsily kicking off his shoes and almost tripping over himself in the process as she helped remove his pants. He was sure any second she'd have second thoughts about the whole thing and say they had better stop before Brook came back, but she didn't. His warm wet tongue drifted down her neck to her breasts, pausing a few seconds to kiss and excite each one a little more if that was even possible and then he continued down her smooth belly and along her thighs kissing and licking every inch. She wrapped her fingers through his jet-black hair massaging his head and softly guiding him where she wanted him most. Soon he was driving her crazy with his tongue darting in and out, in and out, until she couldn't take any more.

"Stop, stop," she whispered pulling him to her lips.

Well, he told himself, she let me go farther than I expected.

"I want you inside me," she whispered taking a hold of him and guiding him into her. Then she put her hands on his hips pulling him tight into her as she pushed hard against him, now she took full control. She wanted to scream with pleasure and let him know he was driving her crazy, but knowing Brook could possibly hear her she bit onto his shoulder muffling the sounds coming from her pleasure, she figured they had at least ten minutes. So she hurried.

They would rather have taken their sweet time but they knew Brook would be returning soon, and because it was the quickest quickie they'd ever had they were both laughing as they quickly replaced their clothing. When Brook returned they managed to hide their laughter as she checked the teeth marks she'd left on his shoulder. Brook began by reminding her she had to be by eight.

"What's so funny, remember I told my mother I'd be home by eight."

"OH shit that's right. I've got to run her home," she cheerfully informed Shawn fighting back another burst of laughter. He swore she acted as if she'd been high on something when she placed her finger on his nose and promised to be back real soon. The look in her eyes told him she wasn't finished with him, and then he remembered what Tony had said. "SHE'S HIGH ON YOU." It was a great feeling and he hoped there was more to come. She gave him a big hug with a long wet kiss before leaving him, both of them wanting and needing more of each other.

"Shell." Brook urged out of jealousy. She knew she couldn't have Shawn, but to watch while Shelly pushed her soft body against him was a bit too much.

"Yes, yes." She said reluctantly pulling away. "Hold that thought," she whispered with another quick peck, "I'll be back soon."

He sat watching her leave hoping she'd return as soon as possible. Something about her was changing, totally changing, and he loved it. He was beyond cloud nine now, and he didn't ever want to come down. Her love for him was escalating, he was sure of it.

For quite some time he sat at his desk in shock. He wanted to ask her again if she'd marry him but he was scared. At this point he didn't want to do anything to scare her away. He knew where Tony was coming from, but this time it felt different. This was wonderful. He couldn't remember ever seeing the look in her eyes he was seeing now. That vulnerable look. Maybe it was just from feeling she was loosing everything her career ment to her, and for a second he realized he could fix that by telling her he had all the money they'd ever need. But he knew she would never accept money over the career she'd prayed for ever since he'd first met her. No, they'd have to play this one out and see what happens. If Hinkley went down like they planned, she'd have her judgeship.

Shelly was still wondering about the answers she'd gotten from Brook the night before and with a bit of fast thinking she came up with an idea. She was going right by the office of her gynecologist and she was sure this time of the morning she wouldn't be busy. She'd tell Brook she only had to stop for a minute, and then she'd talk the doctor into giving her a quick checkup. She knew she could be over stepping things but she had to be sure of everything. She wouldn't go in to court without being ready and she wanted to have all the facts she could get. After talking with her doctor she returned to the waiting room where Brook was patiently reading a magazine.

"Can you believe it, she's been giving free check up's all week to high school students playing sports, are you ready to go?"

"Wait a minute," Brook protested wide eyed. I might try playing sports when I go back to school and mom can't afford to pay our doctor for me. Could I get one?"

"Ya, but what about your mother…?"

"It doesn't take that long, I've had'em before. She'll be glad she didn't have to pay for it. Do you know this doctor very well?"

"She's nice, she's been my Gynecologist for about ten years, I trust her."

"Would you mind if I get the free check up?"

"No go ahead, I'll just sit and read while you're in there." About fifteen minutes later Brook returned to the waiting room with a smile on her face.

"She says I can play any sports I want, I'm in perfect shape." She stepped up to the counter and began filling out the paperwork the doctor requested, and when the doctor finished filling out what she needed to she gave Brook her copy for school.

"Shelly, before you leave I think I have some samples of those Birth Control pills you're thinking about using, that way you can try them before filling the prescription."

"Ok." Shelly replied as if it was something her doctor had just thought of, they went back into the main office while Brook took a seat and continued reading the magazine she'd been reading before. "So what did you find?"

"Well, if she's sexually active it must be orally because she's still a Virgin." Shelly's mouth dropped a little, then it changed to a smile.

"Tough little punk doesn't even know what sleeping with a man means, thanks," she said handing her friend a folded up twenty dollar bill, "and thanks for the samples I'm going to need them." She made sure Brook could see the pills so she wouldn't catch on to her trickery, she wanted to be trusted and excepted by Brook and any mistake could set that back.

She got Brook home a little after eight but her mother had already left the house, leaving no note as to why she wanted her home in the first place. Now that they were alone Shelly took the opportunity to ask Brook more questions that she wanted and needed answers to.

"Why didn't your father help your mother out instead of keeping his wealth to himself?"

"I don't know; they hated each other I know that."

"Do you know why they hated each other so much?" Shelly hoped Brook was feeling a lot closer to her now and the conversation would have more of a sister-to-sister feeling. The disgust she'd been harboring about Brook's sexual freedom was now forgotten about and she was looking at her like the child she was.

"No, I just know they fought a lot when I was little. They didn't even talk with each other the last few years. My mother didn't even know he lived there."

"How did he manage to pull that off?" Shelly asked with great surprise.

"When he first met my mother his last name was Shepard. Sometime after that he changed his name back to his fathers last name, Foust. He looked totally different when he was married to my mother. She wouldn't have recognized him if she was standing right next to him. He used to have real long hair and he was real skinny. He said he used to be a hippy," she finished with a slight giggle. "Then he started lifting weights and got really huge, I don't mean fat but really muscular."

"What did he do for a living?"

"He didn't work, he couldn't, something happened years ago, an accident or something, he hurt his back real bad from it. I remember he had an operation on it. My mother said she hoped he'd croak on the table.

"Come on, how did he pay for everything?"

"He got some sort of insurance settlement, that's how he built the house. Mom was pissed because she thought she should have gotten some of the money. She knew he got a lot of money but she could never get him into court to get any of it, because they couldn't find out where he lived. And because he changed his last name to Foust. He'd been fighting for the settlement for a long time and my mother never knew where he was living. But that was over five years ago. Mom never knew he changed his name. You should have seen him when he was younger." This statement brought some more laughter from her. "He always had long hair and my mom called him a Hippy freak," she giggled. "She knew his voice on the phone so if he called she'd hand it to me or sometimes hang up on him. That's really why she quit paying for the phone I think, so he couldn't call."

"That's probably why she was so mad. But, did he have a steady income from the insurance claim?"

"I don't know, all I know is he always had money. When ever he got done making all his phone calls, we'd go to the races, or sometimes we'd just play pool or other games."

"What do you mean all his phone calls?"

"Mondays, Wednesdays, and Thursdays, he had lots of calls to make for some reason, sometimes other days too, but mainly those days."

He was a freaking bookie, Shelly told herself listening to Brook. That's how he's been doing it. Beth probably found out and went ballistic.

"So are you saying your mother didn't know where you were when you were at his house?" Brook just gave her a blank stare without saying a word.

"Why do you think Beth killed him?" Up till now the conversation had been smooth and interesting, Shelly wasn't at all prepared for what was about to happen.

"She caught us sleeping together and she started yelling, she was swinging the bat when I woke up and she'd already hit him." She stopped there, but Shelly was sure there was more she wanted to say. That was probably when her father grabbed the bat and chased Beth through the house paying her back, Shelly added in her own thoughts, she figured Brook just couldn't get it out. She still needed to hear the rest in Brook's own words though.

She held back the anger hearing Brook admit she'd been in bed with her father, although her emotions were exploding inside. She wanted to scream but she knew he hadn't been having sex with her, she wondered if somehow Beth found out they'd been sleeping together and thought the same thing she had? But Brook began crying. Shelly quickly remembered she'd just been told Brook was still a Virgin. Now she suddenly realized they weren't having sex they were actually just sleeping together.

It was hard to see this tall young lady as a child but she was her fathers little baby and they were probably laying very close to each other and Forest was holding her tight. Beth must have seen them and thought the same thing she had thought when she first heard Brook's words. Beth must have thought Forest was having sex with her too. Forest fooling around with another woman, and a child at that, or maybe she never took the time to find out she was a child. She must have come home unexpectedly and caught them sleeping together. She figuered Forest had sex with her and in her anger she grabbed the bat and hit him with it. But they were only sleeping. Beth must not have known about Brook, Forest had somehow completely hidden her existence from her. Beth didn't know he had a daughter, or if she did, she didn't know that daughter was visiting when she was out. Shelly took Brook into her arms hoping and knowing there was more she needed to hear, but for the moment Brook was finished talking.

"Didn't Beth know you'd been coming over?" Shelly questioned after a brief moment. But before Brook could stop crying and answer her question the sound of the front door opening startled them. They both grabbed tissues and began drying their eyes as the bedroom door was flung open and Brooks mother burst through it.

"Have you seen the news!" she half screamed excitedly.

"No, what happened?" Shelly questioned standing up still wiping her eyes. They quickly followed Karin to the living room where she quickly turned on the television.

"One of our judges was murdered this morning," she continued, "someone shot him."

Only if it could be Hinkley, Shelly thought with streaming humor, and then her hand swept quickly to her mouth.

"Oh my God tell me it wasn't Judge Hinkley," she said sounding very frightened. "Did you hear the name? You didn't hear the name." Now she was rubbing her face in fear. No, he wouldn't, he couldn't have, oh my god tell me it wasn't Hinkley her thoughts begged. She was beginning to sweat profusely. For the first time in a long time she'd left the radio off in the car while she drove across town because she and Brook had been talking.

"No, but I'm sure they'll tell it again soon," Karin replied.

Not even a minute went by before Channel Four news gave the broadcast again. Judge Thomas Hinkley had been shot while sitting in his car and had been announced dead at ST. Mary's Hospital this morning at 7:10 a.m.

The fear shot through Shelly's body like a bolt of lightening striking a tree. She almost bit through the knuckle she had forced between her teeth. Instantly she went cold as the fear gripped at her guts. Had Shawn made good on his promise? Where had he been when she went looking for him at 4:30 this morning she wondered? She'd sat in his office from 4:30 to about 5:00 a.m. just wondering where the hell he was. And then she checked back at 6:30, he still wasn't there. Why hadn't he said he'd been out? He made her think he'd been there all night. He said he fell asleep in his chair. She shuttered inside thinking about what might have happened.

"Can I use your phone?" She had tried to use Shawn's car phone earlier but she couldn't get it turned on, it was a new one and he hadn't showed her how to use it yet. Both Brook and Karin gave her a stupid look as they both said, "we don't have one."

"Oh shit," Shelly blurted, realizing she'd forgotten they had no phone. Brook knew why she wanted a phone; she wanted to call Shawn, she had to know if he knew Hinkley was dead.

"C'mon," she said grabbing Shelly's hand and heading out the door, "let's go to the house." Shelly knew what she was suggesting as they both jumped into the car and headed for the mansion and she wasn't at all surprised when Brook pulled out a key and unlocked the side door when they got there.

"You can't tell anyone I let you in here," but Shelly ignored her order; she just wanted a phone and fast.

Shawn had spent a few minutes floating on cloud nine after Shelly left, than he tried calling his broker. After the second try he left his instructions on the answering machine as he had in the past, then fell asleep. Usually by now he'd have turned on the news, but certain events still had his mind locked in serious thought and he slipped off into a wonderful dream. Now it was almost 9A.M. and he was wondering why Shelly hadn't made it back yet. His body was still begging for her return and the wanting was getting stronger and stronger every minute. Suddenly he heard scuffling outside his office door and figured it was probably the same young boys he'd seen a few days earlier screwing around; so he turned his back to it glad he'd had his new mailbox installed.

When the phone rang he picked it up smiling at hearing Shelly's voice and at that same moment his office door exploded. Two police officers had smashed it in with a large battering ram. He spun around in his chair facing the door with splinters still flying through the air when a flood of Detroit Police Officers busted through yelling, "GET YOUR HANDS UP, GET ACROSS THE DESK, SPREAD'EM; and they were led by none other than James T. Hunter the Assistant District Attorney.

"SPREAD'EM!" Hunter yelled again, kicking Shawn's feet and ankles. He grabbed a handful of Shawn's hair forcing him down onto the desk. "Read him his rights Rookie!" Hunter yelled at one of the officers with him.

"The door wasn't locked!" Shawn yelled over the commotion. "You didn't have to smash it in."

"I said shut the fuck up Cassidy, you're under arrest!"

"What the hell for?" Shawn bellowed back totally confused. Shelly listened on the line and through the commotion she could hear Shawn being arrested and she knew what for, she kept yelling Shawn's name through the phone hoping someone would pick it back up and let her know what was going on but suddenly the line went dead. She called back again but no one would answer. Frantically she headed for Shawn's house telling Brook to stay home.

Hunter kicked at Shawn's left foot again, trying to move it farther purposely kicking his ankle instead.

"Goddamn you Hunter."

"Shut the fuck up, I'll shoot you if I have to!" Hunter yelled, roughing Shawn up as much as he could. The Rookies just looked at each other. They knew Hunter was over stepping his bounds but they weren't about to cross his authority. They both knew Shawn and they knew he could clear the place out if he wanted to. They just hoped he was smarter than that. Shawn was playing in his mind how easy it would be to flatten Hunter and clean out his office, when another bunch of officers came running into the office from the back way and he wondered how much damage they'd caused coming through his apartment. The only thing he could figure was he was being arrested for something to do with the Foust Mansion or the investigation he was conducting.

And now he was sure the client was some judge's wife. This treatment was a bunch of bullshit. Something was probably missing and he was being accused of taking it, or stealing the money he'd been given. His anger was building about taking the case, until one of the Rookies said he was being arrested for the murder of Judge Hinkley.

After hearing those words the first thing he thought about was, now he wouldn't be able to thank him for driving Shelly into his arms but he'd damn sure get to piss on his grave. Then the reality hit him that he was being accused of killing the bastard. Any and all pain disappeared as he smiled from ear to ear. The Rookies immediately knew they had the wrong man; the way he smiled they were sure he didn't even know about it.

"You mean that stupid fuck is really dead?" Shawn asked turning his smiling face to Hunter as Hunter jerked him up from the desk by his handcuffs and his hair.

"You know he is, and you're going to prison for killing him." He pushed Shawn towards the door as he managed to continue kicking him in the heels every third or forth step as they walked to the car. The pain from getting kicked was being masked by the news of Hinkley being dead, but it wouldn't last long, Hunter was pushing his luck.

Hunter let most of the officers go but the two he was riding with and then he loaded Shawn into the back seat of their cruiser and headed for the Fourth Precinct. Hunter wanted him into a cell as fast as possible and the Fourth Precinct was the closest place to take him. When they got him there Hunter pushed the two Rookies aside and walked behind Shawn still kicking him every chance he got. Up the stairs and down through the two hallways Hunter placed a kick against the back of Shawn's left heel again and again. As they walked Hunters face lit up planning each and every kick to Shawn's heels while he jerked at the handcuffs gouging into Shawn's wrists. And with every kick Shawn registered his plan of attack. He knew being at the Fourth Precinct he had a close friend Hunter wasn't aware of, Captain John Redman. When they were about ten feet from the Chief's office Shawn had made up his mind. He'd been timing the kicks Hunter was beating into the back of his feet and ankles. Another one was about to hit and Shawn's plan of action went in to effect.

Going high on his left toe he gave Hunters right foot plenty of room to slide well underneath his foot. Feeling Hunters toe touch under his foot he quickly came down on his heel settling onto the top of Hunters instep. The second he knew his heel was where he wanted it be he put all his weight onto his left leg and did a shove with a twist towards the floor driving his heel towards the floor. This was like putting almost a thousand pounds or more onto that heel driving it straight to the floor crushing everything in its path. Hunter screamed bloody murder. There wasn't an ear within six blocks missing the squall of pain radiating from Hunter's loud mouth. "If you do it right you can shatter a man's foot," Tony had told him. He'd seen Tony do that very thing stomping on a guy's foot while they were in a bar fight a few years back. The man out weighed Tony by at least fifty or sixty pounds; depending on whose scales they were using. This little trick should teach Hunter a good lesson he thought. Hunter continued his blood-curdling scream as he went immediately to the floor; his right foot had been shattered. It was worse than being with a sledgehammer. As he hit the floor he fumbled for the revolver tucked under his left armpit finally getting it from its holster and waving it at Shawn with all intensions of pulling the trigger. As soon as he could hold it straight a large foot came flying out of nowhere kicking the gun from his grasp and sending it flying down the hallway.

"What the hells going on here?" Captain Redman yelled as he stood over Hunter.

"That man is under arrest! And I want him booked and stuffed into a cell immediately!" Hunter yelled.

"Take him into my office!" Redman's order rang out at the Rookies.

Shawn knew Redman very well; as they ushered him away he nodded his head in greeting.

"Red."

"Shawn." Redman replied nodding back with a questioning look of what the hell did you just do? As Shawn was escorted off into the Chief's office.

"Hunter what the hell did you arrest him for?"

"Murder, Goddamn it! He's guilty of murder and he's going to swing for it!" Hunter kept yelling as he lifted himself up onto a chair one of the Rookies had brought him. "Did you call me an ambulance damn it?" Hunter questioned jerking away from the hand helping him into the chair.

"What happened to innocent until proven guilty?" Redman asked. One of the Rookies had retrieved Hunters gun but as he started to hand it back to Hunter Redman grabbed it.

"That's mine!" Hunter blurted.

"You'll get it back when I'm damn good and ready to give it to you!" Redman yelled. "You don't pull a fucking weapon in my Precinct! If you'd have shot him you'd be sitting in a cell of your own, you had no reason to pull that damn thing and you of all people should know that!"

"He was trying to break away!"

"In the middle of my Precinct."

"Shit! You dumb fuck! Are you really that Goddamn dumb?" He turned back to the two Rookies. "When the ambulance gets here you get this piece of garbage out of my Precinct. If you ever go with him again you'd better plan on staying with him because you'll never work for me again! He turned and walked off into his office slamming the door and leaving Hunter sitting in the hall in excruciating pain waiting for the ambulance.

When Redman walked back into his office Shawn was busy tapping on the glass of the large fish tank Red had decorated his office with, the handcuffs that were behind his back were now in front and he was holding his own key in his left hand ready to unlock them. "Is that one a shark?" he asked trying to start light conversation.

"You know damn well what it is," Redman replied throwing Hunter's gun and shells into a drawer. What the hell did you do to him?"

Shawn continued unlocking his cuffs then he tossed them into the same drawer Red had thrown Hunters gun into.

"That prick kept kicking me in the heels, I let him know it was a big mistake."

"That fuck would have shot you, you do know that don't you?"

"Well, I forgot to thank you for that, so thanks for kicking that out of his hand."

"I enjoyed it very much," Red replied with a smile. "And that damn shark you bought me died!"

"I figured that had to be a different one, Shawn said still tapping on the glass and shaking his head. The first one should have been a foot long by now, and he had spots on his head."

"Shit, he croaked two weeks after you put him in there. He tried eating everything that wasn't attached, and then he swam into the mouth of my biggest fish and started eating it from inside out. That fish started flopping around like it swallowed a treble hook. After he killed it he started chewing on the scenery." Shawn just laughed.

"And this one doesn't?"

"Not so far. Would you like to call your lawyer?" he asked turning the phone towards him. "Sounds like the ambulance is here, I'll be right back."

Shawn knew Shelly was probably going crazy wondering what had happened. He called the house leaving a message on the machine but before he hung up she rushed into Red's office quickly wrapping her arms around him.

"I should have known you'd come straight here," he said mumbling through her kiss. You must have flown.

"What's going on?" She was looking straight into his big blue eyes not knowing what to believe or think. She knew without asking he'd been arrested for Hinkley's murder and the fear in her eyes told him she wasn't sure if he was innocent.

"Can you believe it, they think I killed Hinkley. If I'd have killed him, I'd have beaten that bastard to death."

"You know better than to talk like that," she scolded. "Who do you want me to get to defend you?" Shawn pulled his head back looking hard into her eyes. There was a look of shock well pronounced on his face. "I trust you'll do a fine job," he said his look changing to complete assurance.

Tears she'd been holding back began streaming down her face. "I can't do it! You know if I fuck up you could go to prison."

"I trust you. You're the best attorney in the state of Michigan, HELL THE WORLD."

"I've never defended anyone close to me for murder ..."

"Hey! You don't think…"

"I didn't mean it that way, I've never, oh you know what I mean damn it!" She was getting very frustrated and it was showing. She wanted to ask him, "where the hell were you this morning" but she knew any question like that would mean, are you lying.

"Don't cut yourself short. I didn't do it. Get Tony to investigate for you, between the two of you this will never go to trial!" He half shouted.

"You really believe that, don't you?"

"Yes I do. He was probably cheating someone with all the scams he's into and they found out. Find out who it was; dig into his life I know you can do it. He probably has a thousand people wanting him dead. I haven't any motive for wanting him dead! You know I suddenly love that bastard."

"God have you been out of touch," she whispered.

"What do you mean?"

"It's not that simple. You're probably going to sit in jail for months. They won't allow bail, not on this charge. And if by some miracle they did neither one of us could pay a bondsman."

"You just get hold of Tony." She knew, or thought, that Tony had more money than they could raise but she was sure bail would be denied. Christ, he was arrested for killing a District Court Judge.

"I guess I'd better get started then. I'll tell Tony to give you a call." The door opened and Red walked back in. "Who were they taking away in the ambulance?" she asked directing the question to Red.

"You should be asking him about that."

Her neck almost snapped as she quickly turned back at Shawn, "What did you do?" she asked sharply.

"Hunter sort of got stepped on." Shawn said, scrunching his face into a wrinkled mess.

"He's a jackass," Red threw in before Shelly could reply.

"You guy's, he's a district attorney!" she said letting out a big sigh. The only thing we've got going for us is Hinkley won't be the presiding Judge." Both of them laughed. The look on Shelly's face became very angry. "Neither of you are taking this serious! You could go to prison! And you know damn well you'll be charged for attacking Hunter!"

"That'll keep him from putting ANY MORE killer fish in my fish tank," Red wisecracked. Shawn just smiled.

"I'm leaving. I'll do my best. Maybe this will help you start taking this more seriously. Think of big Johnny Black

Man renaming you Shawn Bendover, does that help show how serious this is?"

"IT SCARES ME," Red quickly exclaimed.

"I know it's serious. But I think you and Tony can straighten it out before it goes that far. He's had his hands in dirt for years, the only question that should be asked is how did he keep himself alive this long? And, Honey?"

"What?" she snapped.

"Could you stop by the house? Hunter smashed in the office door, they might have gotten the main door too. Clean out my desk if you will." She knew he was talking about the secret drawer in his desk where he kept quite a few personal items.

"Yes, I'll do that." He could tell she wasn't very happy with him right now, but he didn't know they each had different reasons for thinking it.

"I'm going to start my own investigation." Red added. "I want to know why Hunter honed in on you so damn fast, who the hell fingered you? He's stupid, but I'm sure there's some other stupid ass out there feeding him shit information."

Shelly gave Shawn a big hug with a quick warm kiss before leaving, she had a lot to get accomplished and she didn't want remodeling the house to take up most of her time.

"Oh, how do I turn on your new phone?"

"A little button down on the left side, I usually turn it off when I'm home for the night."

"Thanks," information I could have used earlier she mumbled as she left.

CHAPTER THIRTEEN

When Shelly got to the house she found only the office door busted in. Evidently the person in charge of entering the rear of the house knew how to check the door to see if it was locked or unlocked before entering. There were things knocked over and busted and she'd include it all in the lawsuit she'd start against the city of ST. Clair Shores and Wayne County in Shawn's behalf.

She had heard Shawn talk about the hardware store across the street so she called there to see if they could replace the door, five minutes later the son was there measuring the opening for a replacement. While he worked, she busied herself removing the letters from his secret drawer. When she pulled out the envelopes containing the money he'd received from his mystery client she was sure she'd seen the same identical ones some where before and she knew exactly where. She tucked everything into her purse and called Tony.

"Have you heard what happened?"

"Yeah, I just got off the phone with Shawn, I'm doubling the guard up here, than I'm all yours."

"I'm going to have Shawn's car so I'll have a phone, call me on that line. I want to talk with Judge Thurman."

"Well, you know where you'll find him."

"Do you think he'll be there already?"

"He practically lives there," Tony replied.

"Could you check where the shooting happened and see if you can get anything going?"

"Sure, it's probably the best place to start."

Shelly headed for Harpers, while Tony headed for the scene of the crime. It took only one phone call for him to find out the exact location where the shooting took place. One mile from the Foust Mansion in Warren, right in front of a Quick Stop convenience store. Someone had unloaded the whole magazine of a handgun into his car with the luck of making a couple of the shots fatal. Evidently he'd been sitting there sipping on some hot coffee waiting for someone, but whom.

"What the hell is a District Judge doing out at five in the morning, especially here?" Tony questioned when he arrived in Warren. He questioned everyone he could find within a three-block area of the shooting. Most of the people were either sleeping or not home at the time the shooting occurred. Two men said the shooter was riding a motorcycle, but they couldn't say what kind. A shop owner across from the Quick Stop said he believed the motorcycle was past the intersection when the shots were fired. One elderly lady said she was cleaning the window on her front door when she heard what she thought were gunshots, when she looked out at the street a pickup was pulling away. She had no idea any one had been shot until an hour later. At first they all thought a truck had backfired. It was too dark for her to tell what kind or color the pickup was, she said apologizing. After all it was a little foggy and there was a heavy mist in the air. Tony was stunned; no one else had mentioned any rain or fog. He worked for another hour but was unsuccessful in getting any more information, other people did confirm the fog but most said there was no rain. Other people either couldn't remember seeing anything, or didn't want to get involved. What surprised him most was the police hadn't talked to any of these people, or at least they all claimed so.

Hinkley had been shot sometime between five and six a.m. It was dark and foggy, and there was a white convertible with lots of chrome seen in the area. Tony cringed. What had the judge been doing in Warren at that time of the morning? He wondered if Shawn had been out and about that early but on second thought he was sure he'd been curled up with Shelly. He decided he wanted to see Hinkley's car next so he could see exactly where the bullets had entered, he'd get with Shawn later for that other answer. Knowing at what level the bullets hit the car could tell him if it was from a motorcycle or a pickup. He called Starkway hoping the car had been placed in his impound, it hadn't.

"That was taken to County," Starkway told him. "Hunter said he knew who killed him and he wanted the car under guard. Do you know if they've arrested anyone yet?"

"Yeah, Hunter arrested Shawn for it."

"That stupid ass!" Starkway blurted.

"My thoughts exactly. I'm investigating to see if I can find the truth before they railroad him into prison."

"If you need any help I'll make myself available."

"Thanks, I'll probably have to take you up on it." See Shawn, Tony mumbled in his mind. There are some people that like you out there. He knew there was more than one white convertible in Detroit but the thought of Shawn being in the neighborhood that morning kept creeping into his thoughts. He wanted to hear from Shawn that he'd been curled up with Shelly between five and six that morning. He'd feel a hell of a lot better knowing that.

Shelly walked into Harpers but before she could request to see Judge Thurman she was directed to a table near the rear of the dining hall, and as she approached the Judge waved her to his table as if he'd been waiting for her.

"Hello Ms. Barnes, have a seat," he said softly.

"Have you heard what's been going on?" she asked with fear in her eyes after taking the seat he offered.

"I know we've lost a District Judge," he said in a slow collection of words. She hadn't seen or talked to him in a long time and she thought maybe his slow speech was do to his getting older, he must be in his seventies by now maybe close to eighty she guessed. For a second she wondered if she should have even bothered him.

"Do you know the D.A. has had Shawn arrested for Hinkley's murder?"

"That doesn't surprise me in the least, you are going to defend him of course, aren't you?" Her slow response at assuring him she would, brought him to heated anger. "You've been dangling this man on a string for so, so damn long! And now you're dangling his life. Is it…is it that you haven't learnt by now how to trust him yet? You know he loves you very much." She didn't know how much Judge Thurman cared for Shawn, or about how much he knew about their situation, but instantly she knew it was more than she was aware of.

"Yes I do know. That's why I'm afraid to defend him. What happens if I loose and he goes to prison?"

"Does he believe in you?"

"Yes." She replied, throwing her head like a child being scolded.

"Then believe in yourself. We both know… he couldn't have shot Thomas, break his neck maybe, maybe," he said holding his finger up. "But not shoot'im. Defend him… with everything you can trust, if that's not working, dig deeper." He took her hands into his squeezing them softly. "I don't have many more years on this earth, I can only hope things turn out the way they should. Things will work out, just trust him."

"I wish I hadn't put so much time into my career," she said apologizing for the time she kept from Shawn. Stan did his best to keep me busy."

"I'm sure…" He took a drink of water a waiter brought over, then setting it down he continued. "I'm sure there's more than your career…in his reason for making you work so much. I've talked with Shawn. I'm sure by Monday all this will be cleared up. Our Mr. Hunter has made a grave mistake. You work on your investigation, collect your facts. Red will take good care of Shawn. Monday we'll meet in chambers and try straightening this all out before he's arraigned."

She left the Judge with more questions on her mind than she had before she came. How did he know where Shawn was being held? He knew more than he was offering but he had faith in her and it was time for her to realize it. At least now she knew for sure she could defend Shawn. She knew she had to put her mind into investigating what had happened, not the fear of losing. There was more Judge Thurman hadn't said and she was sure of it, possibly because he wasn't able to. But if a man as important as Judge Thurman had enough faith in her, she knew she'd better pull herself together and fight for Shawn.

"So Shawn wasn't home all night," she told herself, "but he didn't go and kill Hinkley." He would have used his hands, unless that's what he wants everyone to think. "Shut up shut up," she said pounding on the steering wheel. She put a lot of trust in Judge Thurman's words, trust she should have given to Shawn and she knew it. The more she thought about the situation the more confused she became. She was a damn good lawyer, but she never had to defend anyone close to her, not like this not for murder. If she made a mistake she could ruin Shawn's life, and possibly get him killed if he went to prison. She knew she had to work both sides of the case so she needed to know the prosecutors questions before he knew them himself. That way she could have as many answers as possible.

She headed for Stan's office. She needed to know what he knew, most of the time she could read the answers to any questions he was given from the look on his face. He had his link to the D.A's office, and usually knew everything they knew.

Tony stopped at the city garage to look at Hinkley's car, but it wasn't there. He was told it was being held at the county lab. At the lab he was told the car had been locked up and the only way he could see it was with a signed order from the Assistant District Attorney James T Hunter. Tony scowled.

In the past Tony had offered classes in self-defense for free to various officers, officer's wives, and many of their family members, creating a pool of promised favors, which he figured he'd never collect on. The official requesting he set up these classes for free assured him if he ever needed help it was only a phone call away. Now he decided it was time to call that official and collect on a few of those favors. He called his wife Correen.

After giving Correen a couple of minutes to get over her shock she instructed him to go and have coffee at the restaurant on the corner of Crest and Hill, "request a phone be brought to your booth and within a half hour you'll know exactly where that car is and when you can get to look at it. He thanked her said he loved her and headed for Thomas' Restaurant.

Ten minutes into his coffee someone called him, he was sure he recognized the voice but there was no name given, he was given the address where the vehicle was being stored until the lab could get to it, so he'd better hurry because the lab was supposed to be picking it up at three that afternoon. An officer named McKay would meet him and let him in.

"You find what it takes to help him" Correen pleaded, "don't you dare let them put him in prison." Tony promised he'd do whatever it took.

He finished his coffee and headed for the north end of the county. Supposedly there was a large garage the county purchased some months back and it was located up on Eight Mile Rd. and when Tony arrived there were no questions asked, an officer with the name badge McKay was parked in the drive waiting. The only word from his mouth was

"Tony?" Tony said "yes," and the officer unlocked the door and then stepped aside.

The garage was large with six individual stalls each closed off from the others. It was used by the county for hiding vehicles they needed to lock away for safekeeping. Tony found the light switch and flipped it on, lighting a single 60-watt bulb that didn't show him a damn thing. He unhooked the latch and opened the large drive in door, expecting McKay to say he couldn't do it. McKay was nowhere to be seen, the padlock was hanging on the hasp for him to lock back up when he was finished. For some reason he figured the D.A's office didn't even know he was there.

When he looked at the car he yelled for McKay but there was no answer. He was sure he had the wrong one. Hinkley drove a blue Cadillac; this was a white Mercedes convertible with a tan colored top. It looked a lot like Shawn's car in some ways. He pushed the car out into the light so he could get a better look at it. It had lots of chrome on it like Shawn's, and the convertible top was almost the same off white tannish color and that's when Tony began scratching his head. The tires were nice and clean and the rims were real nice chrome looking a lot like Shawn's. And yes it must have been Hinkley's, or someone else had been shot recently.

The driver side window had been shot out so some bullets definitely went through it, and he could see where three bullets had hit the frame of the rag top right at the top of the window. There were three more holes through the ragtop just above the driver's head; it had to be from a pickup Tony figuered. The front seat was covered with blood but for some reason Tony was sure it wasn't supposed to be Hinkley's blood; it was supposed to be Shawn's.

"In the dark at 5:00 a.m. on a fog rainy morning this car could very easily be mistaken for Shawn's convertible, by some half blind stupid jackass," Tony said with a worried look. "This whole thing is just a fucking mistake, he was after Shawn." Suddenly Sherin's words echoed in his mind. "He said he'd kill you too Shawn."

"Shit, a first year forensic student could tell the shots came from above; probably from the window of a pickup. "Ray's still in town and he's after Shawn," Tony blurted. "These shots probably came from the window of his pickup, the old lady was right."

He knew Shelly had Shawn's car and she needed to be warned. If Ray knows he shot the wrong person and he sees Shawn's car he might start shooting again, she had to know her life could be in serious danger. He called Shawn's car phone, but there was no answer. "Shit she doesn't have his beeper." Shawn had his car phone set up with a beeper he carried. If he was out of the car the beeper let him know he had a call. He was sure Shelly never thought about it. "She needs to be warned." He didn't want to scare her so he left a message for her to meet him at the Fourth Precinct, she must be some where near there he thought. He pushed the car back into the garage locking everything up. He needed to talk to Shawn and soon, he headed towards the fourth Precinct.

Stan was in court when Shelly walked into his office, so she helped herself to a cup of coffee and took a seat. About a half hour later she heard him in the hallway bragging to someone about how he'd just won another one.

"Come to beg for your job back!" He asked puffing his chest out when he saw her sitting there.

"Not hardly, I want to know what you know about this mess."

"I know your boyfriend is going to prison, that mess?" he asked plopping his brief case onto his desk.

"What ever happened to presumed innocent?"

"Shit, he called the Judge and threatened to kill him, he told the Judge to stay away from you or his life would be worthless."

Shelly looked at him in shock. She knew everything Stan was saying was a lie. "Did Hinkley tell you that? Its just hearsay."

"He's got a witness," Stan said pouring himself a cup of coffee. "You know, I'll bet you're not even aware of one tenth of what Shawn has been into in the past. There's no statute of limitations on murder you know."

"What the hell are you talking about? He didn't kill Hinkley?"

"I thought so," he said with an arrogant look. "You don't know do you? Remember one-day way back I asked if you really knew Shawn, and you said yes? I figured at the time you were full of shit, but out of respect for you I kept what I know out of the conversation. Now you're going to hear what he and his little black buddy have been hiding in their closet." He sat down in his large over stuffed chair stirring his coffee, knowing she was hanging there waiting. He wanted her to ask him to continue, but she didn't. So he finally went on.

"They killed a couple of men back in the late sixties," he said throwing out the words with a look of total conviction. Shelly's face went white as she listened to Stan shoot off his mouth. "Yeah, they had themselves a little gang, they tried taking over some of the investment businesses around

Detroit. You know, the ones that charge twenty five percent interest every week and break your legs if you don't pay. If the D.A. can tie them into any of the unsolved murders around that time, they'll both rot in prison. We... don't know who saved their Asses," he said playing with a pencil on his desk, but the D.A. will find out. Not only is he going down for Hinkley's death, they're going down for things they've done back then. His little black buddy will be arrested too as soon as he can be tied into Hinkley's death and the D.A. can get a warrant signed. And your boyfriend is also being charged with, flight to avoid..."

"Flight to avoid what?"

"Flight to avoid arrest and assault on an officer," Stan continued, raising his voice well above hers. Both felonies if I must remind you. He won't be released on bail, he won't see daylight for a long, long, time," Stan concluded with a smart-ass tone.

Shelly had heard all she wanted to, she slowly rose from her chair and walked up to about a foot from his face. "So what the hell are you doing helping the D.A.? Stan I stopped to tell you I'm defending Shawn." He started to open his mouth to say something but she quickly stopped him. "Shut up! Both Shawn and Tony have more class in their little fingers than you have in your whole fucking body. YOU!

Better hope the hell YOU! weren't in with Hinkley on any of his scams, because if YOU WERE! You'll be going to prison. HAVE A NICE DAY STAN!"

She left shaking inside but outside she was showing a strength Stan had never seen before. She wanted to scream, she wanted to cry, she wanted to throw things, but she didn't. She wanted to hear the sound of breaking glass from her throwing bottles at a cement wall. She pictured Stan tied against that wall as she pitched the bottles.

Back in the car she listened to the message from Tony on the car phone and was glad to hear it because now she had more questions she needed answers to and right away, things were getting worse. She headed for the Fourth Precinct ASAP.

"I really think Hinkley took those bullets for you," Tony reiterated looking at Shawn and Red's doubtful faces.

"Damn, he not only chases Shelly right into my arms but he takes a few bullets and dies for me. Sorry Tony, I can't swallow that. I mean I believe you about some of these guys liking me but Hinkley. His car really looks like mine?"

"On a shitty fog rainy morning? I can see it happening," Red agreed with Tony.

"I just can't see Hinkley doing that nice of a favor for me, how the hell long has he had this car anyway. He's always driven caddies as long as I've known him."

"Probably all that hard earned money he has if he's been scamming as much as you say he has," Tony added.

When Shelly arrived at the Precinct she was happy to see Tony's car sitting there, maybe she could clear up a whole lot of things she thought. She found Shawn and Tony sitting with Red in his office. Shawn hadn't been booked yet; Red didn't seem too worried about getting that done. They were discussing what Tony found at the garage, and the lack of investigation from Hunter. Tony was certain Ray had gone after Shawn as he told Sherin he would, only his stupidity made him kill the wrong man. What the judge was doing in Warren was confusing to all of them. From the look on Shelly's face when she walked in they figured she was already aware that Ray was still around.

"You look like you already know."

"Know what?"

"Tony thinks Ray killed Hinkley. Did you know Hinkley had a new car?"

"No."

"Well, he was driving a white Mercedes convertible, which at five in the morning could easily be mistaken for my car," Shawn said, hoping the news would help ease her mood.

"You mean Ray could have been looking for you, and shot Hinkley instead?" She plopped down into an old stuffed leather chair like a child being told she couldn't go out to play. She looked very tired. "And I've been driving your car around. So you've been arrested, because you weren't killed?"

The three men looked at each other mumbling, "Yeah," one said, "looks that way," another said "pretty much" the third one said. Then Tony added, "It's probably a good thing Shawn took that tire off his back bumper."

Shelly sat rubbing her hands over her face, then she looked at Red. "Do you go along with this?"

He was nodding his head yes before he spoke. "Yeah, from what Tony's found out, I'd say the shots came from a pickup. We'll get ballistics on Shawn's gun; it's not the murder weapon. If we could find Ray and see if he's got a nine mill, I'll bet you'll have your murder weapon and your murderer, case closed."

"What do you mean about the tire?" she asked turning to Tony.

"Well if it was Ray he'd have known for sure it was Shawn's car, or at least not the Judge's car. Shawn took the tire off his back bumper, if it was still there and Ray saw Hinkley's car without it maybe he'd still be alive and Ray would still be looking for Shawn. He'd be looking for the car he saw at the apartment house, Hinkley would still be alive."

"Sherin did say he was blind as a bat," Shawn added, "and if he was drinking he'd probably never have seen the tire anyway. Hinkley was just in the wrong place at the wrong time."

"Or the right place at the best time," Tony added knowing they all could care less he was dead.

"The D.A's. office couldn't have given much time into investigating this thing, some one pointed the finger at Shawn and Hunter jumped," Red added.

The three of them sat looking at her as if everything was going to be as easy as that. She was getting pissed. Then a fire like burst came out of her that shocked them all.

"Well you guy's get your magic wand out and poof Ray into the fucking parking lot, search his truck and find that Goddamned gun and take it over and shove it up Hunters ass!" She wasn't smiling one lick when she finished.

"I think she's mad," Red said looking from Shawn to Tony. The fire continued.

"I have something else I'd like to discuss with you two!" she said looking from Shawn to Tony. Her tone hadn't eased one bit, and her look would have scared the hell out of any witness on the stand.

"Go ahead, we keep no secrets from Red." Shawn replied.

"It's got to do with the late sixties, like, 1968,1969," she said holding her hands out palms up," like presenting a year in each one.

"Go ahead, we keep no secrets from Red," Shawn replied again.

She looked at him trying her best not to cry, but it didn't work. Pulling her hands back towards herself and crossing them on her chest she started crying.

"Than why do you have so many damn secrets from me?" She spat, doing her best not to cry but tears were flowing.

Shawn quickly looked at Tony and began snapping the fingers on his outstretched left hand.

"Quick, give me a buck." Tony pulled a money clip from his pocket handing Shawn a dollar bill. Shawn nodded his head slightly towards Shelly; Red grabbed a dollar from Tony's money clip too. They all reached out offering her a dollar, none of them smiled. She knew what they were doing; she just didn't want it to be a joke. Slowly she reached out taking the money from each one of them.

"Now ask us anything," Shawn said. "We'll answer any questions you have." He handed her a small box of tissues while the three of them sat looking at her like school children having just been scolded for cheating. She knew the three of them well enough and that was the only reason she allowed herself to loose control of her feelings. If there had been a stranger in the room she'd be gripping on to her courtroom composure as tight as she could, and she was glad there wasn't. She began crying uncontrollably.

The three men busied themselves getting her coffee and working on helping her calm down, they knew she was distraught. A few minutes later she pulled herself together enough to start asking questions.

"Did you two kill someone back around that time in your life?" she asked when she was finally able, certain they'd both say hell no.

"Yes," Shawn and Tony said together. "But can we explain?" Shawn asked, seeing the shocked look on her face. She needed the explanation and quickly Shawn realized hoping she wouldn't start crying again before they got started. She nodded yes; but she was too chocked up to try saying it.

Shawn looked at Tony giving him the chance to begin.

"In the summer of 68, Shawn and I came home from swimming one day and found my father all beaten up. He had taken out a loan from some loan shark's, which he couldn't pay back the way they wanted so they beat him half to death. We waited till they came back to collect another installment and they never collected on another loan."

"You killed them?" Shelly asked in shock.

"They didn't give us any other choice!" Shawn blurted. "They were armed and ready to make an example by killing one or both of us, we negotiated, they lost." Shawn sat waiting for her to absorb what they had said, but she said nothing.

"So we started taking out loans ourselves from other sharks. We would use the money to help people in the hood. When they came to break our legs for non payment, we broke theirs."

Shelly began to smile as she listened to their version of what went down. She shook her head in disbelief knowing it was all probably true, and Stan had it all wrong. They weren't going into business; they were canceling businesses. It didn't make the news they'd killed someone any better though.

"The other two..." Shawn began to say, but she cut him off.

"Other two! Couldn't you two just go to the police!"

"Yeah, a guy shoves a gun in your face, you tell'im wait I need to call the police, that'll stop him," Shawn interjected. She quickly realized how stupid her suggestion was.

She couldn't imagine how it would be to kill someone, especially with your hands. Those same hands had touched every inch of her body. Suddenly fear shot through her just thinking about it, to have the skill capable of stopping any physical threat from someone and making love to her with those same hands. She thought about the many times those hands were around her neck, holding her face, holding her in a way that in a split second he could have snapped the life from her body. Suddenly she didn't know what to think, she had a different perspective for the Martial Arts training he and Tony were skilled in.

"Did you two have a gang?" She asked, her voice quivering.

"Just the two of us, if you want to call that a gang," Shawn replied, looking at Tony.

"Did you ever get caught?"

"Yeah," they both spoke at the same time again.

"Don't tell me, let me guess," she continued. "Because you both were active in Martial Arts you were charged with felonious assault second degree murder, and Judge Thurman presided over your case."

All three men nodded their heads up and down, while looking straight at her, Shawn wondered how all of a sudden she was able to put things together, and then he silently called himself stupid. "And your part," she asked Red.

"I didn't know them back then."

"But you were nodding your head."

"I told you we don't have any secrets," Shawn offered. "After Thurman became involved the charges were changed to misdemeanors, things died down and after a couple years our records were cleared," Shawn said, hoping she didn't know about everything. "But that was on the second two. Nobody but Tony and I know about the first two, 'til now anyway. We dumped them car and all into the Detroit river." Both of her hands went quickly to her mouth as another wave of shock blasted through her. After a couple of minutes of her shaking her head in disbelief she began again.

"And everything they know about, everything you could go to prison for was cleared up?" she asked with a wide-eyed look still wiping tears.

"Yes," both Shawn and Tony replied.

"Is there anyway they can find out about the other two?"

"No, some other thugs were convicted of killing them, they had killed three other people and our great system pinned those on'em too."

"So just where DO YOU fit into all this mess?" she asked turning her attention towards Red.

He started nodding his head no. "I just thought I might need a lawyer," he replied. She finally cracked a smile.

"I need to know one other thing and I need to know it now. Back a couple of years ago why did you come home that night covered in blood?" she asked looking back at Shawn.

"Shawn hoped she'd forgotten about that night, but he was glad to finally tell her the truth. He and Tony knew right away which night she was referring to, Red gave them a questioning look.

"Two years ago Eight Mile Road, the Skin Head Bar," Shawn said looking at him. He nodded his head, indicating now he remembered.

"We rescued…"

"Kidnapped!" Tony blurted.

"We removed an eighteen year old boy, at his parents request I might add, from a Skin Head Bar over on Eight Mile Road."

"DID YOU KILL ANYONE THAT NIGHT?" she asked sharply.

"No," all three said in unison. "We filled a few hospital beds, but no deaths," Shawn continued.

"At least none that we know of," Tony replied quickly. Now she looked at Red, he was pointing at himself like a schoolboy begging to answer the teacher's next question.

"So YOU WERE with them this time?" He began nodding his head no again. Shelly sank back into her chair letting out a big sigh as if exhausted "WHAT THEN?" Her tone told Shawn she was either getting more pissed, or she was awfully tired, his bet was on pissed.

"My job was to work at dispatch and make sure if any emergency calls came from the bar to dispatch they were blocked from the recorders and operators."

"And did you do that?"

"No, no calls ever came in."

"So you really didn't do anything wrong?"

"Well, no. But I was willing."

She wadded up one of the dollar bills throwing it back at him, "You don't need a lawyer" she said, "maybe a shrink but not a lawyer."

"Why a shrink?" Shawn asked.

"Because you three cannot go around using your might to make things go your way!" Suddenly she didn't want to know any more. It would be better if what ever happened in the past was left there, she thought. I'll be there if one of them needs me and that's the best I can do. "ON SECOND

THOUGHT," she said reaching out and snatching back the dollar she'd thrown at Red, "maybe I should keep this for your retainer, the more I think of it I'm sure you'll be needing an attorney some day soon," she ended those words with a smile.

She knew she'd left Brook hanging after the call to Shawn, now she wanted to at least let her know what was going on. Probably what had happened this morning and her reaction the way she had yelled, she knew Brook was probably a little angry with her. She knew sometimes she'd like to take matters into her own hands, but not the way these guys had done. If she allowed herself to do that it would put an end to her practicing law. The three men finally relaxed a little, giving their cheeks a chance to smile. Now she looked back at Shawn.

I need to know about this morning. "Where were you this morning around five o'clock because you weren't home I looked all over for you? I need to know," she asked with a sniffle.

Without a seconds hesitation he began. "When I found you two sleeping I figuered it would be a good time to check the Foust Mansion and see if anyone was there. I knew for sure where Brook was, so if someone was there I could be sure it wasn't her screwing with me. I was going to tell you but Brook was there when you asked me so I lied, I'm sorry."

"So you were in the neighborhood?"

"I didn't…" Shawn started but she cut him off.

"I believe you. What I'm wondering is if maybe Ray saw you, lost you, then thought he found you again and started shooting?"

"That sounds about right," Tony said quickly agreeing with her. Things briefly went quiet while Shelly sat letting everything filter through her mind. Finding out the man she loved had killed someone bothered her. She was telling herself that was a long time ago though, and then Brook's situation quickly popped into her thoughts. She had information she wanted him to know.

"Well you were right, it was Brook hiding in the house, and Forest is her father." Shawn and Tony gave each other silly looks; this information came as a complete surprise.

"And I believe he was a bookie," she continued.

"He was" Tony added. "I was going to tell you that. I found out all the work on that house of his was done by people he'd helped win money on the races and games. Seems he was pretty damn good at what he did and every one liked the hell out of him. He wasn't the usual kind of bookie, he never hurt anyone that owed him money he just called on them when he needed help with something. Besides, he should have a lot of money hiding somewhere because I was told he made a lot himself the last few years."

"So the house and property are all hers now," Shawn said rubbing his chin, "does she know that?"

"I think she does, but there's still more I have to find out yet. She doesn't seem to care about that. She probably doesn't realize it yet but I still need a few more answers from her. But first we've got to get you out of here," Shelly advised.

"He'll be ok here tonight," Red said. "I'm staying. I want to see a headline saying Shawn Cassidy was wrongfully charged for the murder of Judge Thomas Hinkley before I put him back out on the street. If not, some damn rookie is going to be taking shots at him. I'm going to step up the hunt for Ray too, and I'm going to let the State Police know about the new evidence. Anyone in his or her right mind can see Shawn was the intended target. Shawn had no motive to kill that bastard. With the evidence I have about Ray telling Sherin he was going to kill Shawn, and him almost killing her, everything points to Ray. The Judge was just in the wrong place at the right time." A smile quickly came across his lips; there was no mistake that he couldn't care less about the Judge being dead. "We'll have a court order to release him by morning. Besides, Hunter never handed me the warrant, it was on the floor; I touched a match to it."

Shelly smiled. "I didn't hear that, I'm going to go talk to Brook. She needs to be brought up to date on what's going on. Then I'm coming back here and spend the night in jail." The three of them just looked at each other and smiled.

CHAPTER FOURTEEN

Shelly didn't want to leave but the questions she needed answers to couldn't wait. If she were right she'd be able to tell Shawn just who his mystery client was and she knew that would make him very happy. She'd left Brook hanging that morning and now she wanted to touch base with her and let her know what was going on, and hopefully Brook could help her get those answers.

"I'll be back as soon as possible and then we can get started working on your arraignment for Monday morning," she said still drying her eyes.

"You take my car home and park it in the garage," Shawn commanded with a stern but polite look. "It's probably not a good idea for you to be out in it."

So she agreed, she'd drive her own car over to Brook's. If Ray really was looking for Shawn it made it too dangerous for her to be seen driving his car. She completely understood his concern for her safety but she had a feeling it was silly, but she would follow his wish to go and pick up her own vehicle. Everyone else had left the office so she and Shawn could have privacy, now they were locked in each other's arms trying to ease the pain of everything that had happened through the day.

"Did you clean out my desk?" he asked, knowing it was a stupid question.

"They cleaned out everything but your secret drawer."

"See, I told you that would come in handy some day, so they over looked it and you took care of the important things. You did get my newspaper too didn't you?"

"Why did you hide that in there, were you afraid some one would take it before you finished the cross word?"

"How'd you guess?" he replied with a grin. He always kept his previous copy of the financial section so he could compare his moves and follow his next ideas. Even if she had looked at it she wouldn't have know what he'd been up to. She might have seen his notes and short hand scribbling along the columns of stock symbols, but she still wouldn't have under stood he'd been trading stocks.

Shelly softly rubbed her hands over his; she was still having difficulty controlling her thoughts of him killing someone with those same hands. She knew he had always touched her with gentleness, but she felt like she was touching the paws of a tiger and she knew that was silly. She looked at him a little bit different now and she wondered if she was just being stupid. Looking deep into his eyes she could only see the kindness and gentleness she'd always received from him and wondered if he could ever snap and use that killer strength against her. "Never", she told herself as she pulled him close wanting his soft lips against hers.

"So she's the missing daughter?" Shawn questioned with a look buried in fog. Shelly pushed her stupid thoughts away telling herself he deserved all of her attention.

"She's been in the house hundreds of times," Shelly said smiling. She had a look as if she'd just put the last piece in place to a thousand-piece puzzle they'd been working on for days. His shoulders sank as did the look on his face, then he wrenched every muscle of his face into the most disgusting troll like shape he could develop, which always made her laugh. Reaching down into his throat he created the most troll like voice he could produce like when he would mock certain judges.

"What?" He questioned shaking his head in disbelief. "You say she's the missing daughter, are you sure?" He was playing with the phrase as if a judge was getting the news. "Are you positively sure?"

Laughing, Shelly quickly put two fingers up to his lips stopping him from saying anything more. He didn't seem to realize what was at stake with his situation and making her laugh wasn't dispelling her fears at all, she didn't particularly want to laugh right now. Then she quickly replaced the fingers with her lips giving him a warm kiss, and then sounding like a little girl collecting clues to a treasure hunt, she blurted.

"I just need the answers to these questions, and then I'll tell you everything I know." She was playfully trying to reshape his face while he kept making different ugly looks and twisting his head this way and that like a child being corny. They both laughed again as she kissed his distorted lips and tried stopping his crazy facial expressions.

He was surprised at the information she had already collected and he was feeling like a schoolboy being noticed by the prettiest girl in class. It had been a long time since he'd received this much attention from her. She had followed up on his request to find out from Brook what he was unable to, she had put forth the effort to help him and he loved it. Maybe he could talk her into working with him on other cases he wondered? In the past she had always furnished him with priceless research and good common sense information when it was needed, but she had never interacted with any of the people involved in his investigations. Now she was swept up into his way of life and he could tell she was enjoying it. He was sure he had her hooked.

"Let me slip over to Brook's and I'll be right back. I've got a lot to tell you, I just need the answers to these last two questions. And I think we'll both be very surprised, maybe shocked but satisfied, that's if my hunch is right." He knew she was like him when it came to working on a hunch, he wouldn't tell anyone what his was for fear of jinxing it, so he didn't bother asking what hers was. He was so impressed with her help he let her continue out of fear of loosing her. It had been too damn long since they'd worked on anything together, so now he was keeping his mouth shut.

"You just take my car home first, ok?" He was sure Ray had no idea where he lived, so she'd be safe going back to his house it wasn't that far away.

"Maybe we can get Red to let us stay in here tonight?"

"What, you don't want to share a cell with me?"

She gave him a sharp poke in the ribs. "Do you want everyone to watch and listen while I rape you?"

"No, this should be ok," he quickly replied shaking his head and smiling.

"I thought you might agree," she said forcing her best smile.

"Ok, but you watch out for Ray. I can't believe he'd do anything in broad daylight, but you never know. If you see anything that doesn't look right you hide and call Tony."

"I will. When I get back you're going to tell Red to get lost for about an hour." She looked at the stuffed leather chair she'd been sitting in, and then at the desk, she gave a quick look at the six-foot table they'd all been sitting at minutes before and then back to the chair. "On second thought maybe half an hour." He'd been following her eyes as she talked, not believing what he thought she was hinting at. Her smile met his and his thoughts hoped he knew what she was suggesting but he was too afraid to ask. The table was definitely out. All he could say was "hurry back", while he mentally rehearsed telling Red to get lost.

She assured him she'd hurry and when she walked out into the hall she told Tony she'd stay in touch with him, Red was no where to be seen. She left the station hiding the worst fear she'd ever felt in her life; she was hoping Ray would be arrested soon and the gun used to shoot Hinkley would be found in his possession. Shaking her head she still couldn't stop thinking about Shawn killing someone with his bare hands.

Tony was making a quick trip to the hospital to check on Sherin and touch base with his guards; he had assured them he'd be back soon but his soon had been dragged out to a slow return. He wasn't about to miss the poker game

Red and Shawn had set up, so he planned a quick stop at the hospital and then back to the precinct. They were all sure with the information they had collected that the charges against Shawn would be dropped and he'd be free to leave before Monday, if common sense were allowed to enter the picture.

About ten minutes after Tony and Shelly left the station, Hunter called from the hospital, and he became totally enraged when he heard Shawn hadn't even been booked yet.

"RED WHAT THE HELL ARE YOU DOING? I'M GOING TO MAKE DAMN SURE YOU'RE REPLACED, YOU CAN KISS THE FOURTH PRECINCT GOOD-BY!" Hunter screamed through the phone.

"I'm afraid you'll be the one crying after Shawn gets through suing the county for your bullshit."

"What the fuck do you mean? I'm the one gonna sue."

"He'll be booked as soon as I get your arrest warrant signed by the judge. From what I've seen so far you've arrested a man without the proper investigation or the proper paper work. You're a damn fool Hunter, you jumped after getting bad information, and I'm going to find out where you got your leads and crush you both."

While Red argued Hunter tried to remember where the warrant had ended up? "I've got the warrant, it's in my coat pocket," he said lying. He was sure one of the Patrolmen must have picked it up. With all the confusion they'd forgotten to give it to Redman "I'll get it right over to you."

Well, I'm not doing any more till I get it," Red explained. "And I'd like to know how you zeroed in on Shawn so fast, you might not like him but he's no murderer. Besides, if he wanted to kill someone he'd use his hands, not a gun. What evidence do you have?"

"Plenty," Hunter exclaimed. "I'M MOVING HIM DOWN TOWN TONIGHT!" he yelled, expressing his disgust for the way Red was handling the issue.

"I've collected more facts in the last two hours then you have from all your so called informants," Red fired back. "Did you know the Judge bought a new car? His new car looks so much like Shawn's it isn't funny. Did you know there's a man being sought for damn near beating a lady to death yesterday and the same man threatened Shawn's life? It's a case of mistaken identity stupid ass; the shooter shot the wrong man. He was after Shawn. Have you run ballistics on Shawn's weapon yet, no you haven't have you?"

Hunter's end of the line went quiet; he was getting very pissed at Stan. Stan had sold him on the definite guilt of

Shawn for the murder of Judge Hinkley and because he hated Shawn he fell for Stan's lies. As soon as Judge Hargrove heard this news he'd be pissed too. The judge had asked him if he was sure Shawn was guilty before he signed the warrant, Hunter assured him it was true. He wanted to be praised for catching the murderer of Judge Hinkley so quickly, now he knew he'd be lucky to save his job if his news was incorrect. He had to find that warrant, at least then he could say the judge signed it and authorized it. With Judge Hargrove in the stew with him they might be able to pin this on Shawn anyway.

"He's guilty. You just get him booked, I'll have the warrant to you shortly," then there was a loud click on the line; Hunter had slammed down the phone.

Red sat looking at the phone after hanging it up, he wondered what Hunter would do when he couldn't find the warrant. Quickly he called Judge Hargrove.

"Harold, Redman here, you know there's no way Shawn Cassidy could have killed Hinkley?"

"Good day to you too Mr. Redman, I'm sure that's how you feel, but I have a D. A. claiming he has definite proof."

"Proof" Red continued, he told the judge about the evidence he'd obtained within two hours, which the D. A. had none of and only because he hadn't investigated things properly. He explained he was sure the D.A. had put all his cards on an informant but that informant was totally wrong."

"Why did Cassidy try to flee?"

Red couldn't hold back his laughter. "He never tried to flee," Red snickered after calming himself. "Hunter was kicking Shawn in the back of his heals every step from the arrest to bringing him into my Precinct. On one attempt at kicking him his foot missed and ended up right under Shawn's left foot. What the hell's going to happen when a man six three two hundred pounds comes down on the instep of someone's foot?" Red asked. "Hunter said Shawn was trying to break free, yeah, right in the middle of my Precinct, Cops all over hell and he's trying to break free. If he wanted to run he'd have done it when they came to arrest him, he could have beat the hell out of every one of them and ran then if he'd wanted to. Hunter's a jackass and we all know it, he should be out chasing jay-walkers."

Judge Hargrove didn't know what to think. He didn't appreciate Redman's humorous attitude, but he knew if Red were right, there would be a hell of a lot more people laughing and snickering at him. "That might be what he'll be doing if I find out he's been lying to me. I guess because it was a Judge that was murdered I thought he'd make sure his facts were straight, I could be wrong. I guess I shouldn't have signed that warrant."

"Well, your Honor I haven't seen the warrant yet. I guess with all the confusion he forgot to give it to me so he might come asking you to sign another one?"

"Why… Why would he need another one?" the judge asked speaking in a drawl.

"Because the first one might have been lost," Red implied in a mater of fact tone.

"Could I presume if I denied signing another warrant for him that it wouldn't come back and bite me in the proverbial backside?"

"I think you'd be safe going on record with that statement Your Honor." The judge sat shaking his head, he was sure Red had gotten his hands on that warrant and it was no longer available to anyone.

"And he never showed it to you when he delivered Mr. Cassidy to your precinct?"

"No Sir I never saw it," Red shot back crossing his fingers as he lied. There was a long pause before the judge came back on the line.

"Judge Thurman has been trying to get hold of me. I'm sure if he has the same information you have he'll be disappointed in me too. I wanted to be the Judge that put things in gear so we could put Thomas' killer quickly behind bars. Now, thanks to an over zealous District Attorney I'll walk around with egg on my face. I'll talk with Collin then I'll get back with you Red, I thank you for this information, I think were going to put a stop to something very soon."

"I'll look forward to hearing from you sir," Red chirped. He hung up the phone with a big smile aimed at Shawn. "Hunter needs a warrant and he's shit out of luck." Shawn knew Red had touched a match to Hunter's warrant like he said he had, and from what he gleaned from Red's end of the conversation; the Judge wasn't about to sign another one. Hunter was up a creek.

Judge Hargrove was also a District Court Judge and it was said he was the easiest Judge in Wayne County to get to sign a warrant. He'd been ridiculed various times for handing out too soft of penalties. That was why Hunter had gone to him first. Hunter knew his facts were weak, but he'd hoped they could be proven once Shawn was behind bars. Now, his house of cards was falling down. Hunter knew he'd had a warrant signed by the judge; all he had to do was present it to Red and drag Shawn out of the Fourth Precinct and down town. Having that warrant would keep his ass mildly protected.

Shawn listened while Red argued with Hunter and then gave Judge Hargrove his version of what had happened. From the smile on Red's face he knew Hunter's life, as a Deputy D.A. was getting very short. He stood looking out the window while he listened, turning to Red when he finally hung up. It was getting late in the day, a little after six now. Not late enough for the sun to be going down but it had certainly been blocked out over Detroit. Off to the west it was getting pretty dark like a storm was brewing, the sky looked like it was past sundown. It looks like we're in for a bad one he told himself as he watched the light blue sky slowly disappear turning into darkness with lightening darting back and forth between black clouds moving rapidly along.

"So what's up?"

"Aw, that asshole wants to ship you downtown. If he comes back you get in the closet, I'll tell'im you escaped." They both started laughing.

"You want that prick to shoot me, don't you?"

"I want that prick to move far away. Shit he's not going to show up here, he's probably still waiting in emergency. He's no good around here. Detroit could do a hell of a lot better. Didn't you two used to be friends?" Red asked with a twisted look.

"Years ago, until I found out he was a prick," Shawn replied with a grin. "He'd put his own mother in prison guilty or not."

"I thought he'd be out of the picture for a while, he can't walk but that doesn't keep him off the phone," Red declared. "What are you going to do if this goes to far?" he asked, showing deep concern.

"I'll take the stand. What the hell's my motive. Hinkley drove my girlfriend right into my arms. Hell, I was going to send him a thank you card. Red, he's got things going on that'll even freak you out."

Shawn spent the next hour or so telling Red what he thought Hinkley had going on, and about Judge Thurman's investigation. "Actually there could be a hundred suspects in Hinkleys murder," Shawn added. But, he agreed with Tony. It had to be Ray, and he fucked up royally. Now if they could only poof him there and get him caught, he mused thinking of Shelly's words.

Hunter began making calls to get the paper work he needed so he could move Shawn. His main problem was it was Friday night and most of the judges had already gone home. Red was sure Hunter wouldn't be able to find anyone to help him, he knew every judge in the county; they'd call him first to find out what the hell was going on and he'd blast Hunter's plan right out of the water. Possibly after learning about Hunter's total fuck up, they'd wait till Monday. When Hunter got stepped on, the warrant for Shawn had ended up on the floor and kicked unnoticed to the hall, it was never properly delivered and in Red's eyes it was worthless. Especially since it had been issued for Shawn. He knew it was a gray area, but he still wanted Shawn to stay there so he wouldn't end up getting shot. And Shawn knew Hunter would shoot him on sight if he was found outside the precinct, there was no way of knowing how many Patrolman Hunter had on his side.

Shawn and Red sat chewing the fat when suddenly they heard a ruckus in the hallway then Red's office door being clumsily opened and Hunter entering on crutches; two Detroit police officers accompanied him.

"WHY THE HELL ISN'T HE IN A CELL?" hunter's voice boomed.

"I'M INTERROGATING HIM!" Red shot back even louder. "What the fuck is it to you? You don't just walk into my office and start throwing your weight around!" The two officers started to take hold of Shawn.

"Boys, I suggest you get the fuck out of my office, this man is in my custody!"

Hunter quickly removed a warrant from his pocket, shoving it into Red's face. The two officers continued towards Shawn with handcuffs and leg irons.

"I told you two and I will not tell you again, if you want to have your jobs tomorrow, get the fuck out of here. This man stays here. He will remain here until Monday Morning and then we'll see what a Judge says." The two officers looked at Hunter waiting for his next move. Red opened the warrant to see what Judge Hunter had been able to get sign it and quickly a big smile came across his face. "You stupid fucker, you forged Hargrove's signature." Hunter knew Red was right, he just didn't know how he knew.

"The hell I did, go ahead, call'im, see if he didn't sign a warrant for me."

"Oh he signed a warrant, only not this one!" Red exclaimed loudly picking up the phone. "Here call'im yourself, he's up at Houghton Lake," Red added lying. Hunter grabbed for the warrant but Red held it high passing it over to Shawn. "I suggest you all get the fuck out of my office." The two officers needed no more convincing they left immediately, leaving Hunter to fend for himself getting through the doors. Hunter followed slapping his crutches against everything he could knowing he had just sealed the loss of his job.

"How the hell did he get that foot fixed up so soon?" Shawn questioned with a smile.

"I think he just had'em wrap it so he could come after you," Red replied with a shit eating grin. "That damn fool will never be able to walk right again."

Shelly went back to Shawn's house to exchange cars but she couldn't get her car started. She must have left her lights on the day before and her battery had run down. She stood clicking her nails on his kitchen counter debating what she should do. She knew Ray was a definite threat but she figured it being Friday night with all the traffic she could make it to Warren ok without being seen by him if he was out there. Besides, Ray was probably out hitting the bars; he wouldn't dare show himself and try anything. She could be back in an hour or so and then she'd explain everything to Shawn.

So she decided to take Shawn's car anyway, she also needed quick access to a phone so taking his car really made more sense. She'd just go a different route to Brook's house. She could take back streets and stay away from the heavily lit areas, it would take longer but the coming storm would help hide her she reasoned. The coming storm made it darker than usual for that time of day. She was glad though because that would also make it harder for Ray to see the car if she did pass him. She also knew it made it harder to see who was driving it, and that was why Hinkley was dead. She was feeling a bit apprehensive but she needed to see Brook.

Taking the back streets really slowed her down and by the time she pulled into Brook's drive it was quite dark and there was a steady sprinkle of rain coming down. She was hoping she'd find her there and her question was quickly answered when Brook came flying out of the house running to the car looking half scared.

"It's about damn time! I've left a hundred messages on the damn machine!"

Shelly grabbed her by the hand and dragged her back into the house. "Have you seen Ray around here any where?"

"No, why?"

"Is your mother home?"

"No, she's at work."

Shelly told herself she'd made it ok, Ray was probably nowhere to be seen. She spent the first few minutes telling Brook about Shawn being arrested and what Tony had found out. They were sure Ray had carried out his threat to kill Shawn but he found the wrong car and ended up shooting the judge instead.

"Are you stupid?" Brook quickly asked, "why are you driving his car?"

"My car wouldn't start, and I wanted to see you to bring you up to date on what's going on." Brook liked hearing those words, for Shelly to put herself in danger just to bring her news made her feel pretty important. "And I'm sure Ray's hiding someplace, he wouldn't be out running around with every cop in Detroit after him." All she could hope for was the police looking for him he'd be to scared to be out running around. She was hoping the police would quickly find him and put him away before he harmed anyone else. What they didn't know was, Ray hadn't even been considered a suspect in the judge's murder. The warrant for attempted murder on Sherin hadn't even been processed yet. They needed a signed statement from her before they could issue it and her doctor wouldn't let them up to see her yet, so the D.A's office was holding things up. There were no warrants issued therefore none of the police departments around Detroit were even looking for him, except Starkway's office.

When Shelly had related to Brook everything that happened with Shawn she knew it was time to ask her about the other things she needed answers to.

"Ask away," Brook said taking a seat beside her on the couch.

"Can we talk in your bedroom?" Shelly requested. She wanted to take another look at the envelopes on her desk.

Brook took her by the hand and led her to the bedroom; taking a seat on her bed she patted the space besides her indicating she wanted Shelly to sit there.

"I will, but I want to look at something first." Walking over to Brook's desk she took one of the envelopes from her letter holder and then she took a seat beside her.

"You can have it, I've got a lot of them," Brook chimed.

"I don't want it, I just want to take a closer look at it. I saw some more just like this in Shawn's desk today," she said giving Brook a questioning look, "They're very pretty, sort of specially made to order aren't they?"

"I don't know, my dad got'em for me." She was sure other people had envelopes like that, there was no way Shelly could link the ones in Shawn's office to her.

Shelly decided to cut the bull and come right to it. Removing one of the letters from her purse she held the envelopes side by side, they were identical. "Brook, are you Shawn's mystery client?"

"Am I what?" She hadn't thought of being called a mystery client. No matter, she decided to play dumb.

"You know what I mean. I'm sure you're completely aware of what brought Shawn to this neighborhood. But this case has put his life in danger, serious danger. If only he'd see that. I'm not saying he shouldn't have taken the case, but it's only right he knows everything."

Brook turned her head; she didn't want to look Shelly in the eyes now. "I don't know what you're talking about."

Shelly took her by the shoulders and softly turned her back towards her but Brook kept looking down she wouldn't make eye contact, so Shelly took her chin and tipped her head up so they could look each other square in the eyes.

"They look identical to me," Shelly said softly, holding the two envelopes side by side. "Are you?"

Brook still wouldn't speak she just sat there. Finally Shelly reminded her, "I'm still your attorney, you can confide in me." There was a few more seconds of silence, and then she finally gave in.

"No one pays him enough. He's worth a lot more than two hundred dollars a day."

Shelly smiled, it felt good finding out answers to complicated questions. She was beginning to see what Shawn found so interesting about his work. She reached out pulling Brook close, giving her a warm friendly hug she agreed; "you're sure right about that honey." They sat holding each other for a while, and then Shelly went for question number two.

"Honey, I know you think you're in love with Shawn and you'd like to pay him thousands to work for you, but where'd you get the money. I mean you've paid him one hell of a lot of money, where are you getting it? And what is it you want him to find out.

Brook decided it was time to come clean on everything, well almost everything. The game she'd been playing was getting pretty dumb. She knew she was too young for Shawn, and after all he was going to marry Shelly. The money didn't mean all that much to her. And even if she'd have to give some to Shelly for being her attorney she'd still be rich. She stood up and walked to her desk still wondering if she should tell where the money came from and how much she had.

"As soon as Shawn knows it came from you he'll give it all back."

"Why?" she asked quickly turning back.

"Because you're a minor, he won't accept money from you."

"But I've got lots of it."

"He won't care, you could have millions, he wont take money from a minor."

"That's silly."

"What do you mean silly? He has morals and some very strict rules. He wouldn't break them for anything." As she spoke her thoughts sprang back to everything she'd learnt about him earlier that afternoon and a cold chill ran up her spine. "So where did you get it from?"

Brook stepped up onto the chair in front of her desk and reaching up to the ceiling she slid away the attic panel, and then she pulled down a large shoebox and handed it to Shelly. And then she sat back on the bed beside her, "Open it." She gave Shelly a funny look as she helped wiggled the top off of the box so she could see what was in it, and then Shelly's mouth dropped, it was full with bundles of one hundred dollar bills. Brook reached into the box and removed one of the bundles.

"Where'd you get this?" Shelly asked, her words of shock matching the look of total surprise on her face.

"From my dad's office. That was on the desk the day Beth killed him."

"He was a bookie wasn't he!" Shelly almost screamed with delight. "This is probably mob money, how much is in here?"

"There was five hundred and twenty thousand in that box."

"That box, you mean you've got another one, there's more?" Shelly asked, still unable to hide her shock.

"I've got six more boxes hidden up there," Brook replied calmly. Shelly couldn't believe what she was hearing and she wondered how Brook could be so damn calm?

"Have you counted what's in them?"

"Yeah, there's ten hundred thousand dollars in each one of them."

"That's a million dollars! honey, ten hundred thousand dollars is a million," she spat at Brook in a loud whisper still unable to hide her shock.

"Oh I know, then there's six million dollars up there."

Shelly's eyes went slowly from Brooks eyes to the ceiling above, then back to Brook's eyes. "You're kidding me," she said slowly after a few seconds. Brook was nodding her head no, she wasn't kidding.

Shelly couldn't believe Brook would be sitting here with so much money and not spending it. "Why didn't you give some of this to your mother?"

"She'd think I robbed a bank or something and probably call the police, I would have lost all of it and that would have led her to my father. And I promised him I wouldn't tell anyone. He said I could use some if I needed to, but the only money I've taken out is what I've given to Shawn."

Shelly opened her mouth to ask another question but suddenly there was the sound of screeching tires out in front of the house. Brook quickly put the money back into its hiding place then they ran to the front window just in time to hear the squealing of tires as a pickup sped away.

"Oh Christ it's Ray," Brook said turning out the lights and running out onto the front porch. "Now he's just sitting down there at the corner."

"Shit, he saw Shawn's car and he thinks Shawn's here, Get your ass back in here!" Shelly screamed dragging Brook back into the house. The sound of tires spinning on wet pavement made them both hit the floor as soon as she pulled Brook back through the door. Ray's pickup came racing down the street screeched to a halt in front of the house. He sat there looking at the house revving the engine making all sorts of noise with his loud mufflers. And then with tires spinning he raced to the other end of the block. It was still raining and the wet pavement made it easy for him to spin out and slide around when he slammed on his breaks. He was actually having fun terrorizing people on the street.

He'd been around Warren long enough to know the time it took for the police to respond to a call in the neighborhood. He also knew most people in the neighborhood were too afraid to call and report anything to the police. He'd driven up and down these streets for the last few months making all the noise he wanted, it was nothing new for the neighbors to listen to. They feared retribution from the hoodlum's if they reported anything.

"Now he's sitting down there," Brook whispered peeking out the door."

"Damn I wish you had a phone!" Shelly shouted. "I've got to get to the car!"

"Let me!"

"Don't you dare, he could have a gun!" Shelly blurted.

"Then you do it, I'm going to keep him busy." And Before Shelly could stop her Brook bolted out the door heading down the street towards the corner where Ray sat revving the motor in his pickup truck.

Shelly was pissed but she knew she had to take this chance Brook had given her. Running to the car she quickly jumped in and laid down on the front seat. Fumbling in the dark she grabbed the phone and pushed buttons hoping like hell she'd pushed the right ones for Tony, but she failed, she had a wrong number. She quickly hung up. Now she was shaking almost uncontrollably and she wanted to make sure she pushed the correct buttons. She knew Shawn had his number on auto dial but suddenly she couldn't remember how to set it in motion so she turned on the dash lights, which also turned on the parking lights. As soon as she punched in the correct numbers she hurriedly turned out the light. When the phone was answered she began talking hysterically.

"Tony Ray's here Ray's here!" She half screamed into the phone, but he wasn't there, his answering machine had picked up. "Tony, call me please, call me I'm in Shawn's car," then she hung up. She sat in the car pounding her feet on the floorboard hoping Tony would call right back. Then she heard screetching tires again and Ray's truck came sliding to a halt right behind the car. He sat there looking at the house and car, his engine racing like crazy. When he slid to a stop she sank back down onto the floor as far as possible hoping he wouldn't see her, then the phone began to ring. She knew the taillights blinked as the phone rang and she hoped he'd think there was no one in the car that was why no one answered it, they were in the house. She could feel Ray's eyes staring at her right through the metal of the car and she forced herself tightly against the floorboard, the phone kept ringing. She knew if she answered it with him sitting there she'd be in real trouble, he'd know someone was in the car and possibly start shooting, so she laid there listening to it ring hoping Tony wouldn't give up.

Ray also sat listening to the phone ring, with his left hand hanging out the driver's side window; in it he held the nine-millimeter handgun he'd used to kill Judge Hinkley and he was hoping to find Shawn so now he could shoot him too.

Suddenly something hit the right side of his truck with a heavy thud and then another thud and Shelly knew Brook was tossing rocks at him. Tires began to squeal again and she knew he was going away, she hoped he was just getting out of the line of fire but she knew he was probably going after Brook. She quickly grabbed for the phone but because she was shaking so bad she dropped it and fumbled around in the dark getting it up to her ear. The squealing quickly stopped as fast as it started. Her fear that Brook had gotten herself in trouble by drawing Ray away made her shake even more.

Now Ray could see somebody pitching rocks at him from down the street, but before chasing after them he pulled up the gun and put a bullet into each right side tire on Shawn's car. He didn't want Shawn driving it away. The gunshots made Shelly shake that much more and she huddled against the seat literally shaking the whole car she thought, she was sure the next bullet would come ripping through the car any second but then she heard more rocks hitting his truck and she knew that brave little girl was out there doing her best to draw him away. She pulled the phone tight to her ear and started screaming as the squealing started again.

"Tony...Oh God Tony Ray's here and he's going to kill us!"

"Where are you?" Tony screamed back.

"I'm at Brooks!"

"Where the hell's that?"

"1124 Caliper, it's three blocks south of Eight Mile just east of Ryan!" she sobbed. Tony knew where Caliper Street was and he was already on his way.

"I'm close, I'll be there soon. Why do you still have Shawn's car?" He questioned loudly

"I know it's a long story," she replied starting to calm down, but Tony had heard the shots and was hurrying to get there, he'd already hung up.

She'd heard more rocks hitting Ray's truck and she knew Brook was trying her best to draw him away; it had to be pissing him off. She'd been screaming to Tony over the squealing of Ray's tires as he started to go after Brook. Quickly she pulled herself up into the seat so she could look out and see where he was and when she saw him at least a block away she was sure she could make it back to the house before he could turn around. She also wanted to make sure Brook saw her heading back to the house and come back as soon as possible. Maybe they could hide in the house 'til Tony got there she thought. She scrambled out of the car from the side away from Ray hoping he wouldn't see the light come on in the car, and as she searched the area for Brook he slammed on his breaks and spun the truck around so fast she couldn't believe it. He must have seen the light she thought, and as she started to run for the house her right shoe got caught in the mud and she ended up falling face first onto the ground, Ray's truck came to a screeching halt directly behind Shawn's car. She laid there almost frozen waiting for him to get out of the truck and put a bullet in her back, but suddenly a shower of rocks pelted the truck again and with the screeching of tires Ray took off towards the direction the rocks came from. Shelly took a deep cleansing breath then suddenly froze as a hand grabbed her arm, but hearing Brooks voice made her able to breath again.

"C'mon hurry," Brook said as she pulled Shelly to her feet she had no idea Shelly's shoe was stuck in the mud she just dragged her towards the house. Once inside they both stood with their backs against the door hoping Ray wasn't stupid enough to force his way inside, but they were wrong. Seconds after his truck came to another screeching halt in front of the house something heavy slammed against the door and they both jumped, he was breaking the door down. Soon the thin door began to splinter and they knew he was beating it with something heavy, he'd be through it in a matter of seconds.

"C'mon!" Brook yelled again grabbing Shelly's hand and dragging her through the house, they were just going out the back door as Ray stuck his head through the hole he'd made in the front door.

"AW COME ON, YOU'RE NOT GOING TO GET AWAY FROM ME!" Ray crowed as he kicked the rest of the door in. "You weren't afraid of me the other day why are you running now?" He was sure Shawn was with Brook and nothing was going to stop him.

"C'mon!" Brook yelled grabbing Shelly's hand, but with only one shoe it was difficult for her to run.

"Wait!" Shelly quickly yanked off the other shoe giving it a toss, and then they took off running again. She knew where Brook was taking her she just hoped they could get there before Ray figuered out where they'd gone.

Ray placed the gun in his belt when he jumped out of the truck, he knew he wouldn't need it to go through the door, and he was right. It only took about fifteen seconds with the use of his new ball bat to knock the door off its hinges. As he poked his head through the hole he'd made in the door he thought he heard the slamming of the back door. "You bastard, he's nothing but a pussy," Ray bragged thinking he had Shawn on the run.

"I was hoping I could have knocked him out with a rock," Brook told Shelly as they ran down the street towards the mansion. As they ran they heard smashing sounds coming from the house and they knew he was breaking everything in his path.

For the first time in her life Shelly realized how it must feel to have the skills Shawn and Tony possessed. She wished now she had been trained in Martial Arts. Shawn's words rang in her ears. "Yeah call the police, that'll stop a guy shoving a gun in your face." She was afraid like she had never been in her life, and she was afraid for Brook. Now she knew how Sherin and many of the girls she defended felt when they were being abused. She had a pain in her gut brought on by the fear she was feeling, and she didn't know if she'd ever see Shawn again.

"C'mon, c'mon" Brook whispered pulling Shelly swiftly along behind the houses she had been running behind for years. She knew where every rock and hole was and guided Shelly around them as they made their way the six blocks down the street to the Mansion. "I know where we can hide until he leaves," she whispered pulling Shelly along.

Ray returned to his truck and began driving through the yards of the houses going towards the south. The rain had stopped and a bright half moon was beginning to peak through the clouds. He was about to turn around and search for them to the north when he thought he saw someone scurrying along behind a house and they were headed south. So he drove behind the houses to take a better look. He thought he saw someone just making it over a chain link fence between two houses and he realized it was two girls.

"It's that tall slut Sherin told me about, and I know just where the fuck you're headed sweetheart."

She was headed for the mansion on Beckwith Street and he knew it. He made a fast u-turn tearing up someone's lawn and headed back for the street. As he sped out across the front lawn and into the street he had about three blocks to cover, stomping on the gas he was doing about a hundred when he flew across the lawn of the mansion and slid to a stop about ten foot from the front door. They weren't there yet. He knew he probably made it there before the girls had, so now he made a couple of circles in the yard and headed back towards the street looking for them. As he pulled away he looked along the side of the house and saw them entering through the side door, so he quickly turned back to the front door and stopped his truck.

Grabbing his bat he walked up to the front foyer and began smashing through the window in the door. Brook ran her hand along the chair rail in the living room and headed for the corner in the hallway, by the time they reached the corner it had opened and she quickly pulled Shelly inside immediately closing the panel as she had many times before. Once inside a light came on and stayed on, Shelly was totally surprised. Brook pulled her halfway up the stairs and sat down pulling her down beside her.

"Why haven't the police come yet?" Shelly questioned.

"Because it's Friday night. It takes at least an hour 'till they respond on a regular night."

"But there were shots fired, doesn't that make them move any faster?"

"You've got to be kidding?" Brook whimpered. "People around here just go in and shut their damn doors. I know damn well someone heard him beating on Sherin too, you think any of them would get off their asses and help, or at least call for help. Fuck no."

Ray was now walking through the house smashing things with his bat. Brook opened the door a crack but when she heard what he was doing she began to cry.

"He's smashing everything, that fucking prick." Shelly pushed the door back shut and pulled her up the stairs.

"Sit down, sit down damn it. We're safe in here, you have enough money to replace anything he breaks."

"Those things are my fathers, I can never replace them!" Shelly quickly covered Brooks mouth with her hand.

"WHERE IN THE HELL ARE YOU TWO HIDING?" Ray yelled. "WHERE'S THAT BIG PRICK AT"

"See, he's looking for us and if you keep yelling he'll find us damn It." she whispered.

"But he's breaking everything," Brook sobbed. "I can't let him keep doing that. It's all my fault! It's all my God-damn-fault!" She was becoming hysterical and Shelly was afraid Ray might hear her crying, she had to be stopped. She remembered Shawn had said the hidden stairwell went from the basement to the upstairs. Hearing Ray's voice trail off she was sure he was heading upstairs so she pulled Brook down towards the basement level.

"Why do you think this is your fault, you didn't tell this bastard to chase us?"

"It is my fault," she sobbed, "I forgot to set the alarm. If I would have of set the alarm daddy would still be alive and everything would still be the same."

"What do you mean?" Shelly questioned. Brook was now getting worse and she wasn't thinking about anything she was saying. Shelly took her by the shoulders and shook her, hoping she'd start making some sense. "What the hell are you talking about?"

"I was supposed to set the alarm, I thought I did but somehow I must have forgot. Beth came home and caught us sleeping together. She took my ball bat and hit daddy over the head. I didn't mean to kill her, really I didn't. But she killed daddy. She didn't have to do that, did she?" Shelly quickly wrapped her arms around her and started crying too. Poor Brook had been holding this hurt inside for quite some time, Shelly realized. What more is there to know now, she wondered?

Tony drove past the Mansion heading for Brooks house and when he got there he saw Shawn's car with two flat tires, now he knew where the two shots he'd heard were aimed at. He made his way into the house slowly checking every room hoping he wouldn't find what he was afraid he would. He had fears of finding Shelly and Brook both lying dead inside some where and his sadness was quickly exchanged for hope finding nobody there. The vision of that pickup he saw parked in front of the Mansion on the corner and the grass being all torn up told him to get his tail moving. That was Ray's truck, and now he knew where they were.

Ray was walking through the mansion swinging the bat and hitting what ever he felt like hitting, things made of glass were what he really enjoyed smashing. "YOO-HOO

WHERE IN THE HELL ARE YOU TWO HIDING?" he yelled again and again. "C'MON, I'M NOT GOING TO HURT YOU. I JUST WANT TO KNOW WHERE THAT ASSHOLE IS THAT DRIVES THAT FUCKING CAR? C'MON YOU CAN TELL ME!" He walked around smashing a few more items then he realized he'd pushed things far enough. The police would probably be coming soon. "WELL, I'M GOING TO LEAVE NOW! YOU KNOW I'LL BE BACK TO VISIT AGAIN! I SURE WOULD LIKE TO TALK TO YOU, NOW!" He yelled. When he walked back over to the door he smashed out the glass on the opposite side and walked through it. Reaching his truck he tossed the bat through the broken window and climbed in, then he proceeded to tear up as much of the lawn as he could before heading north on Caliper.

CHAPTER FIFTEEN

As Tony headed for the Mansion he put in a call to Red's Office, he related what he'd found at Brook's house and that he was headed for the Mansion about six blocks to the south. He needed backup ASAP and Warren police were nowhere in sight. He was told Shawn and Red had already left minutes before and should be there soon. But they had to drive clear across the County to get to Warren, and on a busy Friday night that could take a while. Warren Police had been dispatched to the area, but there was no telling how soon they'd be there.

The girls heard Ray revving his engine like crazy so they knew he'd left the house, they slowly crept out of their hiding place and looked out the front window, Brook was surveying the damage in the house and trying her best to keep from crying. When Shelly saw Ray drive away she grabbed the phone and quickly called the police. But at that same instance Tony pulled up to the front of the house, he'd passed Ray on the street but he needed to find the girls and make sure they were all right. Brook came running out to his car and surprised him.

"Are you two alright?"

"We're fine, but that was Ray you just passed!"

"I know, stay here!" Then he jumped back into his car and sped out the drive after Ray. Brook quickly joined Shelly on the porch and they watched as Tony headed towards Brook's house. As they watched, they saw Ray had turned around and was headed back towards the mansion. As he and Tony passed each other Tony spun his car around in the middle of the street and started back after him. Ray spun his truck around and the two vehicles came to a sliding halt under a street light about forty feet from each other. Ray was hoping it was Shawn in the car.

"Get the fuck out of here," Shelly whispered hoping Ray would just leave and let the police get him.

The two men sat in their vehicles under the streetlights staring at each other. Tony was hoping Ray would make a move but he just sat there. The girls were slowly making there way closer to the cars when Tony got out of his vehicle.

"Tony he's got a gun!" Shelly yelled.

Ray was wondering who this guy was and why he was sticking his nose in where it didn't belong. He decided to get out of his truck and find out, the ball bat visible in his left hand. "I don't need this to take care of you," he said tucking the gun into his pants waist walking towards Tony with the bat. He started swinging it above his head like when he went after Shawn, but this guy wasn't running either.

"You'd better get the fuck outta here nigger!" Ray yelled swinging the bat. Tony was signaling the girls to get far away but he kept his eyes glued on Ray's every move.

"WHAT'S THE MATTER CAT GOT YOUR FUCKING TONGUE?" Ray yelled at Tony, still getting no response. Suddenly Ray sent the bat spinning through the stormy night air towards Tony's head, hoping to cause considerable damage when it hit. Tony ducked slightly deflecting the bat from hitting him, and Ray knew instantly he was in trouble again.

Tony knew catching the bat would draw his attention away from the gun Ray was carrying and he didn't need anything distracting him. He was not letting Ray leave no matter what. Seeing what Tony had done made Ray think of Shawn's little trick so he quickly yanked the gun from his belt, he was going to leave. But when Ray turned towards his truck Tony yelled.

"You're not going anywhere."

"I'm leaving, try and stop me and I'll blow your fucking head off," Ray yelled back.

"I said you're not leaving," Tony yelled again. "You're going to put the gun down and wait for the police. You have a few things to answer for. You put a young lady in the hospital... Ray pulled the trigger. Tony quickly turned away giving Ray a narrower target while Ray emptied the gun. When Tony heard what he thought was the last shot he moved swiftly towards Ray, he had to cover about forty foot before getting to him and he didn't want to give him a closer target while he was shooting. In less than three seconds Ray had fired the last five bullets he had in the gun. Seeing Tony was still standing he wondered how the hell he'd missed with that many shots. Tony never flinched. When Ray fired his last shot and realized Tony was still standing; his plan was to leave, get the hell out of there fast. But he was too late. Tony covered the rest of the distance in a split second while Ray was asking himself where had the bullets gone. As Ray ran to the drivers side of his truck Tony had leaped into the air at the same time spinning; his left foot caught the left side of Ray's head slamming him into the truck. Tony than gave him a knee to his mid section and as he buckled Tony took hold of his face with both hands giving it a twist, Tony wasn't playing games, he'd snapped Ray's neck.

Brook and Shelly watched in fear as the bat went flying, Tony deflected it and Ray grabbed the gun, the shots were fired and Tony was still standing, then he was moving towards Ray as if nothing could stop him. They saw the spin kick, the strike to Ray's stomach, and they heard the snap of his neck, they knew Ray was dead. When Tony spun around the second time and they heard the cracking of bones they looked at each other knowing exactly what he'd done. It had all taken place in about five seconds.

The two girls quickly ran to Tony's side, both of them grabbing and hugging him.

"I can't believe he missed you," Brook exclaimed.

"He didn't," Tony said, walking around looking at the ground.

"OH MY GOD!" Shelly said bringing her wet hand up from his right side, "you're bleeding c'mon sit down."

"In a minute," he said walking along the truck. He was looking along the ground for something, but she didn't know what.

"What are you looking for?"

"We have to find that gun," Tony commanded.

"Honey I'll Find it, you get over here and sit down." Shelly looked at her hand under the streetlight; it was covered with blood.

"Brook, call an ambulance he's bleeding bad. Tony you've got to sit down."

"There it is," he said bending down and picking it up by the tip of the barrel. "Get this into a bag and don't let it out of your sight. Now I'll sit down," he said leaning against Ray's truck and slowly sliding to the ground.

When the call came in over the scanner on Red's desk Shawn grabbed the keys to Red's cruiser. Warren police were being dispatched to 1124 Caliper, along with any available unit in the area. Shots had been fired. Shawn and Red lost no time heading for the west side of the county. About five miles away from Beckwith Street they heard another announcement, an ambulance was being dispatched to the corner of Beckwith and Armour Streets to rescue a gunshot victim, there were two casualties, one was deceased. Shawn was feeling sick.

He didn't know the first address but he was sure it was Brook's house, now he knew the ambulance was headed for the Mansion, or at least an intersection by it. Armour was the first block running east and west north of the mansion. All he could think of was the two casualties were Shelly and Brook.

Tony had tried calling the Fourth Precinct when he first heard from Shelly but because of the storm his car phone wouldn't work, when he finally got through Shawn had already left.

"I'm going!" he yelled at Red. Either you take me or I'm stealing one of your cars." His last few words were unnecessary, when the first call came in Red was already headed for the key rack.

They arrived at the scene shortly after the ambulance; Shawn was out of the car running before Red was able to stop the car. A sigh of relief waved through him when he saw Brook standing by the road, running up to her he grabbed her by the shoulders.

"Where's Shelly!" Then came the words he was so afraid of hearing. He already hated himself for getting her involved.

"She's in the ambulance," Brook said crying.

Tears began slowly trickling down his face as he turned to chase the ambulance as it backed out of the drive.

"She's ok!" Brook yelled grabbing him by the shirt and twisting him back around. The look on his face asked who than? "It's Tony, he's been shot, Shelly's with him." Shawn looked out into the street at the body covered with a blanket, than back at Brook.

"That's Ray he's dead," Brook mumbled, following him to the ambulance. "Tony killed him." He shot a quick glance at her before opening the back door. The attendant tried pulling the door back shut, but Tony seen who it was.

"Let'im in," Tony demanded. Shawn jumped in taking Shelly in one arm and Tony in the other.

"How bad is it?" The look Shelly gave him told him it wasn't good.

"It's just one," Tony said bravely.

"Oh yeah, and one can't kill you? Damn it, how bad?"

"It's in his right side close to his kidney, he says it missed but we won't know till we get him to the hospital. Can we go now?" the attendant asked somewhat rudely.

Red was now standing at the back door listening to the conversation.

"Shell, give that to Red," Tony whispered quietly.

Shelly took the gun from her purse handing it to Shawn, and he passed it to Red.

"That's what he shot me with, I'll bet it's the same gun Hinkley was killed with," Tony whispered. He took Shawn's hand looking into his eyes. "You go pick up Correen. I don't want her to hear this from anyone else." Shawn agreed then jumped out of the ambulance. Before he shut the door he heard Tony say, "bring me some tea, the good stuff."

"I'm going to run ballistics on this myself right now," Red said, even if I have to drag a lab technician out of bed," he declared. Shawn had a vision of him dragging a lab technician from his home by gunpoint; he knew Red would do it too. Shawn pointed his thumb towards his car. "Go, get the hell out of here, I'll Meet you up at the hospital."

Brook had been standing beside Red listening; now she followed Shawn to the police car getting in with him. They broke the news to Coreen and took her to the hospital. Tony wouldn't let them take him into surgery until she was there.

"Now, can we get started?" the surgeon asked with a disgusted look. "The x-ray shows the bullet missed his kidney, I won't be able to tell how much damage there is until I get in there, but it doesn't look too bad. I've had worse. You're in great physical health; I don't think there's a lot to worry about. So lets get started," he said with a sharp whisper and a quick look at every one standing there. As they rolled Tony into the operating room every one wished him luck and took a seat in the lounge.

The time dragged on and it wasn't long before the lounge became quite crowded. Many of Tony's students arrived and insisted on staying. Ray was dead so there was no reason for a guard on Sherin. Shawn wanted to talk with Shelly in private so they decided to go outside but it was raining.

One of Correen's friends offered the use of her van parked just outside the emergency room door and Shawn accepted taking Shelly along, and Brook happily took her up on the invitation too. Correen declined, she wanted to stay as close to the operating room as possible. Brook fell asleep almost immediately after they settled inside the Van, so Shelly and Shawn felt they could talk quietly and she wouldn't hear.

"I've got a confession to make," he told Shelly once they were huddled in the far back seat.

"And what would that be?"

"I was scared shitless when Brook said you were in that ambulance, God I was scared." A tear began trickling down his cheek again as he thought about the possibility of her being the one in the operating room, and he was glad being in the darkness of the van she was unable to see It. "I'm pissed at myself for getting you involved in this mess." Shelly squeezed him extra tight listening to his words. Tears were also running down her cheeks. "It's not any better Tony getting shot either," he added. "Never again, ne-ver-again." She knew he was beating himself up for what had happened, and she knew it wasn't his fault.

"Honey, I could get shot in a courtroom by some stupid defendant or ran over on the streets of Detroit. Besides, I'm the one that said poof Ray here so we could get that gun. So

God poofed him to the wrong spot," she said smiling. Now she had her tear filled face about an inch from his nose, and she could see he'd been crying too.

"You mean you're not mad?"

"No, I was damn scared but I was never mad, not at you anyway. I was damned awful mad at Ray. Do you realize we solved three cases in one night?"

"Three?" he questioned emphatically.

"Yes," Shelly shot back with a low sharp whisper. "That gun is going to prove Ray shot Hinkley and not you. I'm sure of it. Your mystery client is sleeping right there in that front seat," she whispered, pointing at Brook. Shawn's mouth opened wide his eyes forming a big question mark. "And we've caught the dirty rotten bastard that beat up Sherin." Nothing else she mentioned seamed to enter his ears; he sat pointing into the front seat at Brook and mouthing these words with almost silent voice.

"My mystery client?"

Shelly sat nodding her head yes. "A very rich one at that I might add," she whispered.

"Rich?" Shawn was beginning to feel like he was in a vacuum and everything was happening around him, he had lost control of the investigation. Shelly was still nodding her head yes.

"And another thing, we found out who really killed Beth."

He sank down in the seat resting his head on the back of it. He couldn't believe what he was about to do, but for the hell of it he pointed at Brook again. Shelly nodded her head along with a whisper, "yes."

A look of exhaustion covered his face as he rested his head against the back of the seat. "That's four. You guys solved four cases in one night. What a great private investigator I am. I get arrested and you two solve the case, not one but four. Don't you just love it?" Then he turned quickly facing her. "What do you mean rich, and why did she hire me if she knew she killed Beth?"

"She wanted her daddy vindicated. She knew she killed Beth and it was eating at her knowing her father was being blamed for it. He was a bookie. Why he gave her his money to hide for him I don't know but he gave her about six and a half million dollars to hide. Sure, it could be mob money, but it also could be his winnings. Nobody has come looking for it. And she owns the mansion on Beckwith Street. I know there will be a fight to get her out of trouble but I think I can get her off with a self-defense plea; after all she was afraid Beth was going to hit her with that bat too. Hell, Beth had already killed her father, what was she to think?"

"So he never did wake up?"

"No. When Beth hit him that was it, he never woke up."

"Then where does Brook fit in."

"Brook wanted her father to be cleared, and after seeing you on television when you found that dog she fell in love with you, it gave her a chance to rekindle an old friendship, after all you helped them before."

"I did?"

"Do you remember trying to help a lady named Karen Shepard?"

"You're shitting me, she's little Brook Shepard?"

"Yes. She would spend time at the house with her father playing pool and some times pin ball, while he placed bets and worked on his collections. At some point he began having her take his money, which he packed into shoeboxes one million dollars at a time, and she'd hide it at her house. She's got six full boxes and another with over five hundred thousand in it. That's the one she kept pulling your money from. Evidently he was prone to taking naps every afternoon and she'd lie down beside him after setting an alarm clock so she could be up and out before Beth came home. On the day in question she forgot to set the alarm or the damn thing didn't work, anyway Beth caught them sleeping together.

She made the same stupid mistake I did; she thought Forest was having sex with Brook. If Brook hadn't have woken up when she did, she'd probably be dead too. Because I think Beth would have hit her next."

"So why do you think he had her take the money?"

"He was probably afraid of being watched by the IRS. Or he was afraid Beth would get her hands on it. I don't know, but I don't think he had anything to do with the Mafia." Shelly and Shawn had been cuddling and talking for a couple of hours when there came a knock on the drivers front door then Red jumped in behind the wheel. Flipping on the dome light he began telling them what he'd found out.

"Well, I ran one of the fastest ballistics tests done in the City of Detroit and Ray's gun did kill Hinkley." Shelly gave Shawn a reassuring look and a tight hug. "I've called Judge Hargrove, he's pissed at Hunter for having him sign that warrant. And because I wasn't handed the warrant when he brought you in, he'll probably loose his job. He probably would have been ok, but he forged the Judges signature on the one we took away from him so now he's in deep shit." Shawn and Shelly sat listening, smiling from ear to ear. "I made sure to let Judge Hargrove know about that. They're going to check back on other warrants to see if any more have been forged. I think every Judge in the county is at the courthouse right now. They opened Hinkley's safe this morning too. He had over a hundred grand in there. It was all wrapped in bundles of ten grand each. Hinkley had the common sense to write the amount on each one as he acquired it must be," then Red paused a moment working on his thoughts.

"And," Shawn asked, wondering what the significance was about a judge having lots of cash in his safe.

"Well, Ray had about seven thousand dollars in his glove box. There was writing on the band holding it together. It was a ten thousand dollar bundle from Hinkley's safe. I mean Hinkley had the bundles dated and Ray's bundle fit the sequence, it looks like he may have paid Ray to do away · with you." Shelly gasped as her hand quickly covered her mouth.

"You mean Hinkley paid Ray to kill Shawn?"

"It looks that way. There's more lab work being done, but I'd stake my badge on it. And that other stuff you were telling me, there's a lady over in zoning and permits ready to spill her guts, they dragged her out of bed and told her to get to the courthouse or they'd have her arrested. It seems Stan has some explaining to do too. Oh, and Hargrove wants you and Shelly in his chambers tomorrow first thing to meet with him and a couple of other Judges. It seems there's quite a few people sitting in prison that have to be released ASAP. They're going back at least five years on Hinkley's cases. They said something about you taking over Hinkley's Judgeship," Red said giving Shawn a questioning look. Both Shelly and Red knew it wasn't news to Shawn; his facial expression hadn't changed. The look on Shelly's face said, " You son of a gun, you knew all the time didn't you?"

Shelly let out a big sigh of relief. " Well, that means lacy will be able to go home," she said in a pleasing tone.

"Well, there's more but it'll keep till tomorrow. I kept the best for last," he said with a big smile. Tony's out of surgery, he'll be in recovery for at least a half hour or so. Everything went good, it took a lot longer than they figuered it would but he should be up and around in no time. But, we've got to tell him to stop collecting evidence this way, it could get him killed. I'll see you guy's inside." He gave them both a friendly smile and as he opened his door to leave Brook woke up.

"So much for trying to sleep, wait I'm coming with you," she said jumping out her side. It was beginning to rain more now so they ran into the hospital trying to shield them selves from the water; Shelly and Shawn watched laughing as they ran.

"So you really liked helping me on this case?"

"Yes, I've never been so scared in my life, but I had lots of fun. I'm sorry Tony got hurt though, the danger, the excitement, meeting new people. I think I'm burnt out in the courtroom; this was really different. I've made two new friends, Brook and Sherin. And I've never seen a man killed before my very eyes. I'm not saying I liked that, but now I know why you and Tony are so sure about yourselves. I wish I could handle myself like that without being scared. I think Tony has two new students, God you should have seen him, I couldn't believe my eyes."

" You mean you were that close?"

"Brook and I both were, but you're the only one I'll ever tell that to." As far as I know, Ray tried to kill him and he protected himself. Ray shot at him five times and Tony just kept going towards him. We thought he missed because Tony was still moving like crazy, he jumped in the air and did this crazy spin kick at Ray and that was it. There was nothing more Shelly could tell Shawn, because he knew just what had taken place. The two of them had discussed what the plan of action would be if either of them were to encounter Ray in the future. They both sat there thanking God Tony had been hit with only one of Ray's bullets.

"Do you think you'll try getting your job back, I mean if Stan gets removed?" Shawn asked.

"I don't think so. Not right now. I think I'd like to try going it on my own. Besides, I'm going to have a real close friend that's a Judge." She smiled at him and stared, waiting for his explanation.

"I'm not taking Hinkley's post."

Her mouth dropped again. "You're turning down a judgeship being handed to you on a silver platter, you can become a Judge and you're turning it down?" The shock in her voice didn't surprise him at all.

"I don't want to be a Judge, I told you I like what I'm doing. It's not always as exciting as it was this week, but who knows, maybe it's getting better. Maybe I'll get to solve the next one," he said smiling. "I'm going to suggest they give it to you." He didn't think it was possible but her chin fell even further.

"You'd do that for me?" she gave him a quick peck on the cheek. "Thank you, but they're not going to do that."

"Shit, you'd be better at it than I would. Judge Thurman can get it done, believe me."

Shelly looked at him partially in shock, partially in awe. First, she couldn't believe her ears. The man she'd been pushing away for so long was possibly handing her the career she'd been working towards for so long. Now she didn't know if she wanted it. She wanted to work close to him.

She enjoyed working along side of him again the way it had been back a few years ago. Now, she didn't want to give it up. She wrapped her arms around his neck giving him a long wet kiss.

He'd thought about suggesting this many times during the last few years, but he didn't. Now he was going to go for it. "My office is big enough for two. Why don't we have a sign made, Cassidy and Barns Law office and investigations?" They sat in silence for a few seconds, than he added, "Or Barns and Cassidy...." She turned looking into his eyes, the distance from his nose being about a quarter of an inch now. They sat looking at each other in the darkness; she didn't know why she'd pushed him away for so long. She knew she wasn't going to any more. She didn't want a day to go by without holding him and possibly making love to him. Her career be damned.

"Why not Cassidy & Cassidy Law office and Investigations?" she asked with a smile.

"That means we'd have to be..." his heart began beating with a flutter he hadn't felt since the first time he'd made love to her. She sat nodding her head up and down softly rubbing her nose against his. He didn't know what to say. His body suddenly had a warm feeling all over as she whispered into his ear.

"Yes I'll marry you."

He took her face in his hands and kissed her a long warm kiss. He wanted to hold her, just sit and hold her for a long time, but suddenly Brook was at the window, Shawn rolled it down.

"Tony said to get your ass in there with his tea," she said laughing.

"Tell him we'll be right there." Brook turned and quickly ran back into the hospital. When Shelly and Shawn started to get out of the van Shawn asked her, "How much money did you say she has hidden?"

"Six and a half million give or take a thousand or so."

"Well, you know my uncle Tim."

"Yes, I remember your uncle Tim." She said wrapping both her arms around his right arm as if she was afraid he was going to run away.

"About three or four years back he got it through my head just how to trade in the stock market and make money, not loose it all the time"

"Yeah."

"Well," he paused a few seconds knowing this was surely the time to tell her, "I've got about a third of what she's got," he said walking along beside her. She stopped instantly turning to him right there in the rain and then she grabbed him by his lapels, her mouth wide open unable to say a word. There was a stunned look on her face as if she'd just been hit by something and for the first time since he'd known her she seemed to be completely speechless. Looking at her he smiled a big broad smile, "you'd better close your mouth honey, with all this rain I wouldn't want you to drown before I get to marry you." Her look seemed to be frozen in time.

THE END